Kin-Slayer

The Grandfather gathered itself to spring, but it was too late. Sullivan heaved the two Molotovs at the monster. Both hit their mark, shattering on the hard cartilage and gnarled bone that made the Grandfather's exoskeleton. Flames shot up instantly as the gasoline spread and burned, setting alight the Grandfather's robes as well as the tapestries and hangings decorating the chamber. The Grandfather-thing roared in pain, twisting up to its full height of nearly twelve feet in a futile effort to escape the flames now engulfing it.

Robes now burned clean away, the naked monster stumbled as it slowly walked toward Sullivan. Hate twisted its face as pieces of burned flesh fell to the floor—a burning tower, a pillar of roaring flame, a walking funeral pyre filling the room with smoke dense as pitch.

Then a shadowy figure appeared in the doorway. Sullivan leaped instantly to his feet and stumbled out the door, just as the Grandfather took its final step and toppled over headlong—a crashing, burning *Hindenburg*, glowing ribs showing through incinerated flesh like so many twisted beams and girders.

THE WORLD OF DARKNESS
Vampire

Dark
Prince

Based on
VAMPIRE: THE MASQUERADE

Keith Herber

HarperPrism
An Imprint of HarperPaperbacks

HarperPaperbacks   *A Division of* HarperCollins*Publishers*
10 East 53rd Street, New York, N.Y. 10022

Cover illustration by Kevin Murphy

First printing: December 1994

Printed in the United States of America

HarperPrism is an imprint of HarperPaperbacks.
HarperPaperbacks, HarperPrism, and colophon are trade-marks of HarperCollins*Publishers*.

❖ 10 9 8 7 6 5 4 3 2 1

For my wife Sharon,
who always bears with me.

PRELUDE: THE EMBRACE

I am rather inclined to believe that this is the land God gave to Caine.

—Jacques Cartier,
La Première Relation

1851, San Francisco's
Golden Gate . . .

On a moonless night six men crouched in a wooden longboat hidden along the shore. Straining their eyes against the darkness, they tried to peer through the thickening fog, watching the entrance to the harbor, waiting for a ship coming in with the tide.

"I see it," said Morgan, the tall black man, stripped to the waist despite the cold night air. "She's moving slow. Most of her sails are down."

The leader of the crew, an Irishman named Sullivan, had also spotted the ship and noted it barely moving in the stream.

"Do you see any crew?" Sullivan asked Morgan, scratching at the stubble of his red beard.

"Nothin'," said Morgan.

"Neither do I," he said. "Let's go."

Silently the longboat slipped from shore and the crew dipped their oars, quietly stroking out toward the unnaturally quiet ship.

1

"Douse the lights," Sullivan ordered. One of the men threw a lit cigar into the sea.

"Still nothin'," said Morgan as they slid in closer. "No one on deck."

"Plague ship!" hissed one of the men. There was a stir among the crew.

"It ain't no fuckin' plague ship," spit Sullivan. "Somebody steered her in."

Still, as they drew alongside they saw no movement on deck, heard no sounds from below.

"I don't like the looks of this," said the bearded, black-haired man who had suggested the danger of plague. "Let's leave this one alone."

"No chance," said Sullivan. "I've got a captain looking to get out of the harbor tomorrow and he needs a crew. This bunch should fill the bill."

The men were crimps—agents providing crews for ships outward bound from booming San Francisco harbor. California's Gold Rush was in full swing and ships pouring into the harbor found it difficult to board a crew to get back out; most able-bodied men were headed for the goldfields. Enterprising crimps—like Sullivan—met incoming ships at the Golden Gate and lured the crews off, promising drink, women, and drugs, forcing the captains to pay them off—sometimes at gunpoint—before rowing the crew ashore and leaving the ship adrift. As soon as the crimps had fleeced the sailors of all their money and gotten them into debt, they forced them to sign aboard the next outgoing ship. In times of greatest shortage, Sullivan simply drugged the sailors, robbed them, then sold them to the highest bidder, all in a matter of a few hours. Sullivan had been a sailor himself, so he was familiar with the trade.

Morgan in the lead, the crew quietly climbed up the side of the silent brigantine and over the rail. Although the ship looked in order, it seemed abandoned—a derelict. The only sounds were the lapping of the waves and the bumping of the longboat against the ship's hull.

"Look here!" shouted one of the men from the aft of the ship. "I found something."

A dead sailor was lashed to the wheel.

"I told it you it was plague," said the bearded man.

"This is no plague," said Morgan, grabbing the corpse by the hair and turning back its head. "Look."

The man's throat was torn open.

"Somebody killed him," the man said.

"It looks like it was done by some wild animal," said another member of the crew.

No one mentioned the lack of blood around the body or the deck, despite the pale, ghostlike appearance of the corpse.

"Go forward and check the crew's cabin," Sullivan ordered the black-haired man. "Morgan and I will check the officers' quarters."

Carrying a lantern, Sullivan went down first, descending the narrow ladder to the passageway. Morgan followed behind, pistol drawn, eyes wary. "What do you think's goin' on?" he asked Sullivan, softly.

"Beats me. Unless someone else got here first and already took the crew."

It was not unknown for even captains to jump ship for the goldfields, but the murdered sailor at the wheel suggested otherwise.

"Look," said Sullivan, holding a lantern through the doorway of the narrow mates' cabin.

They saw another corpse, like the first, its throat torn out. It had been dead awhile longer—at least a few days—but instead of being rotted and bloated, the body looked dried and withered—like a mummy's.

"I don't like the look of this thing," muttered Morgan. "Or the smell," he added, sniffing at the air.

A strange odor hung in the air: spicy, like incense, but it only masked another smell—a pervasive stench of corruption and decay.

"Sullivan, I think we should forget this one," Morgan said.

Those were the last words he ever spoke. As Sullivan backed out of the cabin, he saw something dark drop down the ladder to fall straight onto Morgan's back. The black man shouted, grabbed at his attacker, then fell to the deck as a small Oriental man atop him twisted Morgan's head back and sank his teeth into his throat.

Sullivan moved to help his friend, but was thrown violently back against the wall by an invisible force. He tried to get up but couldn't. Paralyzed, he watched helplessly as the door to the captain's cabin at the far end of the passage banged open and a creature—a beautiful Oriental woman clad in silk robes of red and green—glided smoothly toward him out of the darkness.

Again Sullivan tried to rise, but to no avail. He watched helplessly as the beautiful woman bent toward him, parting her lips, revealing small, perfectly formed white teeth. Out of the corner of his eye he saw his friend, Morgan, sprawled on the deck, the Oriental still crouching over him, now lapping noisily at the blood pouring from the fallen man's throat.

Then the woman was upon him. The last thing Sullivan remembered was her liquid green eyes and a sharp, stabbing pain in his neck.

Sullivan awoke later to find himself in the captain's cabin. Sitting weakly on the deck, propped against the wall, he scanned the room. A lantern burned on the desk, illuminating three people talking furtively among themselves on the other side of the cabin. The woman was there, as well as the small man who had jumped Morgan. The third was also Chinese—a tall cadaverous figure dressed all in red. They were arguing, discussing something in what sounded like Chinese. Movement beside him caught his attention. He looked over to find himself staring into the sightless eyes of a corpse—the bloodless body of the ship's captain—hanging by its heels from the overhead. Gently, it swung back and forth with the easy rolling of the ship.

God in heaven, Sullivan thought to himself. *What have I fallen into?*

The three ended their conversation, the woman turning and walking back toward Sullivan while the two men busied themselves opening a hatch in the cabin floor. Sullivan tried to pull away from the woman, pressing himself against the wall in an effort to elude her, but there was nowhere to go. Seeing his distress, she attempted to calm him, kneeling down next to him, gently stroking his brow.

He quailed at her touch, pulling away, croaking, "My crew? Where's my crew."

"They be fine," she assured him in uncomfortable, stilted English. "We taken care of them."

Meanwhile, the two men had managed to open the hatch and were now standing over the opening, looking down into the dark hold. The tall, cadaverous man stomped his foot on the planked deck, then spoke something in Chinese. The two peered into the hold again, watching, while the woman continued to smooth Sullivan's brow with her cool, ivory hands, but she, too, kept her attention on the opening.

The cadaverous man spoke again and Sullivan felt something shift deep in the ship's belly, as though in response, then the vessel rolled slightly to port. Again the cadaverous man spoke and again the ship creaked and pitched as whatever was in the hold began moving aft, toward the opening. Sullivan heard wood creak as whatever it was set foot on the ladder below and then a nauseous odor poured up from the hold, wafting over him, making him gag. He squirmed vainly, tried to cry out, then fell silent as the woman passed her hands down over his face and he fell unconscious.

PART
I

Blood
Puppets

1

If this is the best of all possible worlds, what are the others like?

—Voltaire, *Candide*

At three o'clock in the morning there were few to witness the blond-haired woman in a miniskirt running down the foggy, nearly deserted streets of San Francisco. White high heels clutched in one hand, the woman threw fearful glances over her shoulder as she raced down the sidewalk at full speed, pantyhose snagged and torn, skirt riding up her thighs.

Kathy knew she should never have come to this part of town at night. It was too dangerous. But she couldn't keep herself from taking the risk. She'd needed a fix and couldn't wait for her pimp to show up. The only connection she had aside from Terry lived in this part of town. The risk was necessary.

At Taylor Street she turned left and headed down the steep slope of lower Nob Hill, toward the Theater District and the Tenderloin beyond. She glanced back before ducking around the corner and caught sight of her pursuer when he appeared at the other end of the block. The man spotted her, ran toward her, and Kathy took off like a rabbit. The malevolent, dark-clad figure came after her, increasing his pace, a shadow moving down the street, footfalls silent as night.

Nearing Geary, Kathy spotted the narrow alley leading to Trader Vic's. Exhausted, she dodged across the street and disappeared into the darkness.

The alley was L-shaped, turning left in front of Vic's to open on Geary to the south. The club was closed this time of night and Kathy noticed the row of garbage cans lined up in front: a place to hide.

She listened, heard nothing. There was no sound of her pursuer. Carefully watching Mason Street, she backed toward the garbage cans, sliding quietly down the wall. At the corner of the alley she had to make a break across open ground to reach the garbage cans, but before making the dash she peered around the corner for a quick look down the alley leading to Geary.

From nowhere the dark-clad man rose up out of the alley's shadows, right in front of her. His face glowed an unearthly pale in the dim streetlights: gaunt, rough, and with the stubble of a red beard.

"Sullivan!" she gasped.

Grabbing her by the throat, the man hurled her against the brick wall. She bounced off, was caught by the shoulders, and slammed back again.

"Owwww!" Kathy wailed.

"Shut up," Sullivan said, slapping her lightly, then grabbing her chin in his big hand, turning her face up toward him, pinching her jaw, twisting her head.

"I've been looking for you," he told her. "Where the hell you been?"

"I quit," she said. "I'm out of the fuckin' business."

"Like hell you are," he said, grabbing at the purse she wore over her shoulder.

She tried to keep him away from it but couldn't. He snatched it away.

"What's in here?" he demanded, tearing the purse open and rummaging through the contents, tossing stuff out on the ground: cosmetics, Kleenex, a dried-up ballpoint, a tiny envelope with a small amount of heroin, and a handful of rubbers.

"What are these for, then?" he asked, shaking some of the sealed prophylactics in her face.

She didn't answer.

"Who ya workin' for?" he demanded, taking her by the shoulder and shaking her.

"No one," she protested, squirming in his grip. "Goddamn you, Sullivan, let me go."

She kicked out at him but he dodged her. With almost no effort he mashed her back into the wall, holding her so she couldn't get away.

"Owww," she whimpered.

A strange voice rang out from the far end of the alley. "What the fuck is going on here?" It was a tall black man, almost bigger than Sullivan.

Sullivan ignored him.

Receiving no answer, the stranger repeated himself. "I said, 'what the fuck are you doin'?" he demanded.

"None of your business," he snarled back, keeping his grip on Kathy's shoulder but turning to face the stranger. "Go on. Get the hell out of here."

"Just let the lady go," the stranger said, stepping forward, stooping quickly to snatch up a length of metal conduit.

The stranger meant business.

"Give her up, man," he said.

Sullivan glared at the intruder, eyes burning like red coals in the darkness. He opened his mouth, revealing inch-long glistening fangs.

"Go!" Sullivan ordered.

With that, the black man dropped the pipe and fled.

Sullivan waited until his fangs retracted before turning back to face Kathy, still wriggling in his grasp.

"So who is it?" he finally asked her.

"Terry," she said wearily, going almost limp. The fight was out of her.

Terry was a human pimp working the territory west of Van Ness, bordering on Sullivan's turf. Terry had been a thorn in Sullivan's side for some time now and Sullivan longed to get rid of him, but he'd had trouble pinpointing where he lived—at least up till now.

"What's his address?" he asked her.

"He's got an apartment on the corner of Franklin and Sutter. Number twenty-three."

Kathy no longer made any pretense of resistance. Sullivan released her. She'd worked for him now the better part of a year and knew all too well what he was like. She avoided meeting him as much as possible. Stories were told about this pimp, but she didn't believe any of them.

"You're working for me now, you hear?" Sullivan told her, watching as she hunted around on the ground for the contents of her purse. She didn't respond.

"You hear?" he repeated, louder.

"Yeah, yeah, yeah," Kathy said, picking up the last of her belongings.

"See Tran tomorrow. Get set up with him. Okay?"

"Yeah, sure." Kathy was standing up now, arranging things in her purse. Still, she avoided looking at him.

Sullivan spotted a roll of bills peeking out of the handbag. Before she could stop him he snatched them away.

"Hey," she protested. "Give that back. That's mine!"

"Fuck you," he told her, smiling.

He counted a little over a hundred dollars, then stuffed them in the front pocket of his jeans.

"Terry will kill me if I come home without that," she whined.

"Fuck Terry too," said Sullivan as he walked away. "You work for me now. See you tomorrow night."

She watched him walk away.

"Cocksucker," she swore after him, under her breath.

January 10

In a dark place somewhere deep beneath Chinatown . . .

A tall, cadaverous Chinese dressed in red robes handed a smoldering brazier to the huge figure seated on a mound of silk cushions.

"It is prepared, Grandfather," said the ghoul.

"Thank you, Chi," the thing said, taking the brazier from his hands.

The Grandfather bent to inhale the fumes that rose from the glowing coals, the great wooden demon mask he wore tilting forward as he did so. The fumes entered his body, seeking his mind, opening doors across stretches of space and time.

"Grandfather?" a voice asked, from out of nowhere.

"Yes, my lord," answered the masked figure, speaking out loud, though the owner of the voice was far away and the two could only hear one another in their minds. "I am here," he said.

"We begin now, as we have planned. It is time for the Spaniard to take his leave," the voice said.

"Yes, my lord. We must put an end to Delfonso before it is too late."

"You have chosen your agent?"

"Yes. A childe of mine will do the job."

"Sullivan?"

"He is my choice, my lord."

"Good. Then it is done."

2

The city is the teacher of the man.

—Simonides,
a fragment

At night San Francisco's infamous Tenderloin is Hell, and Sullivan is its keeper.

Lying in the lowlands at the foot of Nob Hill, the Tenderloin has been a "bad part" of town almost since the city's earliest days. Stretching along the north side of Market Street, from the tourist-ridden cable car terminus at Powell west all the way to Civic Center Plaza, the five or six streets that make up this seedy, littered district are filled with adult theatres and porn outlets, and populated by drug pushers, whores, and criminals. Amidst this turmoil thousands of displaced Vietnamese and Laotian refugees try to raise their families. As in the past, San Francisco is still a popular point of entry for Asian immigrants.

Sullivan began his work each evening at sunset, after he had risen, descending from his haven in the Drake Inn on Pine Street, walking down the southern face of the steep hill for five blocks. Here, at the bottom of the hill, he policed the fetid world of the Tenderloin: keeping the whores in line, collecting his share of the take on drug deals, and making sure no poachers—human or Kindred—strayed into his territory.

He had bossed the Tenderloin since the neighborhood was rebuilt following the Great Earthquake and Fire of 1906. All those years he successfully kept the secret of his vampirism. Stories and rumors circulated about Sullivan, and though some of the oldest residents remembered him from years back, none seemed ready to guess the truth.

However, Sullivan did not own the Tenderloin, he was only its keeper. The territory actually belonged to Sullivan's elder: the Grandfather of Chinatown, a secretive, Asian vampire who had dwelt in the city since the middle of the last century. Sullivan had once lived with the Grandfather—and the rest of the Family—in the underground warrens of Chinatown, but since taking over the Tenderloin in 1912 he had dwelt apart and alone. He daily turned over the lion's share of the proceeds to the Family, but otherwise operated in a nearly autonomous fashion. Sullivan considered himself lord of his domain.

And Tran's video store was his operating headquarters.

"Hello, boss." Tran grinned when he saw Sullivan come through the door. "How's tricks?"

Tran was a small, brown Vietnamese, owner of a tiny video rental store on O'Farrell Street.

"Same as usual," Sullivan replied, disinterestedly examining the racks of X-rated videos displayed on the walls. "How've we done tonight?"

"A good night for business, boss, for sure." Tran punched keys on the cash register, popping the drawer open. He withdrew a thick roll of bills and handed it over to Sullivan. "More than two grand already."

Sullivan thumbed the money and grunted with satisfaction. He stuffed the wad into his pants pocket.

"You seen Kathy tonight?" he asked, changing the subject.

"Kathy? No, uh-uh. Why? Is she back working for us?"

"She's supposed to be."

"Nope." Tran shook his head. "Haven't seen her."

Sullivan said nothing.

Tran spoke up. "Loo was in here earlier, looking for you," he said.

At the sound of Loo's name, Sullivan perked up. Loo was his "brother."

"Why? Did he say what he wanted?" Sullivan asked. He was close to Loo, but saw him infrequently.

"Uh-uh," Tran answered. "But he told me it was important and to make sure you got the message."

"Okay. Did he say where to meet?"

"He said he'd been hanging out at Lori's."

"Got it," Sullivan said.

Finished, ready to leave, Sullivan delayed, making a pretense of re-counting the money in his pocket. Growing impatient, he finally asked Tran outright,

"Are you hungry or what?"

Tran grinned. "Yes, thank you." He nodded.

As a ghoul, Tran required sustenance from his master, but, to Sullivan's eternal exasperation, was far too polite to ask for himself, forcing Sullivan always to make the offer.

Locking the door and hanging up the "Closed" sign, Tran followed Sullivan into the back room. Seating himself in a chair, Sullivan rolled up his sleeve, exposing his forearm. Tran knelt before him, gently nipping the flesh with his teeth and sucking up the life-giving blood that oozed from the vampire's arm.

Lori's is an ersatz 1950s-style diner on Mason Street near Eddy intended to take advantage of the tourist trade spilling over from nearby Union Square. Open twenty-four hours, late at night Lori's catered to some of the shadier denizens of the Tenderloin. Made of chrome and red Naugahyde, decorated with pictures of James Dean, Marilyn Monroe, and Brando in better years, it was the type of place that would appeal to Loo.

Another servant of the Grandfather, embraced in China several years before Sullivan met up with the Family, Loo had been taken at the young age of eighteen. Loo measured barely five feet tall, and because of a youthful face and unrelenting good humor, most people guessed him to be about fifteen years old. By contrast,

Sullivan stood over six feet tall and looked to be in his early thirties. Together the two made an odd pair.

Both were children of Kwon, the beautiful, green-eyed woman who first took Sullivan years ago on the death ship in the Golden Gate. She had alternately been mother and lover to both men and they had once vied bitterly for her attention. The rivalry lasted until the earthquake of 1906, ending with Kwon's death at the hands of a terror-stricken mob in Chinatown. After her death Sullivan and Loo became friends. With the source of their rivalry gone, all they shared was a common loss.

Standing across the street from the diner, Sullivan looked through the plate glass front windows of Lori's, spotting Loo at a rear booth. A red ball cap turned backward on his head, feet up on the table to display his Nikes, Loo was chiding and kidding with the waitress who, in return, smiled brightly at the flirtation. Always up-to-date, Loo was dressed in the latest "housing project" styles, including the expensive shoes, pants shackled to the hips, and an electronic pager hung from his waist. A couple of decades ago he'd favored polyester leisure suits. Before that it was flowered shirts and love beads, in the fifties a ducktail and leather jacket, and in the thirties and forties the zoot suit.

But Loo's looks were deceiving. Among other responsibilities, he controlled the numerous Asian gangs in Chinatown who did a booming business in drugs, weapons, fireworks, and the protection rackets. These gangs were descendants of the vicious Chinatown tongs of earlier days. Loo had played a large part in consolidating these tongs in the late nineteenth century, leading his own gang in street wars, fighting viciously with knives, revolvers, and hatchets.

Sullivan still dressed as he always had: jeans, boots, and a navy blue wool jacket—the clothes of the common sailor he'd been before becoming a vampire.

Spotting Sullivan coming through the door, Loo smiled and lifted his hand in greeting. Sullivan walked to the rear of the diner and sat down across from him, waving away the waitress, who returned to the table to take his order.

"What's up?" was the first thing Sullivan said.

"The Grandfather has a job for you."

Sullivan's interest grew. He'd not had direct word from the Grandfather in several years.

"What sort of job?" he asked.

Loo leaned forward, lowering his voice and casting glances to either side.

"It's time to take out our rival, Delfonso," he said softly, smiling at Sullivan. He sat back again.

At first surprised, Sullivan decided it was really no surprise at all. The Grandfather and the Spaniard went back to the earliest days of San Francisco. Alternately rivals and partners, the two elder vampires had often been at odds with each other.

"Why now?" he asked.

"The *Java King* fuckup was the last straw," Loo said. "We almost blew our whole arrangement with the Prince. He threatened to cancel our immigration sanction."

The Grandfather and Delfonso had planned an incoming shipment of illegal Asians. Somehow, Delfonso had failed to make proper arrangements for the pickup at sea. The result was an unregistered freighter steaming right through the Golden Gate in the middle of the night and unloading several hundred half-starved immigrants at the Fort Mason docks before turning about and steaming back out to sea. The Coast Guard quickly captured the freighter but not before two or three hundred frightened Chinese were left running pell-mell through the streets of the city.

A major scandal erupted and there were calls from many of the city's elder vampires to put a stop to these shipments. The Vampire Prince of San Francisco, Vannevar Thomas, had remained cool, despite the turmoil.

"Grandfather has convinced the Prince it was Delfonso's fault," Loo said. "Everyone knows how he's been slipping the last few years."

Delfonso was generally believed to be the city's oldest undead resident, having arrived in the area with the first Spanish Mission in 1776. Although believed to be a quite powerful vampire, he had never shown the inclination to rule and had stepped aside when Vannevar Thomas arrived in the city in the mid–nineteenth century.

"So, what am I supposed to do?" Sullivan asked.

"Grandfather and Thomas want you to make like you're interested in joining up with him. Tell Delfonso you want to leave the Family. Remember how he tried to lure you into his service in the thirties? Tell him you've reconsidered his offer."

"Okay. I convince him I've changed my mind. Then what?"

"Try to find out what he's up to. The Prince told the Grandfather that there is evidence the Fort Mason fiasco was planned. Perhaps Delfonso was trying to embarrass someone—us. If you can expose him, political weight will shift against him and then we can safely dispose of him."

"And what's in it for us?"

Loo ignored him long enough to blow a straw wrapper at the young waitress now scurrying by. She dodged the missile, giggling. Loo smiled a toothy grin at her.

"Sorry," he apologized, turning his attention back to Sullivan. "Anyway, with Delfonso out of the way, the Mission District will be unclaimed territory. In return for our aid, the Prince has promised the Grandfather a sub-stantial portion."

A sprawling flatland of blue-collar homes, the Mission these days was populated mainly by Hispanics. Gambling, drugs, and whores would be worth a lot, Sullivan figured. He always felt that Delfonso had failed to exploit the area for what it was really worth.

"Do you think I'll gain an audience with the Grandfather?" Sullivan asked.

He'd never seen the Grandfather, though snatches of memories from that fateful night aboard the death ship often came back to him in dreams. The Grandfather was a terrifying and awesome figure, but one Sullivan longed to meet regardless.

"Who knows?" Loo answered. "Probably, I guess—if you do a good job. But what do I know? I haven't seen him myself since we arrived in this country a century and a half ago. I take all my orders from Chi."

Sullivan thought for a moment.

"How soon should I begin?" he asked.

"Tonight."

Later, at a pay phone, Sullivan dialed the number of Delfonso's home in the Mission District.

"Hello?" asked the voice on the other end of the line.

It was Domingo, Delfonso's childe.

"Yeah, this is Sullivan. I need to talk to your boss."

There was a moment's hesitation, then Domingo answered: "He's still asleep. He didn't wake up tonight. What do you want?"

"Tell him I need to talk to him—about business—private."

"I'll give him the message." Then Domingo hung up.

Sullivan smiled to himself. Domingo was a draft dodger and an old zoot-suiter from World War II days. Up from LA, hiding in San Francisco from the law and the draft board, he fell afoul of Delfonso one night while mugging an old woman. Turned into a vampire, he had served Delfonso ever since.

Sullivan and Domingo had never gotten along. Domingo had only been taken after Sullivan turned Delfonso down, and Sullivan had always been quick to remind Domingo of this fact whenever they met.

Looking forward to seeing his old rival again, Sullivan headed up the hill to his Pine Street haven, a smile on his face.

January 11

In an expensive mansion in Pacific Heights . . .

Honerius sat at the desk in his study, rubbing his temples in exasperation. The man seated across from him continued to argue, despite everything Honerius had told him. Who was this Don Benedict to think he could dispute with Honerius, head of the Tremere clan of vampires in San Francisco and advisor to the Prince?

"I respect your decisions, fully, Honerius," Don Benedict was saying. "I just don't believe it wise to tempt the Prince. We have been planning this for many years. Why risk its success? Why risk the Prince's wrath?"

"The Prince will never know," Honerius insisted. "There are too many variables in situations such as this. I have duly warned the Prince, and he understands that events may occur that were not evident in our forecasts."

Honerius had spent years forecasting the future, interpreting events to come, and relaying his findings to the Prince. Together they had thought and planned, laying clues through the years that they hoped would eventually destroy two of their potentially most dangerous rivals. The final days were approaching. If all went well, the Family would bring about their own downfall.

"But I, like you, have read the signs of the future," Benedict said. "Already the plan to eliminate Delfonso and the Grandfather is too delicate, too finely tuned. Trying to alter that future is difficult enough. To bring a madman like Phillips into the situation . . ."

"The Prince neither knows, nor suspects. Phillips is my and the Tremere's 'wild card,' if you will. With him, we can adjust events so they favor a desirable outcome. Do you really believe that the Prince divulges to me all that he does? Besides," Honerius went on, "with the Grandfather gone, the Dowager may do with Chinatown as she pleases. Would that not suit you?"

Angered, Don Benedict rose from his chair. His preference for Eastern ways and culture—and Eastern magic—was a never-ending source of friction between him and his more tradition-bound leader, Honerius.

"I will not stand for this," Benedict said. "I must go."

"Then go you must," Honerius said, waving him off. "Leave me alone. The plan reaches a critical phase soon. I must watch over it. I wish you well. Have faith in the all-knowing father."

Benedict left the house without another word. As a member of the magic-practicing Tremere clan he was bound by a rigid code requiring strict obedience to his elders. He could neither speak out nor do anything to interfere with Honerius's plans, no matter how much he disagreed. Though Honerius had never said as much, in his heart Benedict knew that the old Tremere elder hoped to topple the Prince and take the throne for himself, an action Benedict feared would tear apart the city's fragile balance of power, plunging it into chaos. He was split in his loyalty to his clan, the city's Prince, and his personal fondness for the old Dowager.

He shook his head, worrying, as he left the house, walking down the front steps to disappear into the foggy, nighted streets.

3

**When you send a clerk on
business to a distant province,
a man of rigid morals is not
your best choice.**

—Ihara Saikaku,
The Japanese Family Storehouse

Sullivan arrived at the appointed meeting place a few minutes early. Union Square had been chosen—Elysium, neutral ground, where neither was at the advantage. Though nearing midnight, the area was still thronged with tourists as well as a few street people drifting up from Hallidie Plaza. Cable cars clanged up and down Powell Street, passing in front of the posh St. Francis Hotel, where Riley, the hotel's smiling black doorman, whistled cabs from the nearby stand.

Sullivan took a seat on a bench overlooking Geary Street where he could watch for Delfonso's limo and prepared himself for the wait. Spreading his arms across the back of the bench, he adopted a casual pose, though admitting to himself that he felt a little nervous. Making a false advance to another elder was a dangerous move. If Delfonso did not fall for the ploy, Sullivan would be in trouble deep in the Mission, Delfonso's turf, and far from his own territory. If Delfonso smelled a rat, Sullivan might find himself at the old vampire's questionable mercy.

Sullivan had known Delfonso for years, almost since the beginning, though the two had moved in different circles. Delfonso had run with the Toreador clan of vampires and had once kept a spacious suite at the Palace Hotel on Market, where he frequently entertained. But since the destruction following the 1906 earthquake, the Spaniard had retired back to the Mission. He was still seen about town—cruising in his battered limousine— but only rarely showing up at the Vampire Club or other nightspots popular with the undead.

Rumors circulated about Delfonso's odd habits and the things that went on beneath his Mission District house. Some spoke of a religious conversion. Vampires being what they are, Sullivan wondered what Delfonso could have done to cause so much gossip.

Looking up Geary Street, Sullivan spotted Delfonso's black limo working its way toward him through the thick traffic—like a shark on the scent of its prey, he thought. Sullivan could see two people in the front seat: Juan, Delfonso's ghoul chauffeur, and the childe Domingo, already scowling at Sullivan from the passenger's seat. The rear windows of the limo were opaque black, making it impossible to see who rode in back.

The limo glided smoothly to the curb, stopping in front of the bench where Sullivan was sitting. The rear door popped open, the dome light coming on to reveal a bloodred velvet interior. Like a long-legged black spider, the Spaniard Delfonso sat within, facing out toward Sullivan. Dressed completely in black, with cape and perfectly trimmed narrow moustache and beard, the old vampire sat with his cold, pale hands folded over an expensive-looking gold-headed walking stick.

"Do come in," Delfonso said.

Sullivan started crawling into the backseat with Delfonso.

"And take care not to snag your trousers on that broken spring," he warned his guest. Then, turning to the driver. "Juan! I thought I told you to fix this."

"Sorry, sir," answered the Filipino at the wheel. "I got busy and forgot. I'll do it tomorrow."

"See that you do."

He turned to Sullivan and smiled. "I guess it's true when they say 'you just can't get good help these days,'" he joked, casting a knowing glance at the front seat.

Sullivan, taking note of the front seat duo's silence, made a point to laugh. Domingo turned and glared at him over the back of the seat.

"So what's the matter, *gringo*?" he queried Sullivan. "Tired of drinking diseased whores? You need to come down to the Mission to find a little fun?" He grinned a nasty grin, revealing his gold tooth.

"I'll drink your fuckin' mother's blood, greaser," Sullivan shot back, the smile never leaving his face.

"Son of a bitch," Domingo swore, starting to crawl over the back of the seat after his tormentor.

"Gentlemen!" Delfonso spoke, his voice ringing through the car's interior. "None of this. Please."

The commotion ceased.

"Mr. Sullivan and I have business to discuss tonight, is that not true, Mr. Sullivan?"

Sullivan nodded agreement.

"He brings us word from the Grandfather, Domingo. We are to lay plans for a new merger of our families."

Delfonso was blowing a smoke screen for Domingo's benefit. He was a sly old dog and had probably already guessed why Sullivan had contacted him. Sullivan went along with the sham.

"It'll mean big things for us," Sullivan told Domingo, seconding Delfonso's lie.

Somewhat appeased, the Mexican grunted assent and turned back around in his seat. Delfonso closed his eyes and shook his head in exasperation.

Juan expertly wheeled the big car through the night traffic, turning south to cross Market and entering, to Sullivan's mind, foreign territory. These flatlands were out of Sullivan's domain, and an area he rarely visited. Though a guest of Delfonso and, therefore, enjoying a certain immunity, he felt insecure this far from his familiar Tenderloin.

Mission Street was crowded and, as they made their

slow way south, Delfonso reminisced about the landmarks they passed, talking of the "old days." Sullivan listened for a while, but it soon became obvious the old
man was getting lost in his memories. At one point
Delfonso stopped speaking in midsentence, staring out
the window for more than a minute before his reverie
was interrupted by something Domingo said to him.

Twenty minutes later they pulled up in front of
Delfonso's home: a low-priced frame row house, similar
to the rest found in the old lower–middle-class neighborhood. Delfonso had suffered severe losses in the
1906 fire and apparently had never recovered. The small
house in the Mission was one of the few properties he
still owned.

Delfonso led the way up the steps toward the iron-
grilled door, Sullivan behind, but when the Spaniard saw
Domingo accompanying them, he waved him off.

"Go on," he told Domingo. "I shan't need you tonight.
Go with Juan."

"But . . ." Domingo pleaded.

"Please, just go, Domingo. Sullivan and I wish to be
alone."

Dejected, the Mexican turned and got back in the
limo. The auto pulled away from the curb.

Shaking his head once again, Delfonso unlocked the
front door. "I swear," he said to Sullivan, showing him
into the house, "I don't know how much longer I'll be
able to put up with that man."

"Domingo's not what you hoped for?" Sullivan asked,
stepping inside.

"No, I'm afraid not. I thought he might turn out better
than he promised, but it wasn't to be. I should have
trusted my first instincts." He winked at Sullivan, closing
the front door behind him.

Sullivan ignored the wink, instead turning his attention to the trophies, souvenirs, and other paraphernalia
crowding Delfonso's small house. He was fascinated by
the collection of Spanish lances, breastplates, and helmets

hung from the walls; the huge antique globe that stood in the corner; and the faded, ancient map of the New World hung on the wall, water-marked and crumbling behind the cracked glass in its frame. Thick dust coated everything, cobwebs festooned every item.

"You like my collection?" Delfonso asked, stepping up closer to Sullivan. "I have trophies dating back centuries, you know."

Sullivan admitted his admiration, pleasing the old Spaniard.

"I know the house is crowded, but it is so much smaller than the Palace suite where I used to live and I just couldn't bring myself to part with anything. Most of these treasures were saved from the fire, you know."

Sullivan had noticed that many were water-marked, even rusted. Books still held faint traces of smoke odor, even after decades.

Sullivan's attention was drawn to a large oil painting hanging on the wall. Delfonso noted his interest.

"You like that one, eh? I did it myself, years ago."

The picture was grotesque, though fascinating: Christ nailed to the cross, his breast torn open and his heart—aflame—suspended in midair in front of him. Sullivan had seen similar pictures, but none quite like this.

"You are Catholic, are you not?" Delfonso asked him.

"Yeah, sure. Born Catholic."

Sullivan's upbringing had involved little religion. The son of a drowned sailor's drunken widow, he'd run away to sea at the age of thirteen. He hadn't been in a church since he was eight, and that was almost two centuries ago.

"Like me, of course," Delfonso added. Then: "Have you thought much about your religion in recent years? I mean, in consideration of what you and I are, what we've become?"

"Not much," Sullivan answered, honestly.

"I have," was the Spaniard's laconic reply. Then he changed the subject.

"So why are you really here, Sullivan?" he asked.

"I think you know."

"Perhaps I do," Delfonso mused, drawing down a dusty rapier from the wall. He balanced it in his hand, then executed a few quick cuts, demonstrating a skill far less rusty than the blade he held.

Sullivan tensed. What if Delfonso had found out about his mission? As powerful as the Spaniard was—and with that sword in his hand—Sullivan stood little chance if Delfonso decided to kill him. And Delfonso *did* seem quite mad.

"I want to join up with you," Sullivan finally blurted out.

Delfonso halted his demonstration of swordsmanship and smiled warmly at his guest.

"So you've finally had enough of the heathen Chinese, eh? I knew you'd come around, sooner or later. Even under the skin, you and I are very much alike, eh?"

Then, setting down the sword, he hugged Sullivan warmly, patting him on the back.

"We must stand together, my friend. Always."

Sullivan hesitantly hugged the Spaniard back.

"Come," said Delfonso, breaking away. "Follow me. I have something to show you."

Delfonso led Sullivan down the hall, where a narrow door opened on a flight of stairs leading to the basement.

"This way, my childe, I want to show you my secret."

As they descended the stairs, the old vampire returned to the subject of religion.

"You know, for many years after my change I wandered alone in the wilderness, not knowing why, or what, I was. I had come to the New World with Cortés, you understand, and helped him wrest the land from the heathen savages. Unfortunately, I fell afoul of their godless practices and because of them became the vampire I am today. For decades I lived in the wilderness, killing and drinking indiscriminately, knowing no better and believing myself cursed by God. My very soul was in peril and I knew it. Then, one night, understanding came to me and I realized what I was and for what purpose God had intended me."

They had now crossed the gloomy basement and stood before a narrow door in the wall. Delfonso fumbled in his pockets for his key ring. Selecting the right key, he turned the lock then turned to Sullivan and said, "You will now learn the location of my secret haven, Sullivan. It should be obvious by now that I trust you implicitly."

Sullivan acknowledged his appreciation.

Beyond the door lay a narrow passage of ancient adobe, revealed in the yellowish light of a naked, overhead light bulb.

"This, my son, leads to my haven, and to the old basement, long forgotten, beneath Mission Dolores. I had the good father Junípero Serra build it at the same time the Mission was constructed in 1776, and I have made good use of it over the years, helping to instruct the Indians in the ways of Christ. Did you know that over five thousand Indians are buried in this immediate area, in graves unmarked and unremembered."

Sullivan felt a shiver as he contemplated the mass of dead that must be surrounding them in this underground place.

On the left they passed an alcove and Sullivan caught sight of an ornate wooden coffin, presumably Delfonso's sleeping place because the extravagance seemed to fit the vampire's style. On the opposite wall hung a small mirror, where the old vampire checked his appearance before going out in the evening. They passed the alcove without slowing, headed for the heavy wooden door that stood at the end of the passage.

The door was fitted with an antique lock. Delfonso placed a large iron key in the slot but stopped before turning it.

"Listen," he said, cocking one ear. "Do you hear them?"

Sullivan listened but heard nothing. He shook his head.

"The voices of the dead—the pagan dead. They're all around us," Delfonso told him. "They want me, you know.

Sometimes when I lie in my coffin asleep I can hear them scratching at the walls, calling to me."

Delfonso's eyes took on a wild look. From fear? Excitement? Sullivan wondered.

"They seek a revenge, but they shall not have me, oh no," Delfonso chuckled, almost to himself. He turned the lock and opened the door.

"Behold," he announced. "My House of Prayer, my House of Pain."

Under feeble yellow light, a scene from the Spanish Inquisition greeted Sullivan's eyes. Shackles and manacles decorated the walls while nearby a strappado apparatus hung from the high ceiling. A smoldering brazier stood near one wall, next to it an array of branding irons and vicious-looking pincers.

The center of the room was dominated by a huge wooden rack. Made of heavy timbers, it was fitted with a spoked wooden wheel that drew taut the cords that lay waiting to be fastened to a victim's wrists and ankles.

Delfonso strode to the center of the room, setting off scuffling noises in the shadowed far end of the chamber that drew Sullivan's attention. There, nearly hidden in darkness, were three barred cells. Sullivan saw movement within them and smelled the odor of humans.

"Come right in, Sullivan," Delfonso commanded him. "I want you to meet Rosalita," he said, fondly stroking the dark-stained timbers of the rack. "She is my baby." He leaned over and gave the infernal machine a chaste kiss.

"Come," he said, taking Sullivan by the hand. "Tonight we shall drink to our new agreement—and confess a sinner as well."

He led Sullivan to the cells where a motley collection of Chinese huddled away from the doors.

"Escaped immigrants from the *Java King*," Delfonso explained, anticipating Sullivan's question. "Domingo and I rounded up nearly a dozen of them for ourselves that night."

Most of the immigrants had been taken into custody by authorities, but it was believed that many more managed to find their way to Chinatown and safety. How many fell prey to vampires, never to be seen again, was anybody's guess. Tales of gorged feasts had circulated for days afterward.

"Pick one out," Delfonso said, gesturing to his terrified prisoners. "A nice juicy one for the two of us."

Sullivan hesitated. He was not averse to killing—he'd certainly done his share—but he preferred to let his victims live, drinking only what he needed to keep himself alive and healthy. Besides, Sullivan knew that too many unexplained victims in a community often portended dire consequences for the resident vampire population. Rules that required discretion were enforced. The Masquerade must be maintained or the humans, discovering vampires in their midst, would turn on them and destroy them.

Scanning the prisoners, Sullivan avoided the younger, more innocent-looking immigrants, finally settling on a middle-aged male. He was an ugly brute and Sullivan judged him a murderer, or at the very least a thief. At any rate, someone more deserving of the fate Delfonso had in store for him than the others.

"That one," he said, pointing at the reprobate sharing the center cell with a young male and female.

"Ah, good," said Delfonso, unlocking the cell door. "Not whom I would have picked, but a good choice all the same."

He picked up an iron bar and went into the cell, trying to separate Sullivan's choice from the other two. The intended victim, wisely judging this his last chance to attempt escape, bolted for the door, ducking under Delfonso's arm. Delfonso spun around and swung the bar down on him, but too hard. The man fell to the stone floor, dead with a broken neck.

"Damn it," Delfonso swore. Then, casting a quick look around the cell, his eyes fell on the young woman. "Come on," he said, smiling. "It is you that shall be saved tonight instead." And then he dragged her from the cell.

With Sullivan's aid, the woman was secured to the

rack, and the spoked wheel turned until the cords drew her body taut.

"So beautiful yet, regretfully, so pagan," Delfonso said, caressing the woman's soft throat with the edge of his fingernail. He looked up at Sullivan.

"Do you mind if I go first?" he asked.

Sullivan politely bowed and Delfonso bent over the bound woman, sinking his fangs into her throat and drinking deeply. Her eyes went wide in panic, then closed as she began to moan, muttering something in Chinese.

Then it was Sullivan's turn. He bent to the woman's throat and lapped the blood welling from the wounds left by Delfonso's teeth. The blood tasted sweet and warm, cleaner and purer than the Tenderloin dregs that provided Sullivan with most of his sustenance. He drank deeply.

Unknown to him, while he drank Delfonso slipped around behind the rack and, taking a firm grip on the spoked wheel, yanked it down with all his might. The woman screamed as the cords tightened and her left arm separated from the shoulder with an audible pop. The blood that flowed into Sullivan's mouth was now charged with the woman's terror and pain and it hit Sullivan like an intoxicant, pouring from her vessels into his being, carrying him away. He could feel her fear, her terror, and he wanted more, drinking deeply as the scream died in her throat. For a moment he felt the desire to suck her dry but then, with an effort of will, stopped himself, pulling away and staggering back a step or two.

"The blood of a sinner confessed is good, eh?" grinned Delfonso, gratified by Sullivan's response.

"I hadn't quite expected it," he mumbled. "It took me by surprise." Sullivan was shocked by his reaction. As much as he sympathized with the victim on the rack, he had been thrilled by the taste of her blood, and wanted more. He remembered some of the stories he'd heard about Delfonso, but recalled nothing that hinted at this.

Sullivan was terrified: terrified by Delfonso and his mad behavior, and terrified by his own positive reaction to it.

"But that is not the best part," Delfonso spoke up, stepping around the rack to stand over his victim, looking at Sullivan from across her. Without ceremony Delfonso ripped open the victim's blouse, exposing her small breasts and smooth belly. "Soon we will be one step closer to God, my friend."

With that, Delfonso leaned over the woman and placed both his hands over her breastbone. Pressing down, he dug his fingers into the flesh as she screamed, twisting helplessly on the rack. Sullivan watched, horrified, as Delfonso dug his fingers deeper into her flesh, working them up and under the bones of the woman's rib cage while the girl wailed in agony. With his hands locked in place, Delfonso strained, pulling until her chest broke open, blood gushing up to splash and spatter Delfonso's elegant black dinner jacket and snow-white shirt. The woman's screams stopped instantly as she expired before them, legs twitching, breast torn open exposing wet, pulsing organs.

Unnoticed by Delfonso, who seemed enraptured by the experience, Sullivan stumbled backward away from the rack and the horror being committed upon it, trying to put distance between himself and the madman now gloating over his prize.

Greedily, Delfonso reached his hands down into the bloody cavity of the woman's body and, grasping her still-beating heart, twisted and pulled until he tore it free, blood spraying from torn arteries as the heart continued to beat.

"The blood of sinners and the food of God!" cackled Delfonso as he raised the pulsing organ over his head. Slowly he squeezed the beating heart, crushing it, milking it of its juices, sending a torrent of blood spattering down over his face and into his upturned open mouth. "The blood of the lamb!" he screamed, as he guzzled the fluids.

Sullivan, appalled by the behavior of the monster he was with, kept stumbling away from the rack until he came up against a wall, tripping over some equipment and nearly falling before regaining his senses.

"Rejoice sinners, for we have come forth to save you," gurgled Delfonso, his ceremony continuing, oblivious to Sullivan's distress, swallowing the blood as fast as he could. Lost in the madness of it all, he didn't see Sullivan flee the room.

Racing up the stairs and through the house, Sullivan burst out the front door and into the fresh air of the night, fleeing the scene as fast as he could.

January 11, later

In a dark, deserted alley in the Mission District . . .

A man on hands and knees groveled before a tall, caped figure standing in front of him. The tall man's form was unnaturally obscured by shadow and he spoke to the cowering figure with a commanding tone.

"You have had contact from Sullivan?" the tall man asked.

"Yes, my Prince," answered Domingo, meekly, fearing to look up.

"And you know the part you are to play?"

"Yes. It is time for the Spaniard to step aside, my Prince."

"You did well sabotaging the Java King shipment. You will, of course, be rewarded for your service."

"Thank you, my lord."

Domingo dared to look up at the man before him, light from a nearby streetlamp glinting off his gold tooth. "You will not regret calling on me. I assure you," he promised the Prince.

"I trust I won't," the man said, vanishing in a swirl of mist.

Domingo got back to his feet, cursing to himself,

dusting the dirt and bits of gravel clinging to the knees of his pants.

"Goddamn *gringos*," he muttered under his breath. "I'll show 'em all." Domingo was already laying plans of his own.

As Domingo left the alley the shadowy figure reemerged from the darkness, chuckling softly to himself before again disappearing, this time for good.

The smallest worm will turn being trodden on.

—William Shakespeare,
King Henry the Sixth

Sullivan ran several blocks before final-
ly slowing his pace to a walk. Terrified by what he'd seen
in the basement at Delfonso's, he had to make a conscious effort to get hold of himself. Although still blocks
from safety in the Tenderloin, he told himself he had
gotten out of the house without being noticed and had
time to gain a large head start. He was safe—at least for
the moment. Getting back home to the Tenderloin was
the next order of business.

The threat of Delfonso's defending his domain was
not Sullivan's only worry. The Mission District was a vast
territory and poachers of all types regularly raided in and
out of the area, despite everything Domingo and
Delfonso did to discourage them. Most of these poachers were individuals, but a few were vampire gangs, motley collections of undead, a good many of them insane,
who lived and hunted together. Sullivan would remain
wary.

The streets at three o'clock in the morning were nearly
deserted. Sullivan kept his eye open for a cab but found

none cruising in the neighborhood this time of night. Walking briskly, Sullivan made his way north, up Mission Street, through the crowded Hispanic neighborhoods and past the light industries once affording some employment but now mostly closed. Following the curve of Mission Street, he turned northeast, walking parallel to Market. A few more blocks and he'd be home free.

Then he realized he was being followed. There was no sound to tip him off, but Sullivan's unnaturally keen senses alerted him to the presence of another vampire. Whoever it was, Sullivan thought, he was surely stalking him.

Sullivan stepped up his pace. At Fifth Street he turned left, heading north again. Then, halfway up the block, while still out of sight of his pursuer, Sullivan quickly ducked into the recessed entrance of a shoe store and waited.

He didn't have to wait long. A few seconds later Domingo appeared, peering around the corner. Having lost sight of his quarry, the thickly built Mexican cautiously crept around the corner, slipping up the block, keeping close to shadows of the buildings. The sharpened wooden stake he carried in his hand told Sullivan he meant business.

Sullivan crouched in the darkness, waiting.

So intent was Domingo on searching ahead of him that he walked past the storefront without giving so much as a glance. Sullivan waited until Domingo passed before stepping out behind him.

Domingo sensed Sullivan and spun around, raising the stake in his hand, but he was too slow. Sullivan caught Domingo's wrist and twisted it backward, trying to force Domingo around. But the wily Mexican stooped and grabbed Sullivan by one leg, throwing both of them off-balance and sending them crashing through the plate glass window of the shoe store display.

Sullivan fell on his back among the shards of broken glass, Domingo struggling on top of him. The two rolled over and over, through the glass and stylish footwear, until both of them were cut and dripping blood. Sullivan was the stronger of the two, and he finally forced Domingo off him, so he fell from the raised display window to the sidewalk.

Hitting the ground, Domingo dropped his stake. Sullivan scrambled off the Mexican and dived for the weapon, getting to his feet just as Domingo sped off, running up Fifth Street in the direction of the old U.S. Mint. Sullivan caught up with him at the intersection and belted Domingo across the kidneys with the wooden stake, knocking him to the ground.

Unable to rise, Domingo began crawling across the street while Sullivan danced around him, swinging the club back and forth like a scythe, beating Domingo bloody, the sharp crack of the club echoing off the buildings and mixing with Domingo's howls of pain.

Domingo tried crawling up the broad steps of the Mint to get away, but Sullivan was relentless, beating him continually over the head and shoulders while his victim, no longer strong enough to howl, merely grunted and moaned.

A powerful blow finally knocked Domingo over, sprawling him on his back across the steps. His face was a ruin of broken, swollen flesh and gore, bone splinters showing through where Sullivan had fractured his skull. Without hesitation Sullivan brought the club straight down on Domingo's forehead, shattering the skull and breaking the wooden stake in half. He threw the useless weapon aside. Domingo groaned in pain, rolling his head back and forth on the blood-spattered steps.

Who had sent him? Sullivan wondered. Delfonso was his first thought, but he rejected it. Domingo had obviously been waiting for him when he left the house, before Delfonso could have contacted him and set him on Sullivan's trail. But something was up—Sullivan smelled a trap.

He wondered why, if the Prince and the Grandfather wanted Delfonso out of the picture, they didn't simply eliminate him. Unless they needed an excuse, he reasoned. Sullivan's death at the hands of Delfonso's henchmen would certainly provide such a reason. For that matter, if Domingo was killed by Sullivan, the result would be much the same. Were they both considered expendable?

The Family had long kept Sullivan at arm's length. He was an outsider among them, living and working apart, only rarely having contact with any of the members. Loo had once told him that the Family only intended to keep Sullivan around long enough to let them get settled in San Francisco, then eradicate him. When the time came, Kwon intervened on Sullivan's behalf and he was spared. His loyalty over the years had proved Sullivan's worth to the Grandfather, but he remained a fringe member, never feeling wholly a part of the Family.

He didn't want to believe the Family would betray him but had to admit it was possible. Certainly he and Domingo were mere pawns in a bigger game.

Reaching down, he grabbed Domingo by the shoulders, lifting his head up.

"Who told you to come after me?" he shouted into his ruined face. "Talk, you bastard! Who was it? Delfonso?"

Domingo mumbled something, blood pouring from his mouth and nose, gurgling and bubbling down the side of his face to drip on the stone. He was nearly unconscious, uncomprehending. The sight of the blood awoke Sullivan's hunger and he remembered the sweet taste of the blood of the suffering Chinese woman. For a moment he was sorely tempted to sink his fangs into his enemy's throat and drink him dry, but the thought of dia-blerie—veritable vampire cannibalism—revolted him and he denied the thirst.

Sullivan admitted some sympathy for his victim, they were much alike, but knew he could not allow him to live; he would come after Sullivan again.

Grimly, he tore Domingo's head from his body, extinguishing his sullen existence. Depositing the vampire's remains behind the shrubbery surrounding the Mint where it would be concealed until it burned away with the rising of the sun, Sullivan resolved to go to

Chinatown and demand an audience with the Grandfather. He was angry and had some questions he felt he wanted answered, and tonight. Leaving the area, he crossed over Market Street and entered safe territory.

It was nearly four in the morning when Sullivan arrived at the formal gate to Chinatown at Grant Street and Bush. He was ready to make his complaint, but when he reached the entrance he found his passage blocked. Loo stood in the entrance, refusing Sullivan entrance.

"Let me pass," Sullivan demanded. "I want to speak with the Grandfather."

"Grandfather will not see you now," Loo said impassively.

"Yes he will, damn it," Sullivan insisted. He made a move to dodge around Loo but the little man was quicker, far quicker. Sidestepping in front of Sullivan, the silvery, cut-down hatchet Loo used as a weapon suddenly appeared in his hand, glinting in the moonlight.

"Don't make me do it, Sullivan. You know I can't let you pass."

Sullivan decided not to push it. He knew he was hardly a match for Loo, despite the difference in their sizes. Long ago, when they were rivals for Kwon's attention, Loo had nearly killed him in a fight, Sullivan only being saved by the timely intervention of Kwon and the ghoul, Chi.

"All right," Sullivan said, stepping back down from the entrance. "But tell him I want to see him tomorrow night." He shook his finger at Loo for emphasis. "You tell him that, ya hear?"

"Yes, Sullivan," Loo answered.

Sullivan turned and strode off, heading west on Bush up Nob Hill.

Now he'd done it, Sullivan chastised himself. He'd wanted to impress the Grandfather but he'd actually blown his mission, panicking and fleeing when the depraved Delfonso went into his act. Now he was demanding explanations. What would the Grandfather's reaction be?

Walking slowly up the hill toward home, he thought of Kathy and remembered that he hadn't seen her again last night. He remembered Terry, and recalled he had his address. There was still time to take care of business before sunup, he decided.

Sullivan began walking faster, then began to trot; soon he was running across the hill, making a beeline for Terry's apartment ten blocks away, his mind set on vengeance. Back firmly in his world, Sullivan was enjoying a restored sense of control.

At the corner of Franklin and Sutter he found the building, a twelve-story affair made of brick. Locating Terry's number on the tenant list by the front door, he punched the numbers into the intercom. There was the sound of a phone ringing, then someone picked up.

"Hello?" said a man's voice, hazy with sleep.

It was Terry.

"Let me in," demanded Sullivan.

"Who the fuck is this?" asked the scratchy intercom voice.

"Sullivan. We got business."

"What business?" the voice asked. "Look motherfucker, I don't do no *fucking* business at four o'clock in the fuckin' morning, see. Go the fuck away."

There was the sound of a receiver being hung up and then the intercom went dead.

"Son of a bitch," Sullivan muttered to himself.

Racing down off the porch and around the side of the building, he found the fire escape. Though the bottom balcony was a good twelve feet off the ground, it was little obstacle to Sullivan. A running leap put his hands on the lower platform and from there he easily swung himself up and over the edge. Soon he was pounding up the flights, oblivious of the noise created outside the bedroom windows of the building's sleeping tenants.

He stopped at the fifth balcony—Terry's floor—and peered through the window. The pimp was in bed, asleep, a woman lying beside him. Sullivan threw himself at the window, bursting through the glass, sending fragments flying across the room as he crashed his way in.

Terry was instantly awake and scrambling to his feet.

"What the fuck's going on?" he demanded, coming up and off the bed. He came at Sullivan with his fists, his skinny body decorated with tattoos, his lank, greasy hair half covering his ugly face, his flaccid penis flopping ridiculously between his legs.

"Fuck you," Sullivan said.

He snatched Terry by the back of his neck and swung him around, smashing his face into the doorframe. Wood splintered and Terry sagged to the floor. Sullivan rolled him over with his boot, thinking the man's blood might be fit to drink but, spying the needle tracks in Terry's arms, thought better of it. He kicked Terry under the chin, breaking his neck and ensuring his death.

Then Sullivan turned to the sobbing woman huddling under the bedclothes; he could not afford to leave a witness. Tearing the sheets back he saw a blonde, naked but for her panties, cowering, with her face buried in a pillow. Sullivan grabbed her by the hair and pulled her head back, trying get a look at her face.

It was Kathy.

"Don't kill me, Sullivan," she pleaded. "Please don't. I won't say anything."

Oh, fuck, Sullivan said to himself, letting her go.

There was no way he could do it. He couldn't bring himself to kill Kathy now, not after all this. Right now she reminded him far too much of the Chinese immigrant dying on Delfonso's rack. His mind raced, thinking back. Kathy hadn't *really* seen anything, he decided—nothing that would compromise his life as a vampire, anyway.

He tossed the sheets back to her.

"Okay," he said. "But keep your mouth shut. Tell the cops whatever you want, just leave me out of it, all right?"

"Sure, Sullivan."

Sullivan had the pimp's wallet, taking it from the pair of pants hung sloppily over the chair. Sullivan counted out over six hundred dollars, then stuck it in his pocket. Police sirens were now sounding in the distance. People had obviously heard the commotion and called the cops.

"I've got to get out of here," Sullivan told Kathy.

But then, thinking a minute, reached back in his pocket for Terry's money.

"Here," he said, counting off a couple hundred bucks. "Here's the money I took from you the other night." He tossed it on the bed. "Now we're even."

He wasn't sure why he'd done it.

"Okay," Kathy said. "Thanks."

"See Tran and get yourself set up. I want to see you on the streets tomorrow night."

Then Sullivan was out the shattered window and flying silently down the fire escape. A few minutes later he was in his room atop the Drake Inn on Pine Street, behind boarded windows, resting peacefully on the narrow pallet that served as his bed.

January 12

Somewhere in the Nevada desert, east of Reno . . .

An old red Dodge raced across the highway, eating up the miles, headed for the coast. The man behind the wheel reached across the seat and pulled another beer out of the cooler. He expertly popped off the cap while holding the steering wheel steady with his knees. One hand back on the wheel, he tilted his head back and took a long swallow, feeling the cold brew pouring down his throat. Reaching for the dashboard, he turned up the country music station he listened to.

The man's name was Phillips. His face was pockmarked, his long, hooked nose his most prominent feature. His eyes intent on the road before him, he set his sights west.

He had been told to come here, ordered by the voice

in his head. He was on a mission to destroy evil in this world: the evil that had destroyed his family and his life; the evil that he had committed himself to eradicating. He had already destroyed many monsters in various places around the country but now God had intervened and was directing him—telling him where to find his prey and which of them he should destroy first.

He noted that this was his last cold beer. He had more, but they were warm ones in a backseat already half-filled with boxes of Bible tracts, holy wafers, fresh garlic, and a pile of sharpened wooden stakes.

He was heading for San Francisco, following the voice.

To pull the chestnuts out of the fire with the cat's paw.

—Molière, *L'Étourdi*

Sullivan awoke the next evening just after sunset. Even as he sat up he was already remembering the events from the night before: the horrifying scene in Delfonso's torture chamber, the death of Domingo, and his foolish demands at the entrance to Chinatown.

He had been driven by the heat of passion: the excitement and death—and the blood of Delfonso's tortured victim. Appeased by the murder of Terry, Sullivan now felt repentant. What would the Grandfather have to say? He had failed his mission.

Getting up from his thin mattress, he spent a moment in front of the mirror straightening his short red hair before heading downstairs to the Inn's front desk. Sullivan's haven was in a cramped, fourth-floor garret of the old building. Formerly apartments, then a brothel, it was now as upscale as the rest of the neighborhood and converted to an expensive tourist inn. Passing a vacationing couple on the way down, he noted their look of consternation at his appearance. The

Drake charged over $200 a night and Sullivan by no means appeared in that income category. Little did the couple realize that until a few years ago this stretch of Pine Street had been a major part of the red-light district. It had been more lucrative then, before the Prince pushed the business back down the hill with increased police harassment. The Prince favored the income from tourist dollars over the local trade, much to Sullivan's displeasure.

Sullivan found the inn's smiling night clerk, Chad, at the front desk. A ghoul offspring of Loo's, Chad was a blond, smiling Anglo, perfect for the job he held.

"Good evening." He smiled when he saw Sullivan. "I got a message here for you," he said, turning to the mail slots behind the desk. "It's from Loo."

He handed Sullivan an envelope made of blue rice paper.

"Thanks."

He tore open the seal and pulled out the note inside. It read:

> *The Grandfather requests your presence this evening at*
> 10:00 PM.
> *Loo*

At the bottom he'd added a less formal postscript:

> *Be there, or be square!*
> L.

Sullivan smiled at Loo's P.S. but his thoughts clouded, imagining a meeting with the Grandfather. For years he had hoped for the opportunity of a face-to-face meeting with his elder but he had also imagined better circumstances. Sullivan had bungled his assignment, then had the temerity to complain about it. Would the Grandfather be angry?

Outside, he headed downhill into the Tenderloin. Before the meeting he would check his territory and let Tran know he would be off the rest of the evening. At the shop, Sullivan was gratified to hear that Kathy was out working the streets tonight.

Then, down on Golden Gate Avenue, he collected his
share of the crack dealers' income, taking a few minutes
to put the fear of God into a newcomer who thought he
could work the territory for free. A quick sweep back
east, up O'Farrell, and Sullivan was satisfied the neighborhood was in good enough shape to be left alone for
the night. He headed for Chinatown.

Chinatown at nine-thirty in the evening is a busy place,
crowded with tourists, diners, and late-night shoppers.
Chinese-lettered street signs are lit by Chinese-style street-
lamps. Gaudy neon signs advertise souvenir, jewelry, and
jade shops, while the many restaurants do a booming
business till midnight. Single-lane Grant Street is perpetually clogged with traffic inching along as people crossing
from one side of the street to the other dodge between
creeping cars. Asian youths—members of Chinatown's various tong-descended gangs, looking deceptively young and
innocent—hang out on street corners, though the unaware
tourist has little to fear. Prince Vannevar Thomas has forbidden the gangs, as well as other vampires, from doing
anything that would harm the city's lucrative tourist trade.

Loo was waiting at the front gate to Chinatown when
Sullivan arrived. Stopping at the entrance, Sullivan made
a perfunctory bow. Loo returned the bow, tourists walking past them oblivious to the ritual being carried out.
Loo then spoke: "Your purpose here, O brother?"

"I have come to see the Grandfather, brother, at his
request."

"Then enter, childe of the Family."

Sullivan stepped across the invisible threshold.

"Glad you could make it, brother," said Loo, clapping
Sullivan on the back. "You looking forward to it?"

"Yeah," Sullivan answered, smiling, but he felt nervous now. So many years he'd waited for this moment
and now that it was finally happening he had no idea
what to expect, although he noted Loo seemed to have
no qualms about the impending meeting. He expected
that, like himself, Loo was looking forward to meeting
the Grandfather tonight.

Sullivan knew the Grandfather was ancient, and reputedly very powerful. How powerful, Sullivan was not sure. He and Loo, in earlier days, when they were younger, had argued about it often. Loo had insisted that the Grandfather was actually more powerful than Vannevar Thomas, but allowed the latter to rule in his stead because he liked it better that way. Sullivan never believed this, hardly able to imagine a vampire more powerful than the Prince. And if the Grandfather *was* that powerful, Sullivan reasoned, why did he spend his existence living in a hole in the ground?

"So how're things going in Chinatown," Sullivan asked, noticing Loo make a subtle sign to a lounging youth who, upon seeing the signal, scurried off on some unknown errand.

"Not bad," he said. "Things have quieted down again since the flare-up over the Dowager's coffin."

A jade coffin ordered into the country by the old Nosferatu woman had contained an unexpected stowaway. A Tremere wizard, Don Benedict, had finally located the thing lurking somewhere under the ground in Chinatown and dispatched it.

"So the Dowager's still on good terms with Vannevar?" Sullivan asked.

"As good as ever, I'm afraid."

The Family cared little for the Dowager. She had installed herself in Chinatown—with Vannevar's blessing, it was said—following the 1906 earthquake. Since then she had functioned as the nominal head of the territory, though few doubted the power and influence of the Grandfather. The Grandfather had not objected to the Dowager's presence and in return had received several lucrative compensations from the Prince. Technically, Sullivan owed the Dowager his allegiance, but in actuality rarely saw her. It had been at least twenty years since he'd had audience with her, and regardless of her presence, Sullivan had always taken all his orders from the Grandfather and the Family. He was ever loyal.

"Too bad," Sullivan said, idly wishing the Dowager would somehow disappear.

Loo led Sullivan around a corner and into an alley. Waiting for them in the shadows was a tall, gaunt Chinese: a cadaverous-looking ghoul named Chi, dressed in a badly fitting brown suit.

"Welcome, Sullivan," Chi said in his hollow voice.

Chi still looked exactly the same as when Sullivan had first seen him aboard the death ship so many years ago. Sallow of complexion, skin like leather stretched over the bones of his face, he stood at least three inches taller than Sullivan but was skeleton-thin, hardly more than half Sullivan's weight. Though he fed directly from the blood of the Grandfather, he never seemed to gain an ounce.

"Hi, Chi," Sullivan responded, happy to see the old ghoul again. Chi, along with Kwon, had spent many hours helping Sullivan adjust to his new life after he'd been embraced, teaching him the ways of vampires as well as the ways of the Family.

"You are prepared to meet the Grandfather, I trust?" Chi asked.

Sullivan nodded assent.

"Then may the spirits be with you. Lucky is the man who has a Grandfather."

"Lucky is the man," responded Sullivan and Loo, in unison.

"Follow me," Chi smiled. Turning on his heel, he headed down the alley. Sullivan and Loo tagged along behind.

At a T-intersection they turned left and followed Chi through the rear entrance of a fresh seafood shop, whose front entrance was on a main street. A Chinese man stood near the door, chopping huge fish with a cleaver. He nodded at Chi when he saw the group enter, never missing a stroke. Chi led Loo and Sullivan down a flight of narrow wooden stairs into the building's basement, then through a concrete tunnel to the inner chambers of the Grandfather.

Sullivan had never been there before. He had shared apartments with the Family years ago, before the Great Earthquake and Fire, but since then had dwelt alone on the slope of Lower Nob Hill. The air was fetid, humid, thick with the odor of burning incense—a scent that did little to mask the odor of foul decay that seemed everywhere, hanging in the air, permeating the walls.

"Pretty creepy, eh," Loo nudged Sullivan, whispering.

Sullivan grunted an affirmative. Apparently Loo had not been there before either. If Chi heard them talking, he made no sign.

"Wait here," Chi told them after they'd reached a small chamber. "I will call for you." Parting a hanging silk tapestry, he exited the room through a low-arched opening. For a second Sullivan caught a glimpse of light and movement beyond the curtain.

Loo pulled up a chair and sat down, but Sullivan stayed on his feet, examining some of the objects in the room: the jade statuettes and intricately carved ivories that decorated the many tabletops and shelves.

The tapestry parted again and Chi appeared, standing in the opening. He had changed clothes and was now dressed in the red silk robes Sullivan had seen him wearing aboard the death ship.

"The Grandfather will see you now."

He stepped aside and motioned the pair in. Loo went first, Sullivan behind. The short passage opened into another chamber, larger than the first. Lit by dim red light from paper lanterns, the air here was thicker, even more humid and, despite the nearly overwhelming perfume of incense, reeking with the ever-present smell of death and decay. Against the far wall, propped on a mass of cushions, sat the Grandfather.

"Welcome, my sons," he said.

The voice was deep, accompanied by a fluttering, rattling sound that seemed to come from the Grandfather's chest. His face was hidden from view, covered by a grotesquely carved wooden devil mask lacquered black and red. The voluminous robes of red and gold worn by the Grandfather concealed his form. He kept his arms folded across his chest, hands hidden within his sleeves.

"Good evening, Grandfather. Health to you," Sullivan and Loo responded.

"Please be seated," the Grandfather said, his words again accompanied by the odd fluttering sound from his chest. He shifted his bulk, and Sullivan noted how huge the Grandfather was—the size of two or three normal men, he guessed, though the red-and-gold robes hid him well.

Chi took up a position standing next to the Grandfather. For the first time Sullivan noticed that David was in the room as well. A locally born Chinese turned ghoul just a few years ago, David stood behind the Grandfather and to the right, waiting as if in attendance.

"I know you are anxious to learn why I've called you here," the Grandfather began.

"What happened last night with Delfonso, Sullivan?" he asked, turning his head so the hideous mask faced Sullivan.

Nervously, Sullivan explained as best he could the events of the night before: his meeting with Delfonso, the old vampire's overtures to Sullivan, and the depravity he'd witnessed in the Spaniard's basement torture chamber. He also told of how he'd been followed by Domingo, and how he'd slain the vampire on the steps of the old Mint building. He tried hard to leave nothing out. When he was finished, he anxiously awaited the elder's response.

"You have done well, my son," the Grandfather said.

Sullivan allowed himself a sigh of relief.

"And it seems that all we've had heard about our old friend is unfortunately true. He is apparently quite deranged, I'm afraid."

Sullivan, remembering again the previous evening's events, felt renewed revulsion for the lecherous old vampire.

"He is a dangerous man," Sullivan said. "And sick."

"Prince Vannevar agrees," said Grandfather. "As do I. But I'm afraid that Delfonso has brought charges against you in the death of his childe."

Sullivan was shocked to hear the news. He hadn't anticipated this.

"But Domingo attacked me," he protested.

"Nonetheless, you have slain Kindred in a territory outside your own. Delfonso claims he knew nothing of your presence in the Mission last night and says that Domingo was doing nothing more than enforcing their rights to territory."

"He lies, Grandfather! You know that!"

The penalty for such a transgression was sometimes death.

"Silence," commanded the Grandfather, softly. "Prince Vannevar knows the truth, and is on our side. But there are others who, by supporting Delfonso's claim, would seek to weaken both the Prince and our Family by eliminating you. We, however, shall strike first."

Sullivan shot a glance at Loo.

"Do not fear, we have the full backing of the Prince, albeit in secret only, but we must eliminate the threat Delfonso poses once and for all."

The Grandfather paused to catch his breath, the rattling sounds from beneath his robes clearly audible in the intervening silence. Sullivan and Loo waited patiently for the elder to speak.

"My sons," the Grandfather said, leaning his huge bulk forward slightly, "I want you to kill Delfonso. Eliminate him once and for all."

Sullivan heard the words and, as startling as they were, they didn't immediately sink in. Instead, his thoughts were distracted by something else. Seeing movement behind the eyes of the mask, Sullivan tried to catch a glimpse of what he assumed was the Grandfather's eye. He was horrified when the movement turned out to be a fat, white, maggot, which wriggled blindly out of the eyehole and fell into the Grandfather's lap. Upon seeing this, Chi nodded to David who, stepping forward, whisked the vermin away with a small napkin of white silk.

All the while the Grandfather continued speaking as though nothing had happened.

"He is old and a threat to the well-being of all of us. He must be destroyed. I want you to bring me Delfonso's head!"

The words now took on meaning. Kill Delfonso? Sullivan wondered how. He noticed Loo making a formal answer. Sullivan missed the cue but managed to make the ritual humble bow that followed the statement.

"But it must be done soon," the Grandfather said. "Tomorrow night."

Sullivan and Loo bowed again.

"Now go," the Grandfather said. "And know you have the blessings of the Prince, as well as those of myself."

Without further ceremony the pair were shown out of the chamber. Chi escorted them back to the streets.

Back on Grant Street they walked up toward California and entered the Far East restaurant. Sequestered in a private, closed booth, the two spent the rest of the night laying plans for the assassination of their rival, Delfonso. Although they talked at great length, neither mentioned the maggot they both had seen crawl out of the Grandfather's mask.

January 13

In the Pinecrest Diner
on Mason Street in
San Francisco . . .

The man with the pockmarked face sitting in the rear booth took a napkin from the dispenser and wiped the traces of lemon meringue pie from his mouth. Sipping at his coffee, he watched the blond-haired whore sitting across the table from him and pondered his good luck.

First, he'd arrived in Oakland and, knowing no one, followed the voice until he found the Reverend Hayes, a Kindred soul to Phillips—under the skin, anyway.

Then, needing some diversion, he'd cruised into the city in search of a little relief; it had been a long drive from Texas. In town, what kind of whore does he run into? Why, one who knows something about the people he's after. Phillips rarely found he had much use for the whores he met—after he'd finished with them. They were all hopeless sinners in Phillips's book, doomed to eternal damnation, but this one was different. She had information he could use.

"So you say this Sullivan character never comes out in the daytime," he quizzed the whore.

"I've never seen him during the day," the blond-haired woman answered. "I can't think of anyone who has."

Kathy's pie was long gone. The waitress stopped by to refill their cups.

"Anything else," the waitress queried.

"No, but thanks, ma'am," Phillips said.

He watched the whore adding sugar to her coffee, tasting it, adding a little more. What did she say her name was? Katy? Kathy? What's the difference, he told himself. They were all the same.

"And you don't know where he lives?" he asked her.

"I told you," she said, "somewhere up on Pine Street, no one knows exactly where."

"Look," he said, taking out a ballpoint pen, "I'm going to give you a phone number," scribbling an East Bay number on a clean napkin and handing it to her. "If somethin' comes up—anything like I talked to you about—call me here. I'm right over the bridge in Oakland. I can help."

The whore looked at the napkin quizzically, then stuffed it in her purse.

"Thanks," she said, wondering to herself what kind of nut she'd picked up this time. Oh well, San Francisco was full of them, she decided. With more moving in every day.

The odd man said good-bye, and, after paying the cashier, left the diner.

What a nut, Kathy thought to herself, watching him walk down the street.

Man is neither angel nor beast; and the misfortune is that he who would act the angel acts the beast.

—Blaise Pascal, *Pensées*

      The next night found Kathy and Sullivan waiting at the corner of Geary and Jones streets. Sullivan watched anxiously down the street for the approach of the black limo while Kathy shivered in the foggy air, clad only in hot pants and a nearly sheer blouse under a light jacket.

"Jesus," she chattered through her teeth. "Where is this guy?"

"Don't worry," Sullivan assured her. "He'll be here."

"So what's his story, anyway? Tran said he was a 'special.'"

"The old guy's a bondage freak. Nothin' much, but I thought I'd better go along, just in case," he lied.

Kathy was impressed by Sullivan's concern. She'd never known him to take much interest in any of his girls, generally leaving them to their own devices. That was nice, but damn, she told herself, she was really getting cold.

Sullivan paid her no attention; he was intent on the traffic, watching for Delfonso, afraid that at the last minute the crafty old bastard would smell a trap and bolt.

Then he spotted it: Delfonso's black limo. He had apparently taken the bait.

Sullivan had contacted the old vampire, apologizing for running out on him. He tried to explain the death of Domingo but the Spaniard was surprisingly agreeable, refusing to listen to Sullivan's apology and pointing out that Domingo had acted on his own, hinting that the troublesome childe deserved the end he finally met. The complaint to the Prince was a formality, he explained to Sullivan, done merely to protect his interests and easily withdrawn. Delfonso had been more than happy to meet with Sullivan again tonight, and Sullivan promised to bring along a special treat with which to seal their agreement.

"Kathy," he said, getting her attention, "get ready. Here they come."

The limo pulled smoothly to the curb and the back door opened, revealing the bloodred velvet interior and the waiting Delfonso, dressed in his usual formal black attire.

"Hi!" piped Kathy, bouncing into the backseat and quickly snuggling up against her customer for the evening. Quietly, Sullivan climbed in after her.

Conversation while the quartet drove back down to the Mission was sparse. Kathy's constant probings and ticklings kept Delfonso's attention firmly on her while Sullivan gazed out the window, losing himself in his thoughts.

Everything they planned depended on Loo's successfully gaining entry to Delfonso's house while the old man was out. Loo was a master of locks and Sullivan knew of none that could stop him, but if for some reason he failed to get into the basement chamber, the planned ambush would not come off. Sullivan might find himself trapped with the insane Delfonso, perhaps even forced to torture and kill Kathy in the manner he'd witnessed the night before. Though he kept telling himself that Kathy was just another whore, he was not sure he could face an evening like that. He kept thinking of the Chinese girl who died on the rack and for a moment he saw Kathy on the rack. Feeling the unholy lust rising in him again, he quickly blotted the image from his mind.

He looked over at the revolting old lecher sitting across from him, watched him fondling Kathy's exposed breast, and felt disgusted by his presence. It was all he could do to keep a pleasant smile on his face.

Juan dropped them off in front of the house and they went inside. Kathy asked for the bathroom, giving Sullivan and Delfonso some time alone. They waited till she was out of earshot, Delfonso watching her closely as she sashayed down the hall, admiring her figure.

"She's a very nice choice," he said, after Kathy had closed herself in the bathroom. "And very full of sin, too," he smiled.

Sullivan forced a grin to his lips then began apologizing again.

"I'm sorry about the other night," he said. "I don't know what came over me."

"Tut, tut," Delfonso cut him off. "It is nothing to be concerned with. For our kind the true road back to God is fraught with hazards and terror. My first experience with drinking the blood of the lamb was similar to yours, but I learned. You will grow used to it, I'm sure, and like me, come to enjoy it."

Kathy reappeared and Delfonso complimented her lavishly. He then showed the two of them the way to the basement stairs, leading the way down with Kathy following close behind him and Sullivan bringing up the rear. Crossing the basement, they entered the adobe passage that led to Delfonso's haven and the torture chamber. Here Sullivan tried to squeeze ahead of Kathy, hoping to get into position to ambush the vampire, but, knowing no better, she managed to slip around back in front of him, interposing herself between Sullivan and his intended target. Grabbing Delfonso by the hips she executed a little rhumba step as they walked the length of the passage heading toward the big heavy door.

If all went as planned, Loo was waiting in the torture

chamber, behind the locked door. Sullivan and Loo wanted to hit Delfonso at the same moment, but Kathy and her foolishness had gotten in the way.

With Kathy still clinging to him, Delfonso unlocked the door and had it open before Sullivan could figure a way to get himself into position—Kathy continued innocently to thwart him. He wanted to take Delfonso from behind, holding him helpless for a moment while Loo rushed in and staked him.

As Delfonso stepped through the door into the torture chamber he caught sight of Sullivan trying to push his way forward. Immediately suspicious, he turned and spotted Loo rushing toward him, at the same instant realizing he was the victim of a trap.

With a roar, Delfonso swept Loo aside with his arm, knocking him against the back wall and sending the stake skittering across the floor. He turned back to face Sullivan but the Irishman was already charging him, bowling Kathy over in the process, slamming into Delfonso with such force that they were both sent crashing into the wall behind them.

Delfonso recovered first and, with surprisingly superior strength, threw Sullivan hard to the floor. Leaping atop him, Delfonso bared his fangs, a deep hiss pouring from him as he prepared to tear out Sullivan's throat. But Loo, back on his feet, drew his axe and sent it spinning across the room, burying it in Delfonso's shoulder blade.

The wound gushed blood. Howling, Delfonso grabbed at the axe, letting go of Sullivan long enough that he could scramble away and get back to his feet.

Kathy was screaming now, horrified by the bloodshed and the three snarling vampires facing off against one another in a battle to the death.

Delfonso swung about and, snatching a smoldering iron from the brazier, brandished it like a duelist, the glowing red tip making little arcs and circles in the dim, shadowy light.

"So," Delfonso said fiendishly, slowly approaching Sullivan and Loo, who were now backing off. "You and your Asian friends would deceive me, eh?"

Kathy screamed again, aghast at Delfonso's face, now twisted by hate and rage into a mask of monstrous evil.

Sullivan, finally noticing her, shouted, "Get out of here! Go on."

Kathy hesitated a minute then was on her feet and out the door. Sullivan heard her footsteps pounding up the passage.

"I hope you don't think she's going for help?" Delfonso asked, leering at Sullivan.

"Hardly," he answered. "But there's no reason she should die."

"I suppose there'll be plenty of time to take care of her later—after I've finished with you two," Delfonso snickered, advancing again.

The Spaniard made a quick lunge at Sullivan; the Irishman jumped back, narrowly missing being singed by the brand. Loo, meanwhile, had worked his way around the other side of the rack and managed to retrieve his axe.

"I'm afraid that won't do you any good, little man," Delfonso sneered, turning the glowing brand on Loo. He made a deadly thrust at Loo, who was barely quick enough to parry the blow with the axe and jump aside.

"More skillful than I thought," Delfonso said, admiringly. "But not enough, I'm afraid."

With Delfonso distracted by Loo, Sullivan took the opportunity to stoop down and retrieve the fallen wooden stake. Delfonso caught the motion and turned back on him.

"So you think you want to fight, eh?" he screamed, then flew at Sullivan, the smoking iron flashing through the air in a myriad of cuts and flashing strokes. With deft flicks of his wrist he beat Sullivan about the head and shoulders, burning his skin, hair, and clothing. Sullivan, incapable of defending himself against the onslaught, could do little more than try to protect his face and head as Delfonso flailed away. Then, suddenly going to point, he lunged and ran Sullivan through with the hot brand, piercing his side, filling the room with the smell of burning flesh.

Sullivan yelled in pain and clutched at the hot iron, trying to yank it free, but Delfonso was too strong and he continued his thrust, forcing Sullivan back against the wall, twisting the seething iron in the smoking wound.

"You'll die soon, Sullivan. Then you'll answer for your sins," he cried. "Prepare to meet Rosalita, traitor."

Intent on his victim's suffering, he failed to see Loo flash in behind him. With a swift stroke Loo chopped into Delfonso's leg, hamstringing the vampire before jumping back out of the way. Taken by surprise, Delfonso screamed as he fell over backward, his leg giving out beneath him.

Sullivan saw his chance and, yanking out the glowing brand and tossing it aside, he leaped on Delfonso and, with all his strength, impaled him with the wooden stake, driving it through Delfonso's body with so much force that it emerged from the vampire's back and splintered on the stone floor beneath. Delfonso kicked once, spit out a great volume of blackish blood, then lay still.

Twenty minutes later, with Delfonso securely lashed to the rack with chains and cables, Sullivan pulled the stake back out.

"What are you doing?" were the first words out of Delfonso's mouth.

"Just a little payback," Sullivan answered, tightening the last of the cables on the machine. "Then we're gonna kill ya."

Delfonso fell quiet a moment, then, modifying his tone, said, "Sullivan, certainly you can't be serious." He raised his eyebrows as though he were the victim of some practical joke.

"As serious as I can be," answered Sullivan, refusing to look at him.

Stepping behind the infernal machine, Sullivan gave the spoked wheel a powerful yank. Delfonso screamed aloud as the cables jerked tight and the vampire's body was stretched beyond normal limits.

"A little taste of your own medicine will be good for your soul," Sullivan told him.

He kicked open the toolbox he'd dragged in from the basement and selected a long black crowbar.

"This should do the trick," he said, turning back to the helpless Delfonso. "Prepare to meet your maker, sinner."

With that, he drove the broad tip of the crowbar deep into the vampire's side and began to probe around. Securing it under the edge of a rib, Sullivan began to rock and pry the bar, cracking the bone, slowly separating it from Delfonso's spine, and finally tearing it free with his hand while the torture chamber rang with Delfonso's screams.

Sullivan shook the dripping rib bone in Delfonso's face.

"How do you like it, asshole?" he screamed at his captive, then flung the bloody rib aside before beginning again. Delfonso screamed anew with each fresh assault Sullivan perpetrated on his flesh.

Meanwhile, Loo stood aside, watching in fascination as Sullivan went about his work. Delfonso's mind soon broke and he began to babble, reliving his past, once again dying at the hands of the angered Aztec priests who thought they would continue their line by sacrificing one of the white men to their own bloody god. Like his victims, Delfonso had suffered the agony of having his living heart torn from his body; but unlike his victims, Delfonso had been restored to life, cursed to existence as an undying vampire.

Two hours later the pitiful vampire still lay on the rack, a broken, bubbling mass of ripped flesh, exposed muscle and bone, his limbs shattered by mallet blows and his mind destroyed by pain. Too ruined to cry out or make any noise at all, the thing was silent except for the constant flopping of limbs, the occasional creaking of the rack, and the sound of blood dripping steadily to the floor. Loo, having long since grown bored, perhaps even a little disgusted, sat on the toolbox, waiting.

"You better finish up," he said, looking at his watch. "It's nearly dawn."

"All right," Sullivan said. "I'll get the head."

Picking up a hacksaw, he grabbed the still living Delfonso by his bloodied hair. Pulling his head back, Sullivan looked into his eyes and placed the blade on the vampire's throat.

"I guess this is it," he said. "I hope you've confessed."

Delfonso, unable to utter a sound, quivered in fear, his eyes widening, flickering left and right in sheer terror.

Then Loo's axe flashed down and the head jumped away from the body. The eyes glazed over and Delfonso was at long last dead.

"Enough's enough," Loo said. "Let's get out of here."

Coating the severed portion of the head with a paste intended to retard the decaying process, they prepared to leave. Already Delfonso's centuries-old body was corrupting, the remains left on the rack turning black, festering, putrefying, dripping to the stone floor. The two closed the door on the grotesque scene.

"We'd better call a cab," Loo said as they hurried upstairs.

In the kitchen Sullivan wrapped the vampire's head in plastic, then stuffed it inside a grocery bag while Loo called the cab. With Loo pacing the living room, peeping out the curtains in search of the cab, Sullivan sat quietly in the small kitchen with the head resting in his lap.

When first told to bring back Delfonso's head Sullivan thought the Grandfather only wanted proof the deed was done. Talking to Loo, Sullivan had learned that Chi had methods of divining the future using severed heads. Vampires, because of their sometimes great age, were especially valued, their heads often bringing great prophecies. Loo thought the method was similar to the way heated and cracked tortoiseshells were interpreted, only skulls were used in place of shells, though Loo admitted he'd never seen the actual process. As old as Delfonso was, it was believed his head would be of great value.

"I'll take the head back tonight and leave it with Chi," Loo offered, peeking back into the kitchen.

"Uh-uh," Sullivan answered. "I'll keep it tonight, and tomorrow we'll both give it to the Grandfather."

A bit miffed by Sullivan's blunt refusal, Loo chose to ignore him, turning back to watch for the cab. Sullivan, for his part, wanted to be sure he had a chance to attend the reading.

"Here's the cab," called Loo from the other room. "Let's go."

Outside, the two piled into the backseat and ordered the driver back to the city.

Neither of them noticed the old red Dodge parked down the street, nor they did they see it pull out and follow their cab back to the city. The driver was a man with a pockmarked face and the passenger a blond-haired woman, still terrified by the night's events.

January 14

In the dark streets of Chinatown . . .

Don Benedict hurried along, on his way to see the Dowager on a matter of importance. Arriving at the small, unimpressive entrance to the Six Companies, he was shown up the stairs and into the antechamber of the Dowager.

What was he doing here, he asked himself while waiting for the Dowager to call him. He had a responsibility to his clan, his brother Tremere, and his superior Honerius, but he feared what Honerius was attempting to do. His efforts to usurp the throne from Vannevar could throw the city into chaos, perhaps costing his clan dearly. San Francisco was one of the few stable provinces on the West Coast, much of the rest of California having fallen into the hands of anarchs. Without the strength of a Vannevar Thomas on the throne, San Francisco might fall as Los Angeles had, leaving all the Tremeres' plans in ruin.

A servant appeared, and Don Benedict was shown into the chamber of the Dowager.

She sat before him, resplendent in embroidered silk gown, a fan fluttering in her hand. Once considered one of the most beautiful women in all China, she now suffered the misfortune of being one of the Nosferatu clan, that vampiric bloodline supposedly cursed by Caine himself. The Dowager's skin was a sickly blue color, her head misshapen and covered by warts, her hands overgrown and distended, with large claws.

"Don Benedict," she cooed from behind the fan, "what brings you here this evening?"

"Please excuse my untimely visit," he bowed. "And thank you for agreeing to see me on such short notice."

"There will always be time in my schedule for you," she answered warmly. "Now, what is of such urgency that you come to me so distressed?"

"I bring word of the plot to overthrow the Grandfather," he said, uncharacteristically blunt with the Dowager. The two usually held their conversations in a less direct style the Dowager found more comfortable.

The Dowager had been in on this plot from the beginning, though she saw no reason to enlighten Benedict about this fact.

"I have heard the rumors," she said.

Even now she awaited word from the Prince as to how other vampires were reacting to the news of Delfonso's death, and the progress of the plot to unseat the Grandfather.

"All goes well with the Prince's plans, I hope," she added.

Benedict quickly outlined the plot as he understood it. The head of Delfonso, if used in a divination, might give a false indication, because of the odd nature of Delfonso's Aztec-rooted vampirism. The Prince had long ago been advised of this possibility by his chief bodyguard and private counsel, Hortator, an Aztec vampire himself. It was Hortator who foresaw the possibilities inherent in the situation. Honerius was invited into the plot and made use of his magicks to foresee and alter the future, bringing about the events now taking place. They all knew the Grandfather had a strange fear of his "son" Sullivan, and would jump at any chance to denounce him. Sullivan, however, had never given him just cause. A false prediction naming Sullivan as a potential enemy of the Family was believed to be enough to turn the trick.

"So far," Benedict said, "Delfonso is dead." He consulted his watch. "Or soon will be. Sullivan and Loo should return the head to the Grandfather and then the reading will be made."

"I see," the crafty Dowager said, never letting on that she already knew this, and much more. "But I'm afraid I'm unconvinced of its viability," she said. "The old ghoul, Chi, will no doubt aid in the reading and he is not one to be fooled easily. My homeland is a place of countless mysteries, many unknown even to me."

"Vannevar and Honerius are convinced that the Grandfather still looks for an excuse to eliminate Sullivan," Benedict said. "Once the prophecy is made . . ."

"I know, I know," she interrupted. "The self-fulfilling prophecy. Their actions will force Sullivan to become exactly what they fear, thereby fulfilling their own prophecy and bringing about their own demise." The Dowager sighed. She was already well aware that most of life was little more than that. "But there are too many variables."

Don Benedict said nothing, trying to decide whether or not to reveal all he had learned. The Dowager noted the look of indecision on his face.

"There is more?" she asked.

"Yes," he began. "Honerius has brought another to town—a madman, a vampire-slayer, bent on destroying our kind. By himself he offers little threat but . . ."

"You fear he will upset all these plans," she finished the sentence for him.

Don Benedict nodded agreement.

"It is noted," she said.

Benedict thanked her for her patience and left the room. Soon he was back in the streets, wondering if he had betrayed his clan or not.

Back in the Dowager's chamber, the hideous Nosferatu pondered the secret Benedict had revealed to her. She had spent many years in pursuit of her goal and she would not lose control now.

Any plans that have taken years to lay and decades to fruit must be tended carefully, she said to herself. *And I, for one, am a worthy gardener. Have no fear, Don Benedict. Things shall be taken care of.*

7

No young man ever thinks he shall die.

—William Hazlitt,
Table Talk: "On the Fear of Death"

Sullivan awoke the next evening in a chipper mood. Looking forward to presenting his trophy to the Grandfather, he hummed to himself as he put on his coat. Then, stooping over, he opened the dresser drawer where he had placed the head the previous night.

The drawer was empty.

A dark stain—still sticky—marked where the wrapped head had lain, but of the head itself there wasn't a trace. He sniffed the air, noting traces of lingering human scent. Someone had entered his haven while he'd slept and stolen Delfonso's head. The scent bore perfume and Kathy was the first person he thought of.

Racing downstairs, he accosted Chad at the front desk, taking the young man by the wrist.

"Who was up in my room today?" he demanded of the clerk.

"No one, Mr. Sullivan. Honest." Chad was shaking, frightened; he saw the anger in Sullivan's eyes. "A young lady was by a couple hours ago but she just ran upstairs a minute in order to leave a message."

"A blonde?"

"Yes."

"And you're sure she was only up there a minute? You didn't see her bring anything down she didn't have with her went she went up?"

"Well, I actually didn't see her leave," Chad stammered. "She said she'd be right back down. I went outside to water the plants. When I didn't see her leave, I assumed she slipped out while I was busy getting water."

"Or maybe she left by the back stairs—maybe later," Sullivan finished the story.

"I didn't think of that, sir," Chad explained.

Sullivan let go the ghoul's wrist, throwing it away from him as though it disgusted him.

"Call Loo," he ordered Chad as he went out the door. "Tell him I'll be late tonight."

He headed downhill toward the Tenderloin, all the time wondering what the hell he was going to do. If he didn't find the head, what would the Grandfather do? Sullivan shuddered to think. He'd been so sure of himself, keeping the head in his room. Why hadn't he taken precautions?

He stopped in at Tran's and learned Kathy hadn't been seen that night. Sullivan was not surprised. He left the store, failing to offer Tran the feeding he was hoping for. Sullivan turned south, heading deeper into the Tenderloin.

What was Kathy up to? What did she want with the head? Unless she thought she'd hold it for ransom. That must be it, he told himself. Stupid bitch! What was going through her mind? He resolved then and there to teach her a lesson once he caught up with her.

Right now he was looking for Celia, a black prostitute who had been working for him the last two years. She and Kathy had been great chums, off and on, and if Kathy had left a message with anyone, it would be Celia.

He caught up with Celia in an alley off Eddy Street. Leaning through the driver's side window of a white Lexus, she was busy giving the white yuppie businessman seated inside a quick blow job.

"Get out here," Sullivan demanded, grabbing Celia by the belt and hauling her out of the car window. "I want to talk to you."

The yuppie hollered as Celia's mouth was ripped from his erect penis.

"Damn you, Sullivan," Celia swore, wiping her mouth, seeing who had accosted her. "What the fuck you tryin' to do? Make me bite this guy's dick off?"

"Stow it," Sullivan said.

But the yuppie was also mad. Zipping his pants, he opened the car door and started to get out, jawing away.

"Look you . . ." he started to say to Sullivan.

"Shut up!" Sullivan ordered, pushing the man back into his seat and kicking the car door shut. "Look. Here's your money." He counted off forty dollars and threw it in the man's lap. "Now get out of here."

Rethinking the situation, the man started his car and pulled away. Meanwhile, Celia stalked off, mad as hell. Sullivan caught up with her in two strides, grabbed her by the hair and pulled her back.

"Ouch! Goddamn it. What's got into you Sullivan? You fuckin' crazy tonight or something?" She tried to twist loose but he held on tight, keeping her close.

"I'm lookin' for Kathy," he said. "You seen her?"

"She's not working tonight. Ouch! She told me to tell you that," Celia told him. "Let the fuck go."

Sullivan released her. She spun around to face him, eyes furious.

"Yeah. She said that if I saw you I was to give you the message—and this." She fumbled in her purse then came up with a scrap of paper. "She said she's visiting a sick aunt in Oakland. She said to give you this address—in case you needed to see her about anything."

Sullivan glared at the paper. The address was some-where in West Oakland, across the bay, in a poor part of town near the waterfront.

"She said to give this to me?" Sullivan asked.

"Yeah!" Celia said, wincing as she tried to comb the snarls out of her hair. "Why that crazy white girl thinks you'd want to visit her is beyond me, but that's what she said. She told me you'd probably come looking for her."

"Okay. Thanks," Sullivan said, turning and walking away.

He caught the BART train at the underground Powell station below Hallidie Plaza. A couple of minutes later he was whizzing along under the bay, doing seventy or eighty miles per hour through a submarine tube, heading for the East Bay and the city of Oakland.

Emerging on the far shore, the train rose from its tunnel to cruise above the ground on an elevated line overlooking the shipyards, factories, and low-income neighborhoods that make up West Oakland. Looking out the window, Sullivan saw a huge bronze propeller at least twelve feet in diameter lying in the rear of a fitting yard. His eyes wandered toward the bay and the shipyards along its shore, and he was reminded of his earlier life at sea. They were hard days, he remembered, but certainly far simpler than those he lived today.

Then his present situation intruded on his thoughts and once again he was forced to think of the lost head—the head he had promised to the Grandfather. His tension growing as he waited for the train to reach his stop, he unconsciously dug his fingers into the Naugahyde of the seat.

Getting off at the elevated West Oakland station, he descended into the darkened streets below. North of the station, where his destination would be found, was residential: block upon block of single-family homes with small, fenced-in yards, all butted up next to the shipyards and rail depots crowded against the bay. A small neighborhood market, closed this time of night, stood on the corner nearby while down the street, light and music poured from a neighborhood bar. Otherwise, the area was quiet, almost deserted.

A number of houses along the street were vacant, boarded up, some showing signs of fire damage or recent use as crack houses. The remainder, though inhabited, were mostly in bad repair.

Gray, flickering light from televisions lit living room windows, and dogs penned in backyards barked as

Sullivan walked along. There was not another soul to be found on the streets.

Three blocks away, he found it: a corner building, built of cinder block painted white but now covered with layers of graffiti. A faded sign announced the place to be the West Oakland Body Shop, but it was obvious it had been closed for years.

Walking around the corner, he checked for signs of life but found nothing. The building next door, similar in construction, was occupied. An electric sign over the door read: *First African Emmanuel Baptist Church, Rev. Jonah Hayes, Pastor.* Sullivan crept back to the entrance of the boarded-up body shop and peeked inside.

It was the front office, or at least what was left of it. All that remained was a large metal desk overturned on the floor and a file cabinet that had been knocked on its side. Crack vials and other trash littered the floor. The room was otherwise stripped—even the shelving had been pulled off the wall. Sullivan pushed on the door, and with a groan of protest, it opened.

His instincts told to him to get out—that he was walking into a trap—but he was desperate to retrieve the head at almost any risk and shook the feeling off. There was little to fear from Kathy, he told himself, even if she had recruited some friends to help her. She had no idea how truly powerful he was, Sullivan assured himself. Quietly, he stepped inside, ears attuned for the slightest sound.

"Kathy?" he hissed.

He heard a bumping sound, coming from somewhere in the shop, beyond the office. Then he heard a soft groan.

"Kathy?" he repeated, stepping through the doorway to the shop. He scanned the dark interior, his night-sensitive eyes finding nothing but litter, empty cartons, and a few fifty-five–gallon drums of paints and other chemicals. The sounds seemed to have come from the rear of the shop, near the empty paint-drying booth.

Sullivan moved cautiously forward, peering through the dusty gloom, sensitive to any movement or sound. Stepping into the dry-booth he heard a sound above him. He looked up and saw a vaguely animal shape dropping toward him, then it crashed down on his head. Sullivan collapsed to the floor, unconscious.

January 15

At FBI Headquarters, Washington, D.C. . . .

Agent Moynahan ripped the fax off the machine as soon as it stopped printing. It reported the sighting of a suspected serial killer in Nevada and Moynahan made sure it was delivered directly to his superior's desk.

Director Klein took the fax from his agent and scanned it briefly. The suspect had been sighted in Reno, apparently headed for the border and into California.

"It sounds like our man," he told Moynahan. "The description fits."

"What's Phillips got going on the West Coast?" Moynahan asked. "He has no friends out there, no family that we know of."

"Random chance, perhaps?" Klein offered. "He's slain all those he held responsible for the deaths of his family. He's on a crusade now. No telling where he'll show up next."

Phillips was a Dallas, Texas, Baptist preacher suspected of murdering six cult members he accused of killing his wife and two children. The case would never be brought to trial because Phillips had decapitated every single one of them, driving stakes through their chests, then filling their mouths with holy wafers and garlic. After committing the murders he fled the area, resurfacing in other parts of the West.

"We have two murders in Austin bearing his signature," Klein went on. "And another pair of disappearances in Phoenix that look like him."

Klein rummaged on his desk, found a folder, and handed it to Moynahan.

"Here's Phillips's profile," he said. "It includes all the details we know about his religious fanaticism, his alcoholism, his addiction to prostitutes, and a few other unsavory tidbits—including an arrest for spousal abuse. Fax the whole thing to San Francisco, San Jose, and Sacramento. Ten to one our boy'll show up out there somewhere, and soon."

8

"Will you walk into my parlor?"
said the spider to the fly.;

"'Tis the prettiest little parlor
that ever you did spy."

—Mary Howitt, "The Spider and the Fly"

"Good evening, Mr. Sullivan."

At the sound of the voice, Sullivan awoke. Forcing his eyes open, he saw standing before him a man dressed in black robes complete with cowled hood. All that could be seen of the stranger was his face—and that was pock-marked and vengeful.

Sullivan tried to move but found himself hanging helpless by his wrists, suspended a few inches off the concrete floor below. The chain binding his crossed hands was securely strapped to a beam overhead. A feeble light shone from an old oil lantern set atop an empty drum.

"What happened?" Sullivan asked wearily. His throat was parched, his voice scratchy.

"Just a little bump on the head—that's all," said the man, his speech accented with a Texas drawl. "I'm afraid my associate got a little clumsy and fell on you."

"What do you want?" Sullivan asked.

"We want you to die," he said. "Isn't that right Reverend Hayes?" he called over his shoulder.

A black man stepped in from the other room. Dressed

in a suit and tie, he looked fiftyish and conservative. The face behind his wire rim spectacles was stern and disapproving.

"That we do, Mr. Phillips," the Reverend agreed, moving closer to get a better look at Sullivan. "That we do."

"Ya see," Phillips said, "me and the Reverend both got it in for you bloodsuckers. Our reasons are different of course, but it all ends up the same, I guess." He laughed. "Who says whites and blacks can't find something to agree on?" he added, shooting a smile at Hayes that the black man failed to return.

"Where's Kathy?" Sullivan demanded.

"The whore? Why she's long gone by now. The Reverend and I bought her a plane ticket out of town, out of appreciation for all the help she gave us."

So that's how it worked, Sullivan thought.

"Amazing luck of mine to drive all the way across the country then, the first time I get to feelin' itchy, the woman I choose to tarry with just happens to be familiar with one of you vampires. My luck's been runnin' that way for some time now. In fact, that's how I met the Reverend here, just by chance."

"Let's get started," said Hayes, ignoring his colleague.

"All right," answered Phillips. "But first . . ."

Picking up a large bag he reached inside and pulled out the severed head of Delfonso. Propping it atop the drum next to the lantern, Phillips positioned it so that its dead, filmy eyes stared directly at Sullivan.

"Just a little audience for the show," Phillips grinned. "Besides, to be legal, an Inquisition does require a witness."

Then the two men went to work on him.

An hour later Sullivan's body was streaked with blood, his two tormentors overheated, and the Reverend Hayes stripped of his coat and tie, working now in only his shirtsleeves. The pair had questioned their captive endlessly about the vampires in San Francisco: who was the Prince? who was Sullivan's sire? and other questions about the Ventrue, Tremere, and the many different clans and bloodlines of the secret vampire world. Sullivan refused to talk, revealing nothing, never even admitting his own vampirism, even when it was obvious to him that the two knew as much or more about the subject than he.

"I'm afraid we're running out of time and patience, Mr. Sullivan," Phillips finally said, still holding the iron bar he'd been beating the prisoner with. "The sun'll be up in an hour and then you're bound to die anyway. Why not tell us what we need to know?"

Sullivan spit a mouthful of blood at him, striking Phillips on the face.

"Eat shit," Sullivan said.

Phillips stepped back, enraged, then swung the iron bar into Sullivan's midriff, sending waves of pain through his tortured body.

"Watch him Reverend Hayes," Phillips said, leaving the room. "I gotta take a piss."

Hayes now stepped into Sullivan's line of vision. The black man was big, powerful-looking—his white shirt soaked with sweat and stained with the dust and filth of the old body shop.

Sullivan took a chance.

"What are you doing with that madman," he asked Hayes, softly.

Hayes didn't answer at first, busy checking the chains that held Sullivan, making sure they were still tight.

"Sometimes God sends us devils to help fight the work of devils," he finally answered Sullivan.

"He's gonna get you in a lot of trouble," Sullivan argued desperately. "Let me down and I promise I won't say a word to anybody about this."

The black man simply chuckled.

"You don't understand," Hayes said. "I want your white-ass dead as much as that honky back there does. Then when we get done with you, I can take care of him as needed."

Sullivan realized the man's face was familiar. He'd seen it years before, back in the early seventies. His real name was Taylor and he'd been a member of the Death Panthers, a radical splinter group of Oakland's old Black

Panthers. Charged with racially motivated acts of terrorism and murder, most of the members had gone to prison though a few escaped underground, Hayes among them. This man was older, of course, but Sullivan was certain it was he. With the discovery came the realization that his chances with Hayes were virtually nil.

Hayes struck him across the ribs, sending pain shooting through Sullivan's body.

"Talk, whitey," Hayes growled. "Spit it out."

Sullivan grimaced, gritting his teeth. He refused to speak.

"A little more encouragement?" he asked and laid into him again with the rod. "Talk, you bastard!" Hayes shouted as he flailed away.

Sullivan was twisting in the chains now, kicking out desperately, hopelessly. He knew he couldn't last much longer.

Then from somewhere came the sound of breaking glass—a shattered window—and then a shout. Sullivan cracked open his eyes in time to see Loo launching himself from the floor beneath a broken window, right into the much larger black man. Locked together, the two crashed into the wall. Loo disentangled himself first and was back on his feet by the time Phillips, responding to the commotion, came running out of the back room. Before Phillips could even comprehend what happened, Loo grabbed him by the back of the neck and hurled him headfirst into the wall. Phillips crumpled to the ground, lifeless. Loo turned back to the Reverend Hayes—then stopped in his tracks.

Hayes had changed—and was still changing as Loo and Sullivan watched, dumbfounded.

His clothes torn off and tossed aside in ragged shreds, Hayes now crouched on all fours, a deep rumbling growl sounding from his chest while his powerful, naked body stretched and elongated, limbs twisting and changing form as muscles rippled and glossy black hair sprouted all over his skin. A few seconds more and Hayes was gone, replaced by a powerful black wolf, who now snarled menacingly at the two vampires. Turning its attention to Loo, it lowered its ears and began stalking toward him, low to the ground, ears flattened and eyes glowing like fire in the darkness.

Sullivan couldn't believe it—Hayes was a Garou, the race of werewolves who thought that vampires were the blackest blight of the planet.

Lightly, Loo leaped atop a nearby metal drum, then began jumping from one to another toward the other end of the shop. The wolf bounded after him, swiping savagely at Loo as he reached the last barrel and leaped up to swing himself to safety atop a beam.

Below him the Garou Hayes paced and snarled while Sullivan, twisting in his chains, managed to swing himself around and kick out at the animal. The boot caught the wolf in the haunch and it spun around angrily, lunging at Sullivan with its huge maw. Teeth caught Sullivan's leg, shredding his jeans and opening several deep wounds in the calf of his leg. Sullivan yelled and pulled away while the animal turned its attention back to Loo, who now scampered across the beams back toward the other end of the room. The wolf pursued Loo, but as it passed the drum where the lantern stood, its lashing tail knocked the glass-chambered lamp to the floor. It broke on impact, the spilled oil instantly igniting and spreading toward the wall.

The Garou turned to growl at the fire, then turned back to eye Loo looking down at it from above, still far from its reach. With a snarl it began to change into another form, perhaps the nearly unstoppable Crinos form that was half-man and half-wolf, but apparently reconsidered and instead turned and, with a fluid leap, disappeared through the broken window. Dogs all through the neighborhood set up a howl as the beast fled the scene through the darkened backyards of Oakland.

"Get me down," Sullivan pleaded, the flames already licking up the walls toward the ceiling.

Loo was there, leaping back across the beams to unhook Sullivan's chains and drop him to the floor.

Sullivan nearly fell when he was he let down, his right

leg torn and weakened by the wolf's bite, but Loo was there to catch him and help him out the door, just as black smoke began billowing from the sealed windows.

"Wait a minute," Sullivan said, after they'd gotten safely outside. Hobbling back into the building, he emerged a moment later with Delfonso's head. He didn't bother with Phillips's body, leaving it for the flames.

"Let's go," Loo said. "It's nearly sunup."

They found an idling taxi at an out-of-the-way cab stand. Yanking open the doors without warning, the pair jumped into the backseat. The driver, engrossed in his morning paper, was surprised by the sudden intrusion of the passengers and shocked by their appearance.

Smelling of smoke, both Loo and Sullivan were covered with soot and grime, and Sullivan streaked with dried blood. Not only that, but Sullivan was hiding a bulky package under his coat—no telling what it was.

"To the city. Fast," Loo told him, tossing a fifty-dollar bill over the seat.

The driver's fears and suspicions evaporated with the appearance of the cash and they pulled away from the curb, headed for the bridge.

The first thing Sullivan wanted to know was how Loo had found him. Loo told him that Kathy had been spotted at the airport by some of Vannevar's men who, recognizing her, detained and questioned her. When they found out what was up they contacted Loo and he had simply followed Sullivan's trail to Oakland.

"So, what happened to Kathy?" Sullivan wanted to know.

"Vannevar's people took care of her, I suppose."

Although glad she'd been caught—and well aware she deserved whatever treatment she got—Sullivan was surprised to find himself regretting her end. He'd almost started to like her.

As the cab crossed the bridge, the morning sun was peeping over the eastern ridge of hills that separated the Bay Area from the rest of the state. Splashing off the glass towers of the city, it reflected painfully back into the two vampire's eyes.

"Here," Loo said, handing Sullivan a pair of sunglasses. "I brought extras." He already had his own pair on.

"Thanks," Sullivan said, putting the glasses on. "Thanks for everything."

Even with the dark glasses, the bright sunlight dazzled Sullivan's eyes. Noting the TransAmerica Pyramid glowing gold in the early morning light, he was taken by how much it resembled a gigantic stake, pointed upright.

In the city, the driver dropped Loo off at the gate to Chinatown, then continued on up and over Nob Hill before letting Sullivan off in front of the Drake Inn. Sullivan gave him a quick "thanks" and ducked into the building, beating the rising sun by only a few minutes.

Standing up from behind the desk, Chad was startled by Sullivan's haggard appearance. Sullivan offered the ghoul no explanation, instead simply drawing out the battered, filthy head of Delfonso and tossing it to him over the desk.

"Put that in the safe, will ya?" Sullivan told him.

Chad caught it, his mouth agape at the sight of the rotting vampire's head.

"I'll come down for it tonight," Sullivan said as he disappeared up the stairs to his room.

January 15

In a luxurious residential suite atop one of San Francisco's finest hotels . . .

Honerius watched in silence as the Prince paced the floor. The Tremere Primogen had been called here tonight to be ready to take action if some part of the plan showed signs of failing. The loss of Delfonso's head had spelled trouble, though Honerius assured the Prince that even were it lost, Sullivan would still have suffered expulsion from the Family, if not branded "kin-slayer" as they planned, then as punishment for his failure.

"But I'm still concerned, Honerius," the Prince said, still pacing about the room. "Who is this Phillips? Where did he come from?"

"I know not, my lord," he answered. "Many are the variables in a manifold universe . . ."

"Enough Tremere claptrap," the Prince cut him off. "Someone introduced him into the situation," he said, walking behind Honerius, where he sat in his chair.

The old Tremere closed his eyes as the Prince walked behind him, still talking.

"Who pulls the strings on this new puppet?" he said. "That is the question we must answer."

The Prince stepped around in front of Honerius again and the wizard breathed a silent sigh of relief.

"Hortator assures me the reading issued by the head will be skewed, and consequently misread. Do your auguries still agree, Honerius?"

"All the signs are propitious, my lord. The time is right."

"Good," Vannevar smiled. "But keep a close watch on this Phillips. Other problems presently occupy my attention."

"Yes, my lord."

"With Delfonso out of the way we can safely apply pressure to remove the Grandfather and end the long-range threat his presence imposes."

"I understand, of course," Honerius answered. Strange things were reported from the fringes of Asia. The vampires inhabiting that part of the world had long kept to themselves and little or nothing was known about them. Ominous signs and prophecies had long indicated they held designs regarding the North American continent and the Prince and the Camarilla feared invasion. The mysterious Grandfather, here in San Francisco almost since the city's inception, was believed to be a key part of this plan.

His interview with the Prince finished, Honerius made ready to leave.

"Have faith in the all-knowing father," he told the Prince.

He left Vannevar's residence relieved. Called there on short notice, he thought the Prince had uncovered his subterfuge, but all looked satisfactory. And, as he promised, he would be sure to keep his eye on Phillips.

He got in his car and ordered the driver to take him home.

9

**Wide is the gate, and broad
is the way, that leadeth to
destruction, and many there
be which go in thereat:**

—Matthew

Sullivan met Loo at the Chinatown gate
the following night. After the perfunctory, formal greeting,
he entered, carrying under his arm the head of Delfonso
wrapped in a plastic sack. They met Chi at the usual place
and there Sullivan handed over the prize. Chi smiled when
he took possession of the head.

"The Grandfather is in an exceptional mood this
evening," Chi said. "He looks forward to tonight's reading
with great anticipation."

Sullivan smiled. After being distanced from the
Family for so long, knowing that he had finally done well
was gratifying.

"What does Grandfather expect we might learn?" Loo
asked Chi as the ghoul led them down the alley to the
rear entrance of the seafood shop and the dark under-
world below. Sullivan had been interested too.

"It, of course, cannot be guessed," Chi smiled. "But a
head as old as Delfonso's always promises great revela-
tions."

Sullivan noticed the grin on Chi's face. The old ghoul

83

normally wore a smile but tonight he was positively beaming.

Downstairs, they were led directly to the Grandfather's chamber and once again brought before the masked, bulking figure that was their elder. They took their seats as before, watching while David fanned the coals in a charcoal burner set against the rear wall of the chamber. Chi left the room to prepare the head.

No one spoke for a moment, then finally the Grandfather said, "You have done well, my sons, despite the problems that arose."

Sullivan thought he heard the sound of a chuckle from behind the mask. It was good to know the Grandfather had a sense of humor.

"The Prince is pleased, as well," he added. "Our old enemy is gone, our Family stronger than ever, and we are in favor with the ruling powers. All is well."

He made a small bow, returned by Sullivan and Loo in turn.

Chi reappeared, bearing on a metal tray the prepared head of Delfonso. Though cleaned, and the hair and beard combed and straightened, it had suffered badly from the effects of decay: the nose was collapsed and the eyes were yellow and opaque. It carried with it the stench of rot—different, but as pungent as the smell perpetually surrounding the Grandfather. Sullivan had expected to see a skull cleaned of flesh and was surprised at its appearance, but said nothing.

Chi said, "The time is ready, the fruit is ripe."

"Let the ceremony begin," intoned the Grandfather.

The head on its brass tray was placed on the tripod over the now red-hot coals of the burner. Chi and David stepped back and waited.

A smell soon filled the air—the stink of burning human flesh, the rotten condition of the head lending an additional tang to the odor. Heated fluids began flowing from the open wound of the neck, sizzling in the pan, lending their own acrid stench to a room already crowded with odors. Smoke and fumes curled toward the ceiling.

The Grandfather leaned forward as though watching for something. The rest waited, Sullivan keeping his eyes close on the head.

Then it spoke. "Merciful God in heaven, I am repentant for my sins!"

It was the voice of the dead Delfonso, echoing hollowly from the head in the pan. It seemed to be picking up where it left off a couple of nights earlier, when Delfonso died at the hands of Sullivan.

The thing began to move in the pan, working its jaw, grinding its teeth. The smoke continued to pour up from the pan, thickening and taking on a greenish cast. It seemed to be forming shapes in the air.

"Have mercy on my soul!" the head suddenly shrieked. "I burn in the fires of Hell!"

Chi leaned forward, staring at the moving, roiling smoke.

"The fortunes raised from the vampire's blood take shape, Grandfather. They tell us secrets."

"Save me from my torments," Delfonso screamed. "My soul, my soul!"

The thing gnashed its tongue between its teeth. One custard yellow eye slowly swelled from the gathering heat, then broke open with an audible pop and greasy ooze ran down the blackened, hollow cheek of Delfonso's head.

"Look!" Chi said, pointing at the smoke.

Sullivan looked where he pointed but saw nothing except clouds of billowing smoke. Some occasionally formed shapes, almost human, but he could make nothing of them.

"There," the Grandfather said, nodding at the smoke. "It is the sign."

The head continued to cook, Delfonso howling madly. Sullivan still saw nothing in the smoke. Delfonso's pained shrieks made him want to plug his ears but he also wanted to hear what Chi and the Grandfather had to say.

"Wait," Chi cautioned him. "Be not hasty in judgment. The signs are strange, abnormal."

The head was now cooking furiously atop the burner, grease spattering and sizzling. Still Delfonso screamed, and the smoke took more definite forms, enough apparently for some to divine the prophesy.

"Look!" roared the Grandfather. "It is he! The Kin-Slayer!"

Delfonso's head suddenly toppled over in the pan, sizzling madly.

"No," said Chi, "Wait!"

But no one paid attention to him, all the others having turned their eyes to Sullivan.

"It is he! The one who would destroy us! The traitor within!"

The Grandfather was pointing at Sullivan with a huge clawlike hand scarcely human.

"Seize him!" bellowed the Grandfather from behind his mask, his voice trembling with rage. "Slay the traitor before he would slay us."

Sullivan needed no further prompting. Leaping to his feet, he lunged for the door but found Loo already blocking his path, his deadly axe in hand. Sullivan halted, suddenly reaching over and grabbing the stunned David by the shoulders, and throwing the ghoul at Loo, knocking them both off-balance. Looking about for a weapon, he found only the still-screaming head of Delfonso lying in the pan. Snatching it up by the hair, he swung it around and brought it down on top of Chi's head just as the ghoul made a grab for Sullivan.

"I bleed for my sins," screamed the head as Sullivan swung it around at Loo, now coming after him again.

Sullivan slammed the head against Loo, then watched, aghast, as the head clamped its teeth on Loo's throat, screaming, chewing, swallowing Loo's flowing blood only to have it rain down on the floor from the rotten opening of the severed neck. Loo struggled with the still-smoldering head while it chewed away at him, screaming like a banshee.

Sullivan saw his chance and bolted for the doorway, hurdling David, who was still pulling himself up from the floor. Once out of the room he looked back over his shoulder and saw the Grandfather rising from his pile of cushions, crawling forward on hands and knees to give chase. Its mask fell away and Sullivan's heart quailed when he saw the face beneath it.

He ran as fast he could up the passageway, the snarling, snapping thing that was the Grandfather pursuing him, scrabbling after him on all fours. The air filled with the rattling, scratching sounds of its heavy breathing. Sullivan had caught a glimpse of the fluted vanes and ribs that lined the Grandfather's sides and wondered what kind of thing it was that now chased him through these dingy underground rooms.

Sullivan reached the wooden stairs and swung himself around with one hand, taking the steps two at a time. The Grandfather was right behind and, with a huge hand, snagged Sullivan's leg. Sullivan stumbled and, turning around to kick himself free, saw the Grandfather unveiled, a monstrous creature of hard shell and exposed bone, now poised on the bottom step. It opened its giant maw and the head suddenly shot forward on an extendable neck, the jaws clamping down just inches from Sullivan's foot as he broke free to scramble up the stairs.

The man with the cleaver, hearing the commotion, tried to stop Sullivan, but the vampire batted him away before banging through the screen door and disappearing into the night and out into the city.

January 16

During the night shift at the San Francisco City Morgue . . .

Emily Grange straightened her desk, trying to look efficient. She was expecting company, a member of the Primogen, and she wanted to appear her best.

As a supervisor in the city Coroner's Office, Grange

held an important post in the vampire world. A key position with the power to destroy or publicize forensic evidence of vampire activity in the city, her post wielded a considerable amount of power and influence.

The Prince had specifically asked Grange to suppress information regarding a certain corpse recovered from around the U.S. Mint a few days previously and Grange had readily agreed. But she had contacted Alicia McGreb, elder of the Gangrel clan and a chief antagonist of the Prince's policies.

It was a direct violation of the Prince's wishes, but Grange cared little. She had little respect for the Prince and was more than willing to align herself with the opposition in hopes of improving her fortunes. If she could befriend McGreb, and become her ally, there was no telling how high Grange could climb. Totally ruthless, she had succeeded to her present position at the direct expense of her predecessor, a missing vampire whose fate was still unknown to anybody save Grange and a few secret allies.

McGreb showed up a few minutes later, having driven herself to the Coroner's Office in her own car.

"Ms. McGreb?" Emily asked, rising from her desk when she saw the elder enter the office.

"You called me here, Grange," McGreb said, without a trace of friendliness. "What is it you wish to show me?"

Emily was a bit surprised at McGreb's cool attitude but decided she might thaw out when she saw what Emily had to show her.

"Come this way," she said, leading the elder through a pair of swinging doors into the morgue.

Inside, Emily opened one of the refrigerated drawers and pulled out a slab holding a corpse covered by a rubberized sheet.

"Look," Grange said, flipping back the top half of the sheet.

Underneath was the corpse of Domingo, his head torn savagely from his body. Shriveled and dried like an old mummy, his wrinkled face was barely recognizable, though a gold tooth, exposed by a lip that had dried and now curled back, was familiar to anyone who'd known Domingo in life.

"We picked him up from behind the Old Mint building," Grange went on. "Sullivan killed him, of course, as most know, but the Prince asked me to keep quiet about certain particulars of the corpse's condition."

McGreb gingerly picked up one of Domingo's dried, sticklike arms, then let it drop back down to the slab.

"Diablerie?" she asked, looking at Grange.

"That's what I'd call it," Emily said back.

"Thank you very much for this information," McGreb said, preparing to leave. "It's been most helpful. I will remember you. Thank you."

And she was gone. Emily covered the body up then sealed it back in its nearly freezing chamber, smiling to herself the whole time.

Yes, she thought to herself, this would work out just fine. With McGreb in her corner there was no telling how far she could go.

PART II

Kin-Slayer

10

In God's wildness lies the hope of the world—the great fresh unblighted, unredeemed wilderness.

—John Muir,
Alaska Fragment

A gibbous moon hung over the city's Golden Gate Park. A three-mile-long patch of green in the heart of San Francisco, the park stretches from the end of Haight Street in the east to the Pacific Ocean in the west. Created in the late ninteenth century at the direction of John McClaren, it is filled with recreational facilities, paths, lakes, gardens, and planted groves of exotic flora. By day crowded with picnickers, bicyclists, roller skaters, and those out for a stroll, after dark the place grows empty, left populated only by the criminal, the homeless, and other things that move by night.

Sullivan crashed through a stand of ferns and plunged down the hill, trampling the rhododendrons in his haste. Slipping on the torn vegetation, he half slid down the remainder of the slope to land on his feet on the narrow track below.

A motorcycle, engine roaring, headlight flashing, appeared on the rise above him. The rider, dressed in black, was helmetless, his blond hair shaved on one side, the rest tied back in a queue. His right cheek was tattooed with the international symbol for biohazards. The biker laughed at Sullivan, then turned his motorcycle down the hill in pursuit.

The biker roared down the slope, slipping left and right as the spinning rear wheel churned the carefully tended plants to pulp. Down on the path, he wheeled the bike around—one foot down—and screwed the throttle, smoking the tire as he tore after Sullivan, already disappearing around a bend, while the noise of the motorcycle's exhaust split the still night air. The rider carried a large wooden stake across his back.

Gunning down the path after Sullivan, the biker cleared the bend but saw nothing in front of him. The path, though straight and clear, was empty. Then he noticed Sullivan beside the path, his leg braced against a tree as he pulled something back with all his strength.

A thick, black cable leaped up off the road directly in front of the biker. He tried to stop, hitting both brakes and trying to lay the bike down, but there was not enough time. The cable caught him across the chest, ripping him from the motorcycle and throwing him to the ground. The bike traveled another twenty-five yards, ran off the edge of the road, up a slope, and rolled over on its back, engine stalled, rear wheel spinning, headlight still blazing and pointed toward the sky. Silence fell over the park.

Sullivan was out from behind the tree the same instant the rider hit the ground, but by the time he reached his foe the motorcyclist was already crawling to his knees, choking and spitting blood. Sullivan booted him in the ribs, lifting the man off the ground and sending him sprawling on his back. Helpless, the rider watched as Sullivan raised a stake high, then jammed it down through the punk's chest. The wood pierced the vampire's heart and he fell still, thick blood welling up around the wound.

Sullivan stopped, listening carefully for others who might have been with the punk. He heard nothing save the faint hissing of traffic on distant Fulton Street and the soft sounds of night in the park. He was safe. Another attempt to bring him to justice had failed.

"This cannot go on, Sullivan," a voice said from behind a nearby tree.

At the sound, Sullivan started but, recognizing the voice, calmed himself.

"Where are you, Jacob?" Sullivan asked.

"Here," answered the voice.

A black shadow stepped out from behind a nearby eucalyptus tree as the speaker revealed himself. Jacob was tall and dark, his heavy brow mostly covered by a thick lock of black hair that fell across his forehead.

"I can't have these continual disturbances," Jacob said, walking down the slope, coming nearer Sullivan. "I need to maintain friendly relations with the anarchs."

Sullivan had been hiding out in the park for nearly two weeks now, at Jacob's invitation. With tonight's attack, he had already survived three attempts on his life. The trap he used to stop the anarch tonight—along with several others—was set up a few days before, right after the second attack on Sullivan. Although his criminal status was still being debated by Prince Vannevar and others of the Primogen, the Grandfather had already put out a private contract on his life. While most of the city's vampires would wait and respect the council's decision, the anarchs were a different breed—they enjoyed flaunting their insolence. Besides, the reward, Sullivan had heard, was a hefty one.

"He's not dead," Sullivan offered. "I'll leave him where his friends'll find him. He'll be rescued before the sun comes up."

"More than likely," Jacob said. "But nonetheless, I cannot permit this any longer. Meet me back at camp. We'll speak more."

With that, Jacob made a subtle motion with his arms and, as Sullivan watched, transformed himself into a large, black bat that flew off to the west, wheeling and diving through the trees.

Jacob was of the Gangrel clan—the shape-shifters.

Sullivan dumped the unconscious anarch near the edge of a main road before heading to Jacob's camp in the western end of the park. Picking his way through the dense growth, shunning the roads, he was careful to avoid several places Jacob had deemed dangerous.

"These spots are near the Faerie world and should be avoided," he'd warned. "There are many such places in this park, including some, I'm sure, I haven't yet discovered." Apparently, these nexus points had been created by the park's designer, who must have had some connection with that strange, elder world Sullivan knew so little about.

Jacob was relatively new to the park—and the city—having been "imported" into the area by one of the Primogen in an effort to defend the park against the ongoing inroads attempted by the Garou. Of all the vampires in the city, Jacob was one of the few willing to offer refuge to Sullivan. A newcomer, Jacob was unhampered by the political webs the vampires controlling San Francisco had spun over the years. Jacob, Sullivan soon discovered, was an honest and sympathetic man.

Jacob's camp was in the center of a thick stand of pine and eucalyptus trees in a wild part of the park behind the equitation field. The location was further obscured from mundane humans by Jacob's magicks, which twisted and pulled the space around the area, making it exceedingly difficult to find by accident. Jacob had taught Sullivan the path and, using this knowledge, he entered easily.

"Welcome," said Jacob, in human form again, squatting on the ground before a small fire. "Sit down."

Seated next to Jacob was Dwight, an ex–dope pusher from the Haight and now Jacob's ghoul lackey. As much respect as he had for Jacob, Sullivan failed to comprehend why he would choose such a sniveling rat for a companion. Jacob explained that Dwight was "under the gun," so to speak, with a price put on his head by a local dope dealer. As long as Dwight was under the Gangrels' protection it was nearly certain he would meet with no harm. Even the anarchs would leave Dwight alone, so much did they respect the Gangrel. Without that protection Dwight was dead meat. This made for an extremely loyal servant, Jacob explained. Personality had little or nothing to do with it. For Sullivan's money, Dwight was a weasel-faced little scoundrel who couldn't be trusted.

"How's it goin', man?" Dwight squeaked.

Dwight always tried hard to be Sullivan's friend, despite Sullivan's continual rejections. Sullivan half suspected that Dwight was reporting his movements to the anarchs, who were constantly hunting him.

"Not bad," Sullivan responded, sitting down on the ground. "What's up?"

"The Primogen still debate your case, Sullivan," Jacob began without ado. "Some call for the blood hunt."

When Domingo's corpse was recovered it was found drained of blood. Although Vannevar apparently attempted to suppress the information, it somehow leaked to the rest of the Kindred. Although accusations and theories about the crime were numerous, the majority tended to hold Sullivan responsible. If Vannevar was persuaded to call a full-scale blood hunt, all the vampires of the city would be after Sullivan—even Jacob would be required to pursue and slay him. Sullivan knew he probably wouldn't last a night.

"Do you think I did it?" Sullivan asked.

"No," answered Jacob. "But you know that makes no difference if the hunt is called."

"I understand."

It was quiet for a moment as the three watched the fire crackling softly in the night; the warmth was good. Jacob broke the silence.

"In the meantime, I want you to speak with Dirk."

Dirk was nominal leader of the anarchs—or at least the most respected of the bunch. His gang, the Gutters, included vampires, ghouls, and humans, and was one of the largest and toughest in the city.

"You can visit him on Haight Street, neutral ground, where you will be safe from attack. I will make the arrangements."

"What if he refuses to listen?"

"Then you will have to leave. I'm sorry."

Sullivan knew he was right. Jacob was respected by the anarchs and they generally left him alone to do his job, but the continual friction of Sullivan's presence would inevitably lead to conflict.

"I understand," Sullivan said again.

They passed the rest of the night in conversation. Jacob had traveled widely throughout the world, and though Sullivan had visited a fair number of ports during his early years at sea, Jacob had actually lived among the different peoples of the lands he visited. He was a wise old vampire, knowledgeable in many things, and from him Sullivan learned much about the history of their kind, the different types of vampires known to the world, and the origins and history of the codes and rules of the Masquerade, the great deception vampires practice on the human race.

Sullivan admired the sense of ease and composure surrounding Jacob, as well. Most vampires he'd known, including himself, seemed always at odds with their world and their society. Jacob was detached; he shunned material wants, and avoided the seemingly endless pursuit of power exhibited by most vampires. He never lived in one place very long, he said, and hinted that he felt he would not be in San Francisco much longer. "Only until the Primogen can find a permanent resident to watch the park," he told Sullivan. "Then I think I will move on."

Sullivan guessed that Jacob was quite old, but the Gangrel was evasive about his actual age.

Jacob had also spent a good deal of time living among the Garou. A shape-changer, he used his natural ability to take the form of a wolf to enter and run with different werewolf packs. He had to be careful, though. Many of the Garou, discovering a member of the hated race of vampires in their midst, would have turned on him and torn him to shreds.

With the first gray light of dawn, the two retired: Jacob using his natural ability to meld himself into the very earth itself, while Sullivan had to be content with a shallow grave scooped out of the dirt and dead leaves. Dwight lurked in the area throughout the day, making doubly sure their rest went undisturbed.

February 3

**In a luxurious residential suite atop one
of San Francisco's finest hotels . . .**

Donna Cambridge sat on the couch, watching passively as Prince Vannevar argued over the telephone with someone. As the Prince's childe and courtesan, Donna had been close by his side these past few weeks, watching as a complicated plan decades in the making began to unfold. Now something threatened to undo it and Vannevar was working overtime to assure nothing went wrong, even going so far as to work daylight hours—a feat of will and power rarely possible among the Kindred.

Vannevar hung up the phone and came over to sit beside Donna. He look tired, she noticed, and worried he was straining himself. If anything went wrong, the city might be plunged into chaos, and Vannevar would blame himself.

She placed her hand on top of his, his frown quickly replaced by a smile as he looked at her, placing his free hand atop hers.

"Anything wrong?" she asked.

"McGreb's making trouble," he said. "She somehow found out about Domingo."

Alicia McGreb was one of the Primogen. She had managed to learn of the diablerie committed on Domingo, and, accusing Sullivan, was now calling loudly for a blood hunt. Someone had leaked the information.

"Does she have enough support?" Donna asked him, wondering if there were enough vampires siding with McGreb to force the issue.

"No. Not yet, anyway. But it makes things difficult for

us. It is important that we keep Sullivan alive. He has a job to perform."

Donna had heard this before. Sullivan, like many of the other lesser vampires in the plan, had a role to play, but like most, this role was flexible and ultimately unessential.

"Didn't Honerius show that Sullivan was unnecessary from now on? Isn't it assured that the Grandfather will fall regardless?"

"Indeed," Vannevar said, almost absentmindedly. In his own mind, he felt he had little reason to trust the old Tremere, but he never spoke these doubts aloud, keeping them to himself.

"But I prefer to see Sullivan play the role we intended," he said, finally.

Donna heard his words but didn't believe him. Vannevar would be the last to admit it, but she could tell the Prince was growing fond of his little pawn. He was going out of his way to keep him alive longer than necessary.

Another call came in.

11

**The more things change, the
more they remain the same.**

—Alphonse Karr,
Les Guêpes

The next night found Sullivan making
his way cautiously through the eastern end of the park,
heading in the direction of the Haight. Choosing back
routes, he kept his eyes peeled for possible attacks from
the gangs of anarchs who more or less ruled this territory. Jacob told Sullivan he was guaranteed safe passage,
but common sense and past experience had taught him
to trust nothing.

Finally emerging from the thick woods onto the open
green fronting on Stanyan Street, Sullivan felt relieved,
almost surprised, to find he'd made it safely. Haight
Street was within sight, a short block away. Designated
Elysium by the vampires of the city, he would be safe
there, but first he must cross a block of open territory
where the only protection was that promised him by
Dirk. Hesitant at first, he stepped out of the woods and
onto the street. Keeping watch on all sides, he headed
for Haight Street, seeing no one along the way save the
usual mix of hustlers and street people in and around
the McDonald's that faces the park.

Haight Street was once the commercial heart of a quiet

middle-class neighborhood, but with the arrival of LSD and the hippie movement in the late sixties it had been changed forever. It quickly became an international symbol and haven for the counterculture, and at the urging of the artistic, often bohemian Toreador clan, nearly as quickly declared Elysium: a place officially off-limits to vampire strife, where the undead could mix and mingle freely without fear of attack or reprisal. Elysium was a taboo almost everyone feared to break and those who did usually suffered quick punishment.

Despite the security it offered him now, Sullivan knew that if Vannevar was persuaded to call the blood hunt, there would be no Elysium for him anywhere. There was no haven or sanctuary that could protect a vampire condemned to suffer a blood hunt.

The Haight by day is a sunny street frequented by punks, panhandlers, and tourists but by night it takes on a more sinister tone: groups huddling on corners, exchanging whispered secrets while skulkers lurk in the darkened doorways of closed shops. The fashion of the street is still all black, with brightly colored hair popular and nose rings and tattoos common.

As Sullivan walked along he noted almost all the clothing stores displayed fashions in black: window mannequins draped in funereal gauze while skulls, gargoyles, skeletons, and other death imagery seemed the universal ornament.

One shop had devoted its entire display to the upcoming *Festivo dello Estinto* celebration planned for next month in the Mission. It is based on similar days-long festivals and parades held in Mexico that play heavily on death themes. The event had been unofficially adopted by the death-wish denizens of the Haight and many were preparing for the big day and plans were afoot to stage their own, unofficial parade.

This particular shop's display included dozens of different skulls and skeletons, including many papiermâché figures imported from Mexico: skeletons playing musical instruments, bowling and golfing, engaging in any number of normal, everyday activities common to the living. Candy skulls and skeletons of various sizes were also for sale.

Two young girls, dressed in black tights, boots, ultra-minis, and net tops under jackets lounged nearby. One of them, watching Sullivan as he turned from the window display and walked by them, sucked seductively at the head of a candy skeleton as he passed. His mind on the meeting to come, Sullivan failed to notice them. Feeling ignored, the teenager took out her anger on the candy skeleton, biting down and decapitating it with a crunch.

Gene Splice, the club where Sullivan was supposed to meet Dirk, was on the next block. Inside a punk band called Gran Mal thrashed away, bludgeoning its audience with sound while a crowd milled around in front, blocking the sidewalk, talking, dealing, and laughing.

It was the three sitting on a pair of motorcycles parked by the curb that caught Sullivan's eye. Even from a distance he could tell they were vampires—anarchs. One of them was marked by a biohazard symbol tattooed on his cheek and Sullivan recognized the punk he'd staked the night before, the one Jacob called Smash. Obviously someone had found him and rescued him from the sun. He looked tired but otherwise okay. Sullivan felt a little gratified to see Smash sitting on the back of another's motorcycle. Obviously his machine was out of commission after last night's crash.

The three anarchs eyed Sullivan as he approached.

"Dirk's upstairs," said the vampire seated in front of Smash, when Sullivan reached them. Smash himself said nothing.

"Thanks," Sullivan said.

One of the club doorman showed Sullivan inside, then around a corner, where a narrow flight of stairs led to a second floor above the raucous, crowded club.

Sullivan knew Dirk from years ago. He hadn't seen or talked to him in more than twenty years, but he was counting on their old days together to help him work a deal.

Dirk had showed up in the city just prior to World War I,

after spending most of his life back East somewhere. A hellraiser, Dirk told Sullivan he'd been involved in various organized labor activities back east and Sullivan surmised that he'd probably done something that forced him to move. Dirk had wisely presented himself to the Prince and received permission to dwell in the city before he inevitably fell back into his old ways. Soon labor disturbances along the waterfront were on the increase and Dirk was behind it all.

Sullivan and Dirk had first run into each other along the Embarcadero, where Sullivan occasionally went at night to watch the ships loading and unloading. Soon they were running together up and down the old waterfront: frequenting the dives, gambling, chasing women, brawling with sailors, and generally making as much trouble as they possibly could. They were both younger vampires in those days, Sullivan felt.

When Vannevar began raising hell about all the troubles on the waterfront, Dirk was held responsible and Sullivan, known to be running with the anarch, named along with him. At the order of the Grandfather, Sullivan broke off their friendship and kept away from the waterfront, though Dirk continued to remain active in the labor scene, defying Vannevar in every way conceivable and baiting him at every opportunity.

By the fifties the Port of San Francisco was so plagued with wildcat strikes and violence that most shipping companies transferred their operations to Oakland's port facilities across the bay. Dirk, growing bored, moved his activities inland and was, in his own way, responsible for much of what began in the Haight-Ashbury district in the late sixties; he and his biker gang were responsible for some of the first quantity shipments of LSD sold on the street.

These thoughts passed through Sullivan's mind as he followed the stairs up to the dusty hallway above. Here he found a series of cheaply constructed cubicles made of unpainted drywall, used as dressing rooms and for storage. The largest room, at the far end of the hall, was lit and occupied. Behind a battered wooden desk sat a young-looking man. Leaning back in his chair, feet up on the desktop, he was cleaning his fingernails with a large sheath knife. Despite the punk haircut and multiply pierced ears, Dirk looked much the same as Sullivan remembered him.

"Long time, no see," Dirk called out to Sullivan when he saw him appear at the top of the stairs.

Entering the office, Sullivan saw that Dirk wasn't alone; there were three others in the office—members of Dirk's gang, the Gutters. Dirk continued, coming out from behind the desk, "I'd ask you what was up, but that would be a silly question, I suppose." He extended his hand. The two old friends shook hands, then Dirk gave Sullivan a quick hug and a pat on the back.

"Sit down," he told Sullivan. "I'll introduce you to my friends," he said as he returned to his seat behind the desk.

Although Dirk numbered humans and ghouls in his gang, the three present in the room were all vampires. Joe was the tall, thin one with black hair and the penchant for leather jackets and chains. His attitude was cool, detached. Little Mac, the smaller of the two men, had brown hair and kept closer watch on Sullivan, eyeing him somewhat suspiciously. The woman's name was Veronica. Tall, thin, and with a shock of green-dyed hair, her style was casual sleaze and her attitude half-independent adult woman, half-bitch.

"You're here about the price on your head, right?" Dirk asked, when the introductions were over. "I always warned you about Family loyalties, didn't I."

Dirk was Caitiff, one of the clanless. Once treated as outcasts—unclean—the Caitiffs' numbers had grown so large over the last centuries that they now formed something resembling a caste of their own. Long ago, upon learning of Dirk's situation, Sullivan had felt sorry for him, but since the falling out with the Grandfather he found he had reason to envy him.

"You know I had to obey the Grandfather or die," Sullivan explained.

When the Grandfather ordered Sullivan to quit their friendship, Dirk argued that Sullivan should leave the Family, but Sullivan feared defying the great elder. Dirk had chided him, an event signaling the end of their active friendship, leaving the whole thing to end on a sour note. Dirk had felt betrayed by Sullivan's decision and Sullivan was never sure if he'd gotten over it.

"I could have helped you then," Dirk went on. "The Grandfather couldn't have touched you. Now . . ." he held up his hands in a gesture indicating helplessness.

"I'm not asking for your help with the Grandfather—or Vannevar," Sullivan explained. "Just tell your people to leave me alone. Jacob has offered me refuge in the park and I need a place to hide."

Dirk looked at him with narrow eyes, scratching his cheek with the point of the knife.

"It's not that simple, Sullivan," he said. "I'm not these people's leader, you know. They do what they please— they don't *obey* me. There's a big price on your head and who can blame someone for trying to collect."

The old saw, Sullivan thought to himself. Dirk, as usual, never admitted responsibility for anything that went on around him, but Sullivan knew he secretly reveled in the influence he carried with most people he met.

"That's bullshit and you know it," Sullivan told him. "Most of this bunch would kiss your ass if you told them to."

Both Joe and Mac shot looks at Sullivan, but Dirk smiled, knowing it was true.

"I'll tell you what," Dirk said, leaning across the desk. "I can get you three days of grace—and three days only. After that, you're on your own. But first"—he grinned— "you have to prove you're man enough to earn it."

He pushed the big sheath knife across the desk toward Sullivan.

"Oh, Christ!" wailed Veronica. "Not that shit again."

Dirk said nothing at first, merely smiling at Sullivan.

"What do you think, man?" he asked.

Sullivan knew what he wanted. A long time ago the

two had made a great deal of money on the waterfront, betting against sailors in an old game: money on the table, the two contestants placed their forearms together and a lit cigarette dropped between them. The first contestant to move away lost, the money going to the winner. Although the pain was intense, the vampires could usually hold out longer than anyone else, knowing that their unnatural physiology would heal most wounds overnight, repairing and replacing scar tissue with fresh, new flesh and skin. It was the idea of the body being irreparably mutilated, Sullivan had decided, that made pain as unbearable as it seemed. The two grew bored with the cigarette trick and one night, while roaring drunk on the blood of intoxicated sailors, they invented a game of their own, more fitting for their kind. Now Dirk wanted to play again, though both of them would require much blood in order to speed the healing process of the disfigurement to come.

Sullivan picked up the knife and, without hesitation, began sawing away at his own left ear. Wincing as he cut through the gristly cartilage, he managed to keep his eyes on Dirk's and a broad smile on his face while he performed the crude surgery.

"There," he said, tossing the bloody knife and the severed ear on the desk.

Dirk, never taking his eyes off Sullivan's, picked up the knife and proceeded to remove his own ear in similar fashion.

"That does it!" Veronica said, banging her way out of the office and down the stairs. "This is too gross. I'm out of here."

The other two vampires, silent, stayed to watch.

Finishing the job, Dirk laid his ear carefully on the desk next to Sullivan's.

"There," he said. Then: "Your turn," and passed the knife back to Sullivan.

Unflinching, Sullivan picked up the knife and sawed off his other ear, tossing it, too, on the desk. Blood ran now from both wounds, staining his neck and shirt.

Dirk, in his turn, removed his other ear, setting the knife back down when he was through.

"So there," he said.

Sullivan grimaced to himself. Obviously if he was going to prove anything to Dirk he'd have to take this thing all the way.

Picking up the knife, he began removing his nose, sawing and chopping, finally pulling it free and tossing it on the table with the rest of the bloody parts lying there. He tossed the knife down in front of Dirk as though throwing down a gauntlet.

Dirk lifted his arms in surrender. "Concede!" he said, rocking back in his chair and laughing. "You win."

"You're getting soft," Sullivan smirked. They hadn't even begun on their eyelids, lips, and tongues yet.

"I'll get you three days of sanctuary, Sullivan," Dirk said. "But after that you're on your own. I can't ask anybody to wait longer than that."

"Thanks," Sullivan said. The sound of his voice was funny, made reedy and whistling by the lack of a nose.

"I'll send Joe and Mac out to spread the word. Hang around another half hour or so till the message gets out. Then you shouldn't have to worry about getting home safe."

The two spent the time reminiscing, each catching up on what the other had been doing in the years since their enforced separation. Hearing of Dirk's exploits along the Haight in the sixties and seventies, Sullivan began to feel he'd missed a part of life spending all his time in unwavering service to the Family.

The four-block walk back to the park was an odd one. Dirk had sincerely assured Sullivan that no one would pay too much attention to his appearance. The Haight was a place where anything goes, he said, and if someone wanted to go out made up to look like a skull, that was that individual's business.

"Besides," Dirk told him, "you look perfect for the *Festivo dello Estinto*. You just started to celebrate a little early, that's all."

But Dirk had lied. There was no mirror in which Sullivan could check his appearance and, taking Dirk's word, he attempted to stroll nonchalantly back out onto the street. The first woman Sullivan bumped into shrieked and jumped back, terrified by his appearance. As he walked along, the crowds along the sidewalk miraculously parted, clearing a path for him, and Sullivan could only imagine how truly horrible he must look.

He made it back to the park without any real trouble but was more than happy to get back into the woods and out of people's sight. His missing features would almost completely regenerate while he slept, but in the meantime he felt more comfortable keeping himself from view.

Returning to Jacob's camp, he told him of Dirk's decision, which pleased the old Gangrel. But before reaching the site, Sullivan had come upon Dwight, snuffling around a garbage can. Sneaking up on him in the dark and shouting "Boo!" he had succeeded in nearly scaring the living shit out of the little rat.

February 3

On a street named Beacon, atop
Billy Goat Hill . . .

"I bring word from the street," said Gregori, shuffling down the stone stairs leading to the rank, bloodstained chamber Selena called her own. He was dressed in his usual filthy, ragged brown cloak, his face dead white, hair another shade of white, eyes sunken pits, blackened and red-rimmed.

"What is it?" Selena asked, stretching languorously on the pile of silken cushions beneath her. She was bored— the youth brought to her earlier this evening had not lasted her long. He lay dead beside her on the dais, drained pale and lifeless. So few lasted her any length of time these days.

"Tell me," she commanded Gregori.

"The diablerie of Domingo has become known," he told her gravely.

The Prince and a select few had known of the crime since the beginning, but now it had become common knowledge among the vampires of the city. "They blame Sullivan."

"Good," she responded.

As long as Sullivan was suspected there was little chance of her and the Sabbat pack being uncovered. That would not do so close to the upcoming *Festivo dello Estinto* and all they had worked for over the years. One of her members, now dead at her own hand, had stumbled across Sullivan and Domingo that night and lingered long enough to drain the Mexican's corpse after Sullivan left it in the bushes. To their good fortune, the Prince chose to hush the affair up, afraid of upsetting plans of his own, and their presence was as yet unsuspected by most. But now the diablerie was revealed to all. She must do something.

"Is Sullivan still staying in Golden Gate Park?" she asked.

"Yes," answered Gregori. "He dwells with Jacob, under his protection."

"Then here's what I wish you and the others to do . . ."

12

The wretched have no friends.

—John Dryden, *All for Love*

Sullivan had lately taken to spending his nights walking along the broad, windy expanse of Ocean Beach on the city's western edge. Running for more than three miles, it is a breezy stretch of the Pacific coastline cooled by the fog banks often lying just offshore. Two hundred yards of gray sand lay between the waterline and the concrete seawall separating the beach from the Great Highway that runs along this part of the coast. Popular for walking, Frisbee throwing, and kite flying, the beach was usualy lit by a bright sun providing fair sunbathing, but the water is too cold for all but the bravest of swimmers and wet-suited surfers.

Since the area was nearly deserted by night, Sullivan found strolls along the water's edge soothing, the rhythmic action of the breakers a salve to his frayed nerves. Some nights he spent hours just watching the freighters steaming out of the Golden Gate, running lights set, distant ports their destinations. He was growing more fond of recalling his days as a sailor: the

110

toil, sweat, and grime; but he remembered it as a far simpler time, and for that somehow cleaner.

Besides, on open ground such as the broad beach, it was difficult for anyone to sneak up on him and attack.

Tonight he was intent on feeding. Ocean Beach had become his regular hunting grounds since taking up residence in the park. Late night dog-walkers or diners coming out of the Cliff House restaurant on the rocky bluffs at the north end of the beach were the most common fare. Sullivan usually drained only a portion of their blood, leaving them alive but unconscious, their memories of the event blurred by amnesia, but healthy all the same.

Spotting what looked to be potential prey coming down the promenade overlooking the seawall, Sullivan slipped down the stairs to the beach and, like a lizard, ascended the sheer concrete wall until he hung just below the lip, out of sight of the couple walking his way.

As he waited patiently, his thoughts turned to his current situation. He had only three days in which to find a new residence. After that the anarchs were sure to come after him and then Jacob would be forced to drive him from the park if Sullivan did not leave voluntarily. Even tonight, upon emerging from the western end of the park by the ocean, he had come across Smash, sitting on his motorcycle parked overlooking the beach, waiting for Sullivan to appear. They said nothing to each other but as Sullivan passed him, Smash held up three fingers, meaningfully. Sullivan was sure he could take Smash in any one-on-one fight but knew the next time the punk came after him he would bring friends. Dirk had confided to Sullivan that he had little or no control over Smash and the people he rode with.

Sullivan calculated he was rapidly running out of time—and friends.

The sound of footsteps coming nearer focused his attention back to the matter at hand. The young couple spotted a few minutes ago were still coming this way, walking back to their car after an evening up at the restaurant. He was Anglo, well-groomed, and in a suit—some sort of businessman, Sullivan guessed. The woman was dark, more exotic—a blend of Hispanic and Asian maybe. Sullivan's hunger gnawed at him as he listened to their approach. Young, vibrant, and healthy, these people were very much unlike the Tenderloin fare Sullivan had long since grown accustomed to: a diet where the possibility of infectious blood diseases was always a concern. The diseases most often were not fatal, but could linger indefinitely, and there was also the concern of passing the disease on to the next victim.

The couple was now very near and Sullivan hugged the wall a little tighter. They talked on, oblivious to his presence. The man had a set of car keys out; Sullivan heard them jingling in his hand. The couple had apparently parked way down here earlier in the day, when the beach was crowded and parking places near the restaurant hard to find.

Sullivan waited until they passed, then smoothly vaulted up and over the wall, landing behind them on silent feet. Neither heard him approach nor guessed his presence until Sullivan sent the man sprawling with a blow to the back of the neck. The woman attempted to scream but Sullivan was already on her, clamping his hand over her mouth and bending back her head to expose her soft throat. He sank his fangs deep in the flesh, lapping up the blood that poured from her throat, quenching the thirst that drove him.

Her blood was sweet and Sullivan allowed himself to sink into the warmth that flowed from her into him. As always, there was that moment he thought he would let himself go and drain her to the depths, consuming her life along with the last drop of her blood, but he pulled away, refusing to be seduced.

He looked down at the small woman in his arms, unconscious, vulnerable. Lapping at the wounds in her throat with his tongue, he gently closed them, his saliva healing them without trace of a scar. Setting her down gently, he checked the man's registration, and, assuring himself he had the right car, loaded the woman into a Toyota parked nearby. He then went back and retrieved her companion from where he lay on the cement, and, carrying him back to the car as well, Sullivan placed him behind the wheel. Sullivan noticed the man's forehead was marked by a wound where he'd struck the concrete, but his pulse was strong and Sullivan judged the injury a minor one. In a few moments one or the other would waken and in the end neither of them would remember a thing. Closing the door, he left the couple where they sat.

It was some time later, nearing the hour of dawn, when Sullivan, toiling up from the south end of the beach toward the park, saw Dwight running toward him. The slender ghoul was waving his arms, calling something that Sullivan could not make out over the roar of the breakers.

"What is it?" Sullivan asked after Dwight finally reached him, taking the panting ghoul by the shoulders.

"It's Jacob." Dwight puffed. "We got attacked in the park. I think they killed him."

"Who?" Sullivan demanded, shaking the ghoul roughly. "Anarchs?"

"Uh-uh," Dwight answered. "Vampires, I think, but not any that I've ever seen before."

"How many *were* there?" Sullivan asked Dwight, puzzled.

"Four or five—I don't know, man. They were everywhere. Coming out of the bushes and everything. I tried to save him, Sullivan—I did, honest. But there were too many. I barely got away with my life."

"Which way?" Sullivan asked, not believing Dwight's stories of selfless heroism for an instant. He was certain the little coward would run at the first sign of trouble.

"Over behind the golf course, in the woods."

Sullivan took off at a run, crossing over the beach and up onto the Great Highway, where he could make better time. Dwight, already winded, tried to keep up with him but rapidly fell behind. By the time Sullivan reached the park Dwight was a couple of hundred yards back and Sullivan had to wait for him to catch up.

"Lead the way," Sullivan ordered him, when the ghoul finally reached his side.

Dwight hesitated, looking up at Sullivan wide-eyed.

"Get the fuck in there," Sullivan said, pushing the ghoul into the woods. "I don't know where this happened. You've gotta show me."

Cautiously, but continually spurred forward by Sullivan, Dwight plowed through the thick growth in the direction of where the attack took place.

"It was up here—somewhere," he said.

Along the way Sullivan questioned Dwight more about the attackers. Dwight's descriptions were sketchy: they were dressed in black, he said, and at least one of them had long, scraggly white hair; but when pressed for details Dwight had no answers. It was apparent that he had not stayed around very long after the attack began.

They found Jacob's head first.

"Shit," said Sullivan when he picked it up to examine it more closely. He had grown fond of Jacob in a very short time. The old Gangrel had befriended Sullivan when he most needed it. Now, looking at the remains of his friend, Sullivan began to feel very alone. Jacob had been the first friend he'd had outside the Family in decades, something he found he needed.

They eventually found all the parts of Jacob's body, some of them distorted and canine in form, indicating the Gangrel had tried changing to wolf form attempting to escape. Sullivan was shocked by the savagery of the killing—even the individual pieces had been torn and gnawed.

But there was evidence of something even worse.

"There's no blood in Jacob's body," Sullivan announced grimly.

"Diablerie?" asked Dwight.

The very word was fearful on the ghoul's lips and Dwight stepped back from the mangled pieces of the corpse, as though Jacob's remains themselves were somehow tainted by this act of blasphemy.

"It's all gone," Sullivan said flatly. "Someone drank it. The marks are all there."

It was over, Sullivan was thinking to himself. It didn't matter what he said now, he'd be accused of this crime for sure. The Primogen would not sit still for the death of Jacob. The blood hunt would be called and Sullivan would be tracked down and killed—extinguished.

"What are we going to do?" Dwight asked, expectantly.

Sullivan looked at him blankly for a moment, not comprehending Dwight's meaning. Then he said, "I don't have the slightest idea what *you're* gonna do. I've got to get out of here, and fast."

If news of Jacob's death got around quickly enough, the blood hunt might be called as early as next evening. Sullivan couldn't risk staying in the park.

"But what about me," Dwight whined. "You know that as soon as people find out that Jacob's dead they'll come looking for me. What'll I do?"

"If I were you," answered Sullivan, "I'd do a real good job of hiding Jacob's remains. The way I figure, the longer it takes for people to find out he's dead, the longer you'll stay alive."

Without another word Sullivan turned and walked away from him, heading north out of the park. Dwight continued to scamper after him.

"But after that," he pleaded, "what do I do? I need food, you know." He took hold of Sullivan's arm, compelling him to stop. "Take me with you, man," he begged. "I got no place—no one. I'll die out here."

"Fuck off," Sullivan told him, shaking the ghoul's arm loose. "You're on your own now."

He walked away.

Dwight stood momentarily frozen in his tracks, undecided what to do.

"Shit," he said, under his breath, then turned and sprinted back to where Jacob's dismembered corpse lay in the grass. By the time Sullivan reached the woods along the northern edge of the park Dwight was already burying the first of Jacob's remains.

February 4

In the secret chambers of the
Primogen Council . . .

Eight of the city's most powerful vampires were meeting in emergency session. Prince Vannevar sat at the head of the huge, polished oak table, members of the Primogen seated on either side of him.

Alicia McGreb was growing impatient. She had heard enough of the Prince's lame excuses and double-talk. She wanted action.

"Vannevar," she shouted from the far end of the table, standing up. "Enough of this. I demand you call the blood hunt, and now. Sullivan cannot be allowed to live."

Despite all the Prince's arguments to the contrary, McGreb remained convinced Sullivan was responsible for Jacob's death in Golden Gate Park.

"I have told you once," the Prince said, his countenance darkening. "There will be no blood hunt!" He was on his feet, pacing around his chair, as he had been since the session began. "Sit, McGreb," he ordered.

Angrily, but silently, the Gangrel elder took her seat.

The Prince returned to the table. He took a moment to consider his options, in the meantime making an effort to bring his temper under control. "We have no conclusive evidence of Sullivan's guilt," he said. "It would be a great crime to condemn an innocent man."

He looked at the vampires seated round the table, taking measure of his support. Nickoli, his finance minister, he could count on, as well as the Tremere Honerius and, of course, the old Dowager seated on his right hand. McGreb, his long running enemy on the council, had enlisted the backing of the Brujah leader Tomaine and the Toreador elder Allanyan Serata. The eighth member of the council, the insane Malkavian elder calling herself Bloody Mary was, as usual, uncommitted.

"And what about the body of Domingo?" McGreb asked.

"What about it?" the Prince questioned her back. "We know Sullivan slew Domingo in self-defense. There is no crime there."

"Domingo's body was drained of its blood," McGreb announced.

Whispers and mumbles went around the table.

"I'm currently conducting an investigation regarding the death of Domingo," was the Prince's answer.

"Not good enough!" McGreb shouted. "You are protecting Sullivan," she accused. "Why?"

He wasn't protecting anybody, the Prince thought to himself. He merely needed to keep Sullivan alive long enough to ensure the fall of the Grandfather. But he couldn't tell McGreb that; she knew little or nothing about his long-range plans.

"I have made my decision," the Prince declared. "Unless the Primogen decide to override by vote."

It was a challenge. McGreb took a quick count: Nickoli, Honerius, and the Dowager would all support the Prince, while she, Serata, and Tomaine stood opposed. The insane Bloody Mary, barely paying attention to the discussion would, as usual, abstain, leaving Vannevar to cast the tie-breaking vote. She could not muster the votes to force her opinion on the Prince.

"Then let the contract stand," McGreb said. "Sanction it."

The Grandfather had put out a private contract on Sullivan's life. An illegal act, it was a law often violated in the vampire world. Family matters were just that and few vampires felt it right to interfere in disputes between an elder and childe. These internal disputes were best settled by the individuals involved.

"I see no harm in that," the Dowager said, suddenly speaking up.

Vannevar was shocked. He had counted the old Nosferatu among his followers, now she was siding with the opposition. For what reason?

"Sanction the contract!" shouted Tomaine, seconding the motion.

A quick vote was taken, the Dowager's desertion to McGreb's camp resulting in a 4–2 vote that resulted in legalizing the Grandfather's contract. Now any vampire could kill Sullivan for the reward with nothing to fear from either the Prince or the Primogen.

"Very well," Vannevar said. "It is done."

"Thank you, my lord, and fellow Primogen," McGreb said, getting up to leave. "I will leave it at this for now. But," she added, "I must warn you, Vannevar. If another Kindred falls victim to diablerie, trust me when I say that I will lead every effort to replace you on the throne."

With that, she left the room, the council members stunned by her words. Few had ever dared speak to the Prince in such a manner and none guessed what his reaction might be. After McGreb was gone Vannevar tried to make light of the incident while the others readied to leave, but it was obvious to all that McGreb's words had angered him.

13

Rattle his bones over the stones!

He's only a pauper, whom nobody owns!

—Thomas Noel,
"The Pauper's Drive"

Sullivan caught a Night Owl bus rolling down Fulton on the northern edge of the park and rode it all the way downtown. Hopping off on Market Street, he headed south, into the flatlands and down into the Mission. With a blood hunt about to be called at any moment he could not afford to be seen by anyone who'd recognize him.

The demise of Delfonso and his henchmen Domingo left the Mission wide-open territory. As yet to be divided amongst the ruling factions of the city, the territory was currently ruled by no one. Although Sullivan might be spotted here by other vampires poaching the district, he felt his chances were better there than trespassing on someone else's territory.

Near Sixteenth and Portrero he found a deserted commercial bakery and kicked his way in. Upstairs he located a reasonably secure resting place in a loft. Covering himself with old tarps, Sullivan spent the day asleep.

That evening he was up early, slinking into the streets as soon as the sun had set. Hungry, he decided to feed first, then look for a better temporary haven for himself. The busiest parts of the Mission were south and west, but Sullivan drifted east and north, avoiding the more populated areas, where other vampires might be loitering, and wandered deeper into a desolate and nearly deserted neighborhood of old, empty warehouses near the bay, called China Basin.

Once an area bustling with stevedores, sailors, warehouses, and cartage firms, the Basin had specialized in shipments to and from the Far East. In the old days Sullivan and Loo had made many trips down to the Basin to pick up special shipments that came in for the Grandfather. With the demise of the city's shipping trade and the closing of the wharf, however, the warehouses were soon emptied and abandoned, the area thereafter becoming one of the most desolate in all San Francisco.

Sullivan felt safest here. Prey would be difficult to locate and more often than not of questionable quality, but at the same time it would be difficult for any stalking undead to hunt Sullivan without his knowing it.

Moving carefully and silently through the shadows, Sullivan crept down the deserted streets like a cat, his senses attuned to the slightest sound or movement.

After skirting a long warehouse for the length of a block, Sullivan carefully peered around the corner, checking out the old concrete loading dock he found there. At the far end of the dock stood an abandoned Dumpster. Behind it Sullivan sensed a presence, a living human being. He saw a foot sticking out past the edge of the Dumpster.

It looked to be a wino, trying to tuck in for the night. He would serve Sullivan's needs.

Gently he crept around the building, sneaking quietly, planning to take his intended victim unawares, avoiding any undue noise. But sniffing the air he noticed something wrong. Among the odors of unwashed human, soiled clothes, and cheap wine he detected the scent of blood. The man was injured, and badly. Hurrying to the spot, he found the wino groaning his last, dying even as Sullivan watched.

Examining the body, Sullivan found that the man had been beaten nearly to a pulp, his face smashed and battered beyond recognition. Massive bruises covered much of the rest of his body and he was so stained with blood that at first Sullivan didn't notice how deadly pale the body was. Two small wounds in the wino's throat confirmed Sullivan's fear: he was not the only vampire in the area.

The most inexplicable thing about the corpse was the regulation-sized softball that had been stuffed in the man's mouth—no easy task. Getting it back out—without cutting either the ball or the corpse—looked even more difficult.

Slowly backing away from the body, Sullivan scanned up and down the dark streets, looking to see if he was being watched. Overhead and to the north, the span of the massive five-lane double-decked Bay Bridge was a constant river of traffic carrying thousands of travelers in cars, trucks, and buses back and forth between the city and the East Bay; but down here, on the ground in China Basin, Sullivan was isolated and alone.

He began working his way out of the area, backtracking toward the Mission, moving as quickly and quietly as he could, hoping to get out of the neighborhood before anyone discovered his presence.

All hope of that was lost when he heard a voice somewhere behind him.

"Cuc-koo," piped the voice.

Sullivan spun around, searching for the source of the sound, but saw nothing. He again moved on, more quickly now.

"Cuc-koo."

This time the sound came from somewhere on his right—a different voice echoing from a nearby darkened alley, or maybe from the rooftop above—he couldn't tell. He moved more quickly, clinging to the left side of the street, as far as possible from where he heard the last sound.

"Cuc-koo."

Another one, this time in front of him. Sullivan stopped, standing still in the middle of the street.

"Cuc-koo," from the left.

"Cuc-koo," in front again.

"Cuc-koo! Cuc-koo! Cuc-koo!"

A veritable chorus of cuckoo birds sounded all around him, echoing off the brick walls of the empty warehouses, ringing again and again, filling the air with their sounds. Sullivan turned in all directions, frantic to spot the source of the unnerving sounds.

Then it fell quiet.

He strained his ears and eyes, searching for any sign of his tormentors.

"Hee-hee-hee."

He saw a head emerge over the edge of a roof across the street: round, white, and bald, its mad leer the product of grease paint and pencil. It giggled again.

"Hee-hee-hee."

The Blood Clowns! Sullivan's worst fears were realized.

He broke into a run as the chorus of cuckoos sounded up again, pursuing him up the street. Shrieks and giggles rent the air around him as he ran, surrounding him, behind him, in front of him.

The jig was up when one of the Clowns stepped out in front of him a couple of dozen yards away, blocking his path. Sullivan now knew he was hopelessly surrounded.

"Hey, mister! What did you do to our ball?" the strangely dressed character demanded of Sullivan, walking toward him. He was swinging a baseball bat.

The clown, painted in whiteface, was costumed like a little boy of the last century, sort of a parody on the Little Lord Fauntleroy look, complete with hat and oversized tie. All this despite the fact the clown was over six feet tall and had to weigh at least 250 pounds.

"I don't know what you're talking about," Sullivan responded, trying to decide how one talked to a madman.

The clown continued walking toward Sullivan, who noticed the two-foot-long plastic penis strapped to the vampire's waist. Dangling between the clown's legs, it bounced off his knees with every step.

"You took our ball, you meanie! Give it back!" demanded the clown. He raised the bat as if to strike.

"Stop!" Another clown jumped into the fray. A woman, decked out like a little girl with pigtails, stepped from a nearby alley to get between them.

"Cut it out, Kyle," she ordered the other clown. "He doesn't have the ball."

She turned to Sullivan. "Our last ball's name was Ed," she explained. "At least that's what he kept telling us, until Kyle went and hit a *home run*." She glared at her companion, giving him a rueful look.

"Pow!" shouted Kyle, swinging the bat. "Boy, I hit the old pumpkin a good one. Right over the fence."

Sullivan thought of the battered wino and the softball shoved in his mouth, and winced.

More clowns kept creeping forward. There were six of them now.

"Our ball didn't work so good anymore after that," the girl clown explained. "So we started using him for home plate." Sullivan noticed the clowns all wore cleated baseball shoes.

"We're gonna join a softball league this year," said one of the clowns who hadn't spoken till now.

"Yeah," said another. "We're gonna call our team 'The Serial Killers.'"

"We're all changing our names," said the girl clown. "We're gonna be famous serial killers with our names written right across the backs of our shirts so everybody can read 'em."

"I'm Ted Bundy," said one clown, proudly.

"I'm Henry Lee Lucas," said another.

"And I'm David Berkowitz, Son of Sam," said the clown standing next to Sullivan.

And without further ado the clown yanked out a huge revolver and, before Sullivan could react, fired it point-blank into the side of Sullivan's head.

The .38 roared in the night, the barrel so close to

Sullivan's face that his skin was scorched and his hair singed by the muzzle flash. The slug crashed through his skull, into his brain, knocking Sullivan off his feet and hurling him to the ground.

"Random violence! Random violence!" the clowns began shouting, kicking and beating Sullivan as he lay nearly helpless on the ground. He tried to crawl, lifting himself on one arm. His eyes were swimming; he couldn't think straight. His left side felt funny and neither his arm nor leg seemed to respond to his commands.

When the clowns saw him trying to get up, they changed tactics.

"Monkey pile!" they all shouted, then began jumping and climbing on him, smashing Sullivan back into the dirt. Hands pulled at him, at his clothes, his ears and lips.

Then they began feeding. One pulled off Sullivan's boot and sank his fangs into the big toe, lapping up the blood that poured from the wound. Others also attacked with their teeth, drawing out his blood and, with it, his life. The pain throbbing in his brain soon eased as consciousness began to escape him. He would be dead soon, he realized quite calmly, and that would be okay, too, he thought.

Then he felt the weight lifted from him and light poured down so he could see. Now lying on his back he saw the clowns scattering in all directions, whooping and laughing as a beautiful silver-haired figure clad in white robes floated above him. An angel had come to take him away to heaven, Sullivan thought, closing his eyes . . .

February 5

At the Federal Building in downtown San Francisco . . .

With a flourish, Special Agent Simmons put his signature on the bottom of his report and put it with the stack of paperwork to be filed later. Special Agent Markowitz stopped by his desk.

"How goes it?" he asked Simmons.

"I'm tired," Simmons said, leaning back in his chair and stretching his arms over his head. "I'm due for vacation soon. I'm taking Julie and the kids to Tahoe next month."

"Any sign of Phillips?"

The suspected serial killer had been reported seen in Oakland, in the company of another man, a local black preacher named Hayes. Somehow involved in a fire that destroyed an abandoned body shop and a next-door church belonging to his companion, Phillips had next been spotted in San Francisco, around Chinatown.

"Nothing," Simmons answered him. "We've checked with the locals and nobody's seen hide nor hair of him for more than a week. You know how that neighborhood is."

Chinatown kept its secrets.

"You think he's left town?"

"Could be." Simmons said. "But who knows?"

It was nearing five o'clock in the afternoon. The two agents started getting ready to go home for the day. A few minutes later they were gone.

14

Extremes Meet.

> —Louis-Sébastien Mercier,
> *Tableaux de Paris*

Sullivan awoke lying on his back, coughing, spitting clots of blood from his mouth, his head pounding. Eyes still closed, he lifted a feeble hand to gingerly touch the wound in the side of his head. He was surprised when his fingers touched a soft bandage, expertly tied, covering his injury.

He felt a hand on his wrist and his arm was gently pulled away from the wound. He was too weak to resist.

"Don't touch it right now," someone reprimanded him. "You'll be fine if you just leave it alone and stop fussing at it."

Sullivan opened his eyes, his vision swimming for a moment before settling down and focusing. He found himself in a comfortable-looking living room, lying on his back on a couch, feet up with shoes off. Directly before him stood a large, ceramic table lamp shedding a yellowish light. Hung on the wall behind it, to the right, was a landscape painting his blurry vision couldn't identify.

He tried to turn his head to the right, toward the voice that spoke to him, but the pain made him stop. He closed his eyes again and groaned.

"Don't try to move yet," the voice said, now coming from directly above him.

Sullivan cracked his eyes open again and found himself looking up into the face of the very same angel he had seen in China Basin.

His first instinct was to leap to his feet but he found his body unwilling to obey his commands.

"Just relax, now," the angel said. "Your left side's still partially paralyzed, but you'll heal. We're a hard breed to kill, you know. Just give it some time."

The angel stood up, the face swinging out of Sullivan's view. He heard him call out, "Will, have you got that compress ready yet?"

The voice that answered him came from somewhere else in the house.

"Noo!" someone said. "How could anyone expect to find anything in this kitchen?"

The response was followed by a crashing noise, the sound of several pots and pans falling to the floor, followed by someone's cursing.

"I'll be there. Hold on," the angel said, then to Sullivan: "I'll be right back." Sullivan heard him leave the room.

By now he thought he'd recognized the face of the angel: it was Eddie Conlan, he was sure of it. Formerly a female impersonator working down in the old Folsom district after World War II, Eddie had been befriended and eventually embraced by Sebastian Melmoth, the Toreador operator of San Francisco's secret Vampire Club. Eddie was queer as a three-dollar bill, Sullivan knew, but then it seemed to him that half the Toreador clan was some sort of deviant or other, or so he figured. He'd heard Eddie had picked up a dose of AIDS somewhere and soon after dropped out of the social circle and out of sight. That was years ago. He still lived somewhere in the Castro, Sullivan knew, continuing to suffer from the effects of the disease.

An ongoing argument was running in the other room—the kitchen, Sullivan supposed—then Eddie the Angel came back.

"Here we are. I'll put this on the side of your head. It'll make you feel better."

Sullivan felt the warmth of the compress flooding his injury, soothing his nerves.

"Better?" Angel asked, leaning over him again so Sullivan could see his face.

Eddie still looked young, but his face was too lean: too lean for the always–whippet-thin Eddie, too lean even for a vampire. The flesh, hidden under the thick pancake Angel wore, was parched and dry-looking, his cheekbones too severe, his pursed and painted lips coarse and wrinkled. Sullivan noticed two raw sores on his cheek, partially disguised by the makeup.

"Better," Sullivan managed to answer.

Angel fussed with the compress.

"Here," he said, lifting Sullivan's right arm. "You'll have to hold this in place while I get some tape."

Sullivan held the compress close while Angel left. Already the warmth was driving the pain out. He could feel his body repairing itself, grafting bone, regrowing lost tissue. He moved his head slightly, the pain now subsiding a little, and checked out the rest of the room. Not overly large, it was tastefully decorated and clean. Books stored on rows of shelves indicated a reader lived in the house.

Angel came back into the room and saw Sullivan had moved his head.

"We *are* feeling better, aren't we?" He had with him a spool of adhesive tape. "This will fix us up. I used to work in a hospital, you know."

Sullivan, now seeing him full length, realized why he'd first thought him an angel. Draped in white gauzy robes, barefoot, his hair long, curled, and tinted with silver and gold, the effect was positively ethereal; pale and wispy, Angel seemed hardly there at all. Thinking about it, Sullivan recalled the Blood Clowns—and the attack.

"What happened?" he whispered, while Angel taped the compress down.

"I'm afraid you fell afoul of everybody's favorite Malkavians."

The Malkavian clan of vampires were all, to one degree or another, insane. The Clowns were some of the most violent of the lot, a street gang operating on the fringes of the Masquerade, barely tolerated by the Prince and the Primogen.

"You saved me?" Sullivan asked, still unclear about what went on after the gunshot.

"More or less," said Angel, taking a seat in an upholstered chair facing the couch. "You see, the Clowns—insane as they pretend to be—fear me just as much as the rest of them. In their case, they flee at the sight of me. It's really all a joke. I think they know I don't intend them any harm."

He raised his arms and fluttered his robes, bugging his eyes to startling effect. "Ooooo! They call me the Death Angel," he said.

Eddie had dropped out of sight soon after contracting the disease. Though nothing much was ever said, it was plain that most of the vampires preferred not to associate with him. Sullivan was no exception, though he and Eddie had never associated anyway.

Feeling began to return to Sullivan's side as nerves and tissue continued to regenerate at abnormal rates. Feeling better, he carefully swung his feet down and tried to sit up. Angel jumped up to help him, but Sullivan waved him away, preferring to do it by himself.

"Oh, you always *were* the 'butch,' weren't you," Angel said, sitting back down, crossing his legs while he watched Sullivan struggle to a sitting position. The effort left him woozy, but he felt better for having made it.

"What time is it?" he asked Angel.

"Nearly four in the morning. You were unconscious for almost four hours."

Angel told him how he had stumbled upon Sullivan after he'd fallen into the hands of the Clowns. Angel roamed many territories in search of victims these days, usually unhampered by local ruling lords, who ordinarily prosecuted trespassers. They knew a single nip from Angel would be enough to transmit the disease and, fearing infection, allowed him his little indulgences—provided he brought no trouble down upon the local lord. It was only by chance that he wandered into China Basin last night and came upon Sullivan and his playmates.

"You know, of course," Angel said, rather abruptly, "I only feed from the already infected."

Sullivan wondered why Angel brought it up. Did he sense Sullivan's unease? Was he trying to reassure him? Still partially crippled and nearly helpless, the thought of the "deadly poisonous" vampire seated across from him made Sullivan think of a cobra.

"I made that decision years ago—after I learned I was sick," Angel continued. "I was one of the very first to promote 'safe sex,'" he smiled, ruefully. "You have nothing to fear."

Angel sat back in his chair and called over his shoulder: "Will, will you please come out and say 'Hello.'"

The racket in the distant kitchen that had been ongoing throughout their conversation now stopped.

"I want you to meet Will," Angel said to Sullivan.

A small man in his late thirties appeared in the doorway. Thinning of hair, he was once probably pudgy, Sullivan guessed, but he was quite thin now—though looking positively well fed next to Angel. Will, like Angel, also bore signs of the dread disease.

Will was scowling at Angel when he appeared in the doorway but seeing Sullivan sitting up beamed a sincere smile at the patient.

"Hello," he said.

"Will helped us out tonight," Angel explained. "He came and picked us up in the car after I found you. I'm rarely feeling well enough these days to perform the kinds of feats our kind are used to," he added. "I really didn't think I could carry you all the way home."

"Thank you," Sullivan told Will. "You saved my life."

"It was no problem," Will assured him. Then, turning to Angel, he said, "I'll finish up in the kitchen now, if it's all right with you?"

"Please. Go ahead." Angel waved him away.

"Will's really a dear," Angel confided, when his companion was out of earshot. "We've been together for nearly three years now. It's just that's it's been one of *those* nights, you know."

"He's a ghoul?" Sullivan asked.

He was unsure. Will's unhealthy pallor confused his condition.

"Yes. I did him not long after we met. He was very unhealthy at the time and I originally planned to take him all the way. You know—put him out of his misery and all that."

Sullivan nodded his understanding.

"Anyway, he was so nice I thought maybe this would stop the progress of the disease. It's seemed to slow it, but not really halted it, I'm afraid. I don't think it's a permanent fix."

Angel looked over his shoulder to make sure Will was still out of the room.

"If I thought I could get away with it," he whispered, "I'd make him a vampire and be done with it. But I'm sure Vannevar would never approve. I don't even bother to make the request."

Sullivan wondered aloud why Angel just didn't do it anyway. Who would stop him, he argued. Most of the other vampires were deathly afraid of Angel.

"They would exterminate me without another thought," Angel told him. "They kill what they fear, Sullivan. As long as I offer no threat to them they'll allow me to live. But should I do anything to frighten them—should I dare to create another like myself—they would feel compelled to eliminate me."

Sullivan understood. He then asked Angel if he'd heard of a blood hunt called by the Primogen.

"None that I know of," he answered. "I'm sure I would have heard if there was. I can check it out tomorrow and see what I can find out," Angel offered.

Dawn grew near and Angel suggested bed. Sullivan, feeling better all the time, was able to get to his feet and, with Angel's help, shuffle the few yards through the hallway to a back room that served as Angel's haven.

"I'm afraid our sleeping arrangements may be a little cramped today," Angel apologized as they entered the room and closed the door.

The room was empty, save for a large coffin lying on the floor. Sullivan couldn't believe it.

"I know its a bit melodramatic," Angel said, "but a lot of show-biz people have made a habit of sleeping in coffins. In my case, it seemed perfect. I can make other arrangements for you tomorrow," Angel said. "But for today this is the best we can do. None of the rooms are light-tight. I never needed to bother." He opened the lid.

Sullivan looked at the open coffin before him with trepidation, contemplating the situation. Already the first gray light of dawn was peeping through the sheer curtains. Soon the sun would be over the horizon and he had to be out of reach of its burning rays.

"Come on," Angel coaxed gently, moving him toward the coffin. "I won't bite. I promise."

Realizing he had no choice, Sullivan allowed Angel to help him lie down, then watched helplessly as Angel clambered in next to him and closed the lid, surrounding the pair in darkness.

February 7

In an overcrowded, dusty book shop on Haight Street . . .

It was nearing ten o'clock and Marty Chin was getting ready to close when the last customer of the day stepped through the entrance, setting the little bell over the door to ringing. Marty, wishing he had flipped the sign on the front door to "Closed," turned to see who the late-night browser would be. He was a little surprised to find a tall, handsome woman in a tailored suit looking at him.

"Mr. Chin?" she asked.

"Yes," he said. "Marty Chin, that's me."

"I'm looking for information," she said, opening her hand and showing Marty the tiny statue she held.

Chin was known around the city as an information broker. One of the few humans in San Francisco aware of the control the undead had over the city, he was privy to a great many secrets. Only the fact that most believed he held secret damaging evidence against them allowed him to survive. It was a dangerous business, but a profitable one.

Upon seeing the recognition symbol he nodded, smiling. He should have guessed, he thought to himself. This woman wasn't even human.

"Of course, madam," he said obsequiously. "What can I help you with tonight?"

"I'm looking for a man named Sullivan," she told him, handing him an envelope stuffed with hundred-dollar bills.

15

**What is a friend? A single soul
dwelling in two bodies.**

—Aristotle, attributed

The first evening Sullivan slept at
Angel's house he awoke with a start. Finding himself
cramped in the strange coffin, Angel's arms around him,
a chill passed through him as his memory reassembled
events of the night before. Angel awoke as well and,
opening the coffin, let in some light. Seeing the expression on Sullivan's face he said, "Don't worry. I told you I
don't bite. And I didn't."

Sullivan still looked ill at ease.

"And if *you* had tried anything," Angel went on, "I
would have awakened and stopped you."

Sullivan had not found food the night before and had
gone to bed hungry. In his current condition, he'd worried about what he might try in his sleep. Awake, the
gnawing, empty feeling soon returned.

Angel helped him up from the coffin. Once on his feet
Sullivan discovered he could stand and walk unaided.

In the living room the pair found a brand-new box
spring and mattress, procured by Will during the day.
Sullivan felt relieved when he saw it. Will looked pleased
at his response.

"Did you call Ross like I asked you to?" Angel asked Will.

"All done," said Will.

Angel explained to Sullivan that they had contacted a friend willing to provide sustenance for Sullivan. Ross was a trustworthy soul and HIV-negative. Although either Angel or Will could have fed Sullivan the night before—and would have—the risk of infection was too great.

Ross, a tall, good-looking man in his early thirties, arrived a half hour later. A tennis player and golfer, he was tanned and in fine shape. Standing next to Angel and Will, he positively radiated health and vitality.

Ross and Sullivan retired to the privacy of the back room to feed while Will helped Angel prepare for the evening. As usual, Angel would float through the streets of San Francisco seeking his particular brand of victim, those hopelessly struck by disease and facing death's door.

Ross and Sullivan emerged after a short time, Sullivan looking a good deal stronger and fit while Ross showed obvious signs of exhaustion from the blood loss he'd suffered. Ross sat down heavily in a chair, leaning his head back and closing his eyes while Will went to get him something to eat and drink. Two marks, barely noticeable, showed in Ross's forearm.

"I'm sorry I took so much," Sullivan apologized as he sat down across from Ross, looking only a little stronger than the drained human. "I didn't mean to."

"That's okay," Ross said, waving his hand at him. "You needed it more than I did. Besides, it wasn't completely unenjoyable."

Sullivan fell silent, frowning slightly.

Will brought tea and some cookies on a tray. Ross gratefully accepted the offer.

"The Red Cross always gives their donors this sort of thing," Will said. "I don't know if it really does any good or not, but it seems a fine excuse, anyway."

Ross thanked him again.

"Well, I'm off!" announced Angel, appearing from nowhere, flouncing through the room, heading for the front door.

His appearance was similar to that of the night before though Sullivan noticed the different cut of his robes, and altered makeup and hair. "I'll see you boys later," he chimed, then he was gone.

Sullivan noticed how Ross and Will watched Angel as he departed. The affection the two men felt for the vampire was apparent.

"He really is quite remarkable, in his own way," Will told Sullivan, guessing the latter's thoughts. "A bit of a pain in the ass at times, but still quite remarkable."

Ross laughed at Will's remark.

"He's become a bit of a legend in the Castro," Ross offered. "A lot of non-Kindred know about him—because of what he does and all."

Will explained that Angel particularly sought out victims near death—those for whom the suffering had grown intolerable. So many had he dispatched this way, and so well known was he among the gay community, that he had been dubbed the "Death Angel," an almost mythical figure of mercy believed to visit the sick and dying. Angel had quickly adopted the nickname.

Ross told his story.

"I accidentally met up with Angel when he visited my brother," he said. "Jim was dying at the time and Angel had come to take him away. I was staying at Jim's house taking care of him, and accidentally stumbled onto Angel just as he finished him off."

Ross stopped a moment, lost in thought.

Will said, "Angel says that Ross nearly pissed his pants when he came into the room and saw him standing there." He laughed.

The somber mood that had threatened their conversation was broken and Ross smiled again.

"Anyway," he said, going on, "I've been friends with Angel and Will ever since—nearly two years now."

They talked a bit more but Ross left a short time later, feeling strong enough to drive home. Sullivan and Will talked a little, then Will retired to the den to read, leaving Sullivan to entertain himself. He soon found himself growing bored. He couldn't remember the last time he had spent a whole night trapped in a house. He watched television for a while but, finding nothing of interest, shut the machine off.

Angel came home an hour before dawn with good news for Sullivan.

"I checked around," he announced. "And there's no blood hunt. Vannevar has refused to call one, citing a lack of proof of your involvement."

Sullivan sighed with relief.

"The bad news, however," Angel continued, "is that Vannevar has sanctioned the Grandfather's contract."

That meant that although the Primogen had declined to name Sullivan outlaw, they would not disapprove of the Grandfather's contract nor attempts made by anybody to kill or capture Sullivan, as long as the Masquerade was not endangered, of course.

"You can stay here as long as you wish," Angel told Sullivan, noting the concern on his guest's face. "You're safe here. Believe me, most of them are too scared to come anywhere near me or my haven."

Sullivan slept that day on his new bed, placed in the light-sealed room next to Angel's coffin.

Sullivan spent the next few days recovering. Nearly daily visits by Ross were reinforced by blood given Sullivan by a man named Richard and one or two other of Angel and Will's human friends, but Ross was there nearly every day, and it was from Ross that Sullivan drank the most often. During their private moments together the two struck up a friendship. The subject of AIDS was brought up. So many of the people Sullivan had met lately were infected, or at least knew many who were. Sullivan mentioned how lucky Ross was that he had escaped the virus.

"I guess so," Ross answered him. "But testing negative is an odd feeling—sort of like being the only survivor of a plane crash that kills all your friends and family. You keep asking yourself: 'Why me?' It's lonely, and somehow you almost feel guilty."

Sullivan knew the feeling. He had felt the same way after the loss of his crew aboard the death ship that night in the Golden Gate. Of all those men, he had been the only one to survive. In those early years, he had often asked himself, "Why?"

Evenings were spent with Will, who Sullivan learned had formerly owned a used book store. Sullivan had never been much of a reader but was intrigued by the collection of books on vampirism Will owned. Most of them, Will explained, were apocryphal—written by cranks and pretenders, the information no more than a collection of half-baked folktales and old legends. A few, however, were more reliable and accurate.

Will was well-read on the subject it turned out, and surprised to discover how little Sullivan actually knew about the shadowy vampire world he lived in. Sullivan was intrigued by all the different vampire clans that Will knew about, some of which were familiar to him, others which he'd never heard of. Many facts, Will explained, were obscured by secrecy and rumor—a result of the Masquerade, perpetrated by the vampires of the Middle Ages in an effort to escape the persecutions of the Inquisition.

Sullivan read some of the books Will recommended, though slowly, and only off and on, but he did get interested in some of the myths about vampire origins—particularly those that traced the race of vampires all the way back to Cain, the accursed son of Adam and Eve and the murderer of his brother, Abel. Just as normal humankind believed they had inherited the original sin of Adam and Eve, Sullivan learned that he and his kind likewise bore the "Mark of Caine," the curse of the original kin-slayer.

Sullivan also grew interested in his own vampiric roots. He did not have a clan, as far as he knew. While most of the vampires he'd known were members of one of the dozen or more known and identified clans, Sullivan had never thought of himself as anything but a member of the Family. Will told him that little was known about the vampires of

Asia and that although most believed that all vampires were descended from common ancestors, the evidence coming out of Asia indicated that many of the undead of that continent were of strange and mysterious types unknown anywhere else. Sullivan remembered what he'd seen of the Grandfather in the basement that night and shuddered.

Friday was Ross's thirty-first birthday and Will planned a little get-together at the house. It had been four days since Sullivan had been shot by the Blood Clowns and he was now nearly completely recovered. The last couple of nights had seen him growing bored and restless, wanting to get out of the house, but kept inside by the knowledge that he was in no condition to face off against another vampire. Talking it over with Angel, Sullivan had decided he should wait another night, then venture out, with Angel along to help protect him.

Tonight Sullivan helped Will in the kitchen, peeling the potatoes while Will prepared food for the party guests who partook. In the dining room Angel and Richard hung streamers and inflated a few balloons. Ross, unsuspecting, arrived right on time to a chorus of "Surprise!" and the festivities began. Wine and food were served and conversation was lively, the jokes many.

An hour into the party the doorbell rang and Will got up to answer it.

"I don't know who that is," he said, leaving the table. "Everybody that's invited is already here."

The conversation picked back up, but Sullivan kept an ear cocked for trouble. He heard Will open the door and then some conversation taking place between him and the caller. Although he couldn't hear what was being said, the voices were calm and Sullivan assumed all was well. He turned his attention back to the discussion at the table.

Talk abruptly stopped a moment later when Will appeared in the doorway accompanied by a guest: a tall, elegant, blond woman in an expensive, tailored suit. She looked around the room, her blue eyes eventually alighting on Sullivan, seated on the other side of the table.

She looked familiar, but Sullivan at first couldn't place her. Then, with a sudden flash of recognition, he jumped up from his seat.

"Kathy?" he asked in disbelief.

"Hi, Sullivan," Kathy said.

February 9

On a street named Beacon, atop Billy Goat Hill . . .

Lounging on the pillow-covered dais, Selena heard someone opening the heavy wooden door above.

"Who is it," she called.

"Gregori," called a voice. "I bring a gift."

Selena sat up, watching as the little vampire hopped down the steps, dragging a bound captive behind him. The man was dressed in ragged clothing. Large-nosed, his pockmarked face was scarred by fresh burns. Barely conscious, him head banged on the stone steps as Gregori dragged him downstairs by his feet.

"I caught him lurking around Angel's house," Gregori explained.

Gregori had been sent to spy on Sullivan's activities.

"He was hiding in the bushes across the street. He didn't see me coming," Gregori snickered, his snake tongue flickering in and out of his mouth.

"Who is he?" Selena said, getting to her feet and walking over to examine the captive. There was a rumor going round that one of the Primogen had for some reason lured a vampire-hunter to the city.

"All is well . . ." mumbled the man on the floor, his head rolling back and forth. "Have faith in the all- knowing father . . ."

He was delirious, but his words sounded somehow familiar to Selena.

"I wonder . . ." she mused. "Take him to the rear chamber, Gregori. We'll make him talk." She turned and strode from the room, heading for a special chamber kept out of sight. "We'll find out who he is and maybe, after some persuasion, find a way to turn him to our own uses."

Gregori followed behind Selena, dragging the poor captive roughly over the stone floor.

"Of course," he said.

16

And a woman is only a woman, but a good cigar is a smoke.

—Rudyard Kipling,
Departmental Ditties: "The Betrothed"

Kathy was asked to sit down, and Ross got up to help her with her chair. Sullivan, surprised to find himself on his feet, sat back down.

He marveled at the way Kathy looked; and it wasn't just simply the expensive hairdo and clothing, nor the tasteful makeup, so unlike how he was used to seeing her. She was a ghoul—he realized that right off the bat—but even more than that, she looked vibrant and healthy. Sullivan wondered if she was off the dope; her blue eyes were so clear, her voice even and her speech modulated.

Kathy joined in the party, talking and laughing, telling the others only a little about her and Sullivan's former acquaintance, alluding to the fact that they used to work together. Sullivan went along with it, revealing nothing of their former pimp–prostitute relationship.

Later, Sullivan got Kathy off by herself in another room and was able to question her.

"I work for Vannevar these days," she told him, explaining how, after being picked up at the airport, she had been brought back to the city to face the Prince.

"He's not really that bad a guy," she said.

He had helped Kathy get off the dope, she explained, and now had her set up working for him. She had her own car and everything. Sullivan mentioned how much better she was dressing and actually complimented her on how good she looked.

"Thank you," she said, flattered by the attention.

Then she proceeded to explain why she was here.

"Vannevar's been looking for you. He has a deal to offer."

"What sort of deal," Sullivan asked, wary.

"The Prince really has nothing against you," she said. "He'd like to help you, in fact, but you need to help him, first."

"What could I do?"

Sullivan was puzzled.

"He wants you to kill the Grandfather."

Sullivan didn't answer; he didn't know what to say.

"Vannevar promises you protection if you do the job. With the Grandfather out of the way, Vannevar and the Dowager consolidate Chinatown, increasing his power base. His Primogen enemies on the council will be unable to muster the power to oppose him.

"Of course," she continued, "the Prince assumes you have your own reasons for wanting the Grandfather out of the way, as well. The contract on your life is a personal one. It dies with the Grandfather."

Sure, Sullivan thought. Get rid of the Grandfather. But how?

"Can Vannevar offer me any help? Any kind of aid?"

Sullivan had no idea how he might destroy a creature as powerful as the Grandfather.

"None," was the answer. "Vannevar can in no way be perceived as helping you. The slightest hint that he has made overt moves against one of the local lords could topple him from power. It must never be known that he had anything to do with it. Once the deed is done, however, he can openly support you—and will."

Sullivan thought about it. He could conceive no way

of pulling off such a stunt, but on the other hand, he couldn't see where his life offered much in the way of alternatives.

"Where do we go from here?" he finally asked.

"The Prince wishes to meet with you," Kathy said.

Sullivan's eyebrows went up. The Prince? Facing Vannevar in the flesh was an awesome prospect.

"Where?" he asked. "When?"

"I'll make the arrangements, now that we know you're interested. I'll telephone tomorrow and let you know the details."

Kathy left a few minutes later, driving off in a shiny new Lexus. Sullivan watched the car until it was out of sight. He couldn't get over how good Kathy looked compared to the old Tenderloin days.

He also couldn't get over the idea that the Prince wanted to meet with him.

He went back to the party and joined in, but his thoughts were distracted by the unexpected events of the evening, and the anticipation of meeting the Prince.

The next night Angel and Sullivan left the house together. It was Sullivan's first taste of freedom in almost a week and the night air tasted sweet and intoxicating. He was still a little stiff from the gunshot wound but otherwise felt strong and alert, ready to test himself. He spent a couple hours in the company of Angel, following him on his rounds of AIDS patients, but soon grew restless and decided to move off on his own.

"Are you sure you'll be okay?" Angel asked, before allowing him to leave. "There's still a contract on your head, you know, and people will be looking for you."

"I'll be fine," Sullivan assured him.

He felt strong and fit enough to meet most challenges, he thought to himself as he slipped through the streets. Nonetheless, he was careful to steer clear of China Basin and the maniac Blood Clowns.

He worked his way along the western fringes of the Mission, stopping once to feed on a secretary walking home late from work. Sullivan's quiet attack made her later still, but he released her for the most part unharmed, though a little weaker for the experience. Afterward, he continued roaming north, drawn always toward the glittering spires of downtown.

An hour later he was skulking along the south side of busy Market Street, peering across the traffic at the hilly streets the other side of the city's main thoroughfare. Still hungry after the secretary, he had taken yet another victim a few blocks to the south, just a half hour earlier. His healing body demanded the additional vitæ, the extra blood further accelerating the healing process. A night spent out walking the town had also helped to exercise some of the stiffness out of his joints.

Now he lingered on the edge of forbidden territory, watching, wondering, wishing he could somehow return to his own familiar world. On a sudden impulse he dashed across the street, ignoring the traffic signals, feeling an odd exhilaration as he once again set foot on his old home territory. He knew coming here was foolish, unforgivably risky to even think about, but without further hesitation he headed north, in the direction of Chinatown, driven by a deep need to take the risky chance.

Hiding in the shadows of Grant Street south of Bush, across from the Chinatown gate, Sullivan watched the tourists moving in and out of his old haunts. The scent of exotic foods brought back memories of the old days, when he'd actually lived on this street—then called DuPont. Sullivan had been known as the "white devil"— the Grandfather's heathen enforcer—in the days before the earthquake and Sullivan's subsequent move to Pine Street. For a while he had bossed a string of opium dens and fan-tan parlors, catering to the dope addicts and gamblers of the old city.

Then he spotted Loo, moving through the crowd across the street. Hurriedly, Sullivan stepped back into a darkened doorway, out of sight. Carefully, he watched.

Loo took up position in the center of the gate, waiting, peering down Bush Street. It was obvious he was

waiting for someone to arrive; he was prepared to con-
duct the official ceremony of entrance that Sullivan had
undergone on the nights he'd visited the Grandfather.

A Yellow cab pulled up at the curb and a woman got
out of the back. She turned to pay the driver and Sullivan
got a glimpse of her face, but he already knew who it was
as soon as she pulled up—Kathy! She and Loo quickly
performed the ceremony of entrance and then she
stepped inside Chinatown. Talking together, the two disappeared among the crowd.

Sullivan arrived back at the house to find Angel waiting for him.

"How'd it go?" he asked. "We were starting to worry."
Will was also up and around.

"Fine. No problem." Sullivan said, distracted.

"Kathy called a while ago," Will said. "She says the
meeting's all set for tomorrow night. She'll pick you up
at ten."

"Did she say where the meeting was?"

"No," answered Will. "I didn't think to ask."

"Look," Sullivan said, turning to Angel, "something's
happened. I need your help."

Angel listened closely as Sullivan explained.

February 10

In the Mayor's Public Relations
Office, City Hall . . .

The phones on Jayne Hallender's desk were ringing off the
hook. Her boss, the mayor's press agent, was holding
down as many calls as he could while the other assistant,
Mike, dealt with the crowd of reporters storming the door.

Exasperated, she grabbed the nearest phone.

"Hello, Mayor's Press Office," she said, dreading what
was coming next.

The voice at the other end of the line yapped loud

enough to be heard halfway across the room, forcing Jayne to hold the phone an inch or more away from her ear. She closed her eyes and listened. Christ, she thought to herself, this was only her second day on the job.

"Yes, sir," she said as politely as she could. "That's right. The mayor has delayed the *Festivo dello Estinto* as you've obviously heard. How long? I don't know, sir— probably no more than a week or two . . ."

The angry voice cut her off.

"I understand, sir," she continued. "Many people are upset by the cancellation, but the mayor assures us it is only temporary."

The phone went dead, the angry caller hanging up on her in midsentence.

It had been like this all day, ever since the mayor's unexpected announcement postponing the long-planned event. Merchants and community agencies were up in arms: money had been spent on publicity, printing, etc., now all to be lost? She had no answers for the callers, able only to tell them what little she'd been told.

The phones rang on. Jayne grabbed another one.

17

The first blow is half the battle.

—Oliver Goldsmith,
She Stoops to Conquer

Kathy pulled up in front of Angel's house at ten o'clock on the dot. Sullivan was ready for her and out the door at her approach, quickly getting in the front seat of the car.

"Good evening," she smiled.

"Hi." Sullivan said, adjusting the seat, trying to appear nonchalant.

Kathy backed out of the drive and wheeled the Lexus around, heading back down the hill. Soon in traffic, their conversation was light, meaningless. Sullivan made a show of adjusting his seat, pulling himself up and around, glancing out the rear window in the process, trying to see if they were being followed.

"You all right?" Kathy asked. "You seem fidgety."

"Yeah. Fine," he answered. Checking, he'd seen the headlights of Will's dark blue Hyundai behind them. He was relieved to find his backup on their tail.

As an afterthought he added, "I guess I'm nervous. It's not every night you meet the Prince."

Kathy smiled and nodded, not taking her eyes off the road.

Lying bitch, Sullivan thought to himself. After spotting her with Loo, he and Angel had done some checking. No one had seen or heard of anyone matching Kathy's description working for Vannevar. There were, however, numerous reports placing her in and around Chinatown the last couple of weeks.

"So, where we goin'?" Sullivan asked.

They had been heading east along Army Street, on the southern end of the Mission, traveling in the direction of the bay.

"It's a secret," she said. "You know I'm not supposed to tell."

"Well, I think I got a right to fuckin' know," he said, testily.

The tension was wearing him thin, he noticed, fraying his nerves. He tried to calm himself.

"After all," he said, "what difference can it make now?"

"It's up ahead a little ways," Kathy pointed. "Along the channel."

She turned the car down a narrow street running between rows of old warehouses. Sullivan threw a glance over his shoulder as they went round the corner; the Hyundai was still there, but way back. Will had let too much space open up between them. Sullivan hoped he'd seen them make the turn down the side street.

Islais Creek Channel is an old natural stream, now dredged straight and square, lined with concrete and surrounded by gravel. Unused, the area is barren, devoid of structures and people. The warehouse district just north of it is as desolate as any in the city, and it offered Sullivan little in the way of reassurance. Blithely allowing himself to be led into what he was sure was a trap, he could only hope that his backup was still in tow.

As they drew nearer the channel, now visible past the last rows of warehouses, Sullivan began to feel somewhat annoyed that Loo and the Family thought him stupid enough to walk into such an obvious trap. Then he recalled his close brush with death in the deserted Oakland body shop. He felt pleased to note that he had grown at least a little wiser of late. Or maybe he was just luckier, he thought.

Arriving at the bank of the channel, they saw a darkened car parked near the water's edge: a Mercedes.

"Is that Vannevar?" Sullivan asked innocently, pointing at the car.

"That's him," Kathy answered.

Sullivan asked the stupid question just to watch Kathy lie. Hearing the deceit rolling from her lips made everything he had to do that night just that much easier.

They rolled past the parked Mercedes, then Kathy turned the car and nosed it up to the channel and parked about thirty feet from the Mercedes. Killing the lights and engine, she opened the door and hopped out.

"Let's go," she said.

Sullivan got out too and looked back up the street, searching for any sign of the Hyundai. He saw nothing, but that was to order. Sullivan had told them to wait out of sight until they were sure it was a trap—just in case it really was Vannevar that Sullivan was meeting.

Kathy and Sullivan walked toward the darkened Mercedes, their footsteps crunching in the gravel. The far side passenger door of the car opened and a tall figure emerged, silhouetted in the night.

Vannevar? wondered Sullivan. He still had a little hope.

Then he recognized the man's movements, his cadaverous look. It was Chi, the ghoul. The nearer door opened and Loo got out. He faced Sullivan.

"Good evening, brother," he said.

Sullivan stopped in his tracks. Kathy stepped away from him to take up a position next to Loo. Chi joined the pair on Loo's other side. The ghoul carried a bronze bowl in his hands, covered by a lid.

"So what's the deal?" Sullivan asked, still playing stupid. "I thought I was supposed to meet the Prince."

There was no sign yet of Sullivan's compatriots: Will, Angel, and Ross. He began to worry they'd gotten lost.

"The Grandfather wants to see you," Loo answered.

Loo's face was grim, Sullivan noted, even angry. Loo had always maintained a cheerful, chipper attitude, but tonight he was different.

"Well, I don't want to see him." Sullivan continued to stall, hoping his friends would appear.

"You really have little choice. I am ordered either to bring you back or kill you."

"I don't want to kill you, Loo," was Sullivan's response.

"You won't. Chi has brought something here to ensure our success."

Sullivan glanced at the bowl Chi held. There was no telling what secret thing that bowl contained—Chi was a master of many conjurations. Sullivan continued to stall, watching desperately for any sign of his friends. He saw Chi's hand inching slowly toward the lid of the bowl.

"What's the Grandfather want of me?" Sullivan asked, trying to buy time.

Then the Hyundai appeared from out of the alley, turned toward the group, and bore straight down on them. It skidding to a stop a few yards away, spewing gravel, and the doors flew open. Ross clambered out of the passenger seat, the pistol in his hand pointed at Chi. Will got out from behind the wheel, followed by Angel crawling out of the cramped backseat.

Chi and Loo had remained calm at the approach of the car and at the sight of Ross and Will, but when Angel emerged, Loo's attention was distracted. It was then Sullivan saw his chance. With two quick bounds he closed the distance between them and before Loo could get away Sullivan had both hands around his neck. The force of Sullivan's attack drove them both back against the Mercedes, Loo's head smashing through the glass of the window. Shards of glass fell to the gravel as Sullivan yanked Loo back out and spun him around.

Chi, meanwhile, stepping back from the fracas, lifted the lid on the bronze bowl, releasing long tendrils of curling black smoke that twisted and wriggled forth, lengthening, writhing as though alive.

Angel rushed at Chi to stop the ghoul, but Ross's pistol was faster. Chi was hit by three quick shots and, dropping the brass bowl to clatter on the gravel, stumbled backward and fell over the edge of the canal into the chilly waters below. Angel rushed to the edge, stopping at the brink to stare down after the fallen ghoul.

Kathy, seeing Loo attacked, leaped to his defense, jumping on Sullivan's back, sinking her teeth into his neck while Sullivan struggled to hold on to his slippery, twisting opponent. Howling in pain, Sullivan reached a hand behind him and grabbed Kathy by the scruff of the neck, tore her loose, and slammed her headfirst into the side of the car. She slid to the ground in a heap.

Angel, still staring after the fallen Chi, searching for some sign of the ghoul in the black waters, didn't notice the fallen bronze bowl behind him, nor the black whip-like tentacles that continued to grow and spread, now lashing and twisting their way across the ground toward the unsuspecting Angel's ankles.

"Look out!" Will shouted, rushing forward and booting the bowl across the gravel. It bounced and rolled toward the canal and, with a final hop, disappeared over the edge, dragging the flailing tendrils behind it. The bowl splashed into the water eight feet below, where it immediately erupted, sending up a wall of glowing green water that momentarily towered over Will and Angel before plunging back down, drenching them.

Meanwhile Loo, his axe in hand, had squirmed partially free of Sullivan's grip and managed to lay his blade deep into Sullivan's forearm before the bigger man managed to twist the weapon away from him. Suddenly spinning Loo around and lifting him off his feet, Sullivan bent him backward over his knee and, with a loud snap, broke Loo's spine.

Dropping the paralyzed vampire to the gravel, Sullivan picked up the fallen axe. He fell on Loo's chest with both knees and, taking hold of Loo's hair with one hand, raised the axe above his head.

"One of us would lose, the other win," Loo said weakly. "That was known a long time ago. I congratulate you on your victory, brother." He stopped to cough blood, then said, "But the loser gets a consolation prize. He gets to die."

•

Sullivan brought the axe down with a crunch, separating Loo's head from his body.

"Are you all right?" asked Ross, rushing to aid Sullivan, already getting back to his feet.

"I'm all right," he said. "I won."

Will and Angel were checking the fallen Kathy.

"She's still alive," said Angel, checking her throat for a pulse. "But just barely. Her skull's badly fractured."

Sullivan had spared none of his might when he smashed Kathy against the car. He'd enjoyed the opportunity to punish her betrayal.

"So?" was all he said.

They loaded Loo's decapitated corpse into the front seat of the Mercedes, then pushed the vehicle over the edge of the canal into the water. Watching it slowly sink amidst a gurgling froth of bubbles, Sullivan asked if anyone knew what happened to Chi.

"I didn't see him," Angel said. "He must have sunk like a stone."

"He may have died in the explosion, after I kicked in the bowl," Will offered.

Sullivan thought they might be mistaken. He knew the wily Chi far better than any of them.

Sullivan drove the Lexus back to Angel's house, accompanied by Ross. Will and Angel took the Hyundai, with Kathy's unconscious form carefully loaded into the backseat.

"What do those two intend to do with her?" Sullivan grumbled to Ross on the way home.

"We couldn't just leave her there," Ross said.

Sullivan had voted to dump her in the Mercedes with Loo's body and be done with it.

"The woman's a liar. A traitor," he said. "She doesn't deserve to live."

"Angel said the wound was pretty bad," Ross offered. "He doesn't think she'll survive more than a couple of hours anyway, if that makes you any happier."

Rebuked, Sullivan said nothing. They made the rest of the ride back home to the Castro in silence.

At the house Kathy was placed gently on the couch, the same one Sullivan had rested on the night he'd almost been killed by the Blood Clowns. Sullivan knew that Angel had rescued him that night for no particular reason other than that was simply the way Angel was. He guessed he couldn't really blame him for trying to save Kathy now.

Angel and Will bathed the wound and bandaged it while Sullivan paced and fretted. Killing Loo had left him upset, but with no time to mourn. He knew there was no hope for him now unless he managed somehow to kill the Grandfather. Actually, he thought, accomplishing it should be easy. With Loo out of the way, and possibly Chi, the Grandfather had little to protect him from an outright assault. Escaping with his life, Sullivan knew, would be the hard part. The more he thought about it, the more he became convinced that the sooner he did it the better. Waiting even a night would only give the Grandfather more time to prepare for him. If he hit him tonight, Sullivan reasoned, he might even get to the Grandfather before he learned of the deaths of Loo and Chi.

"I don't think she'll last another hour," Angel announced, coming back to the hall, where Sullivan was doing his pacing and planning. "The fracture's only minor, but there seems to be a serious concussion."

Lost in his own thoughts, Sullivan barely noticed what Angel was saying.

"How about a hospital?" Ross suggested, joining the pair in the hall. Will was still in the living room with Kathy.

"Too late," Angel said. "There's nothing anybody can do, I'm afraid."

The three were silent for a moment, then Ross spoke up.

"You could save her, couldn't you, Sullivan."

Sullivan looked at him askance, not catching his meaning. Then it dawned on him what Ross was driving at.

"You mean, turn her?" he finally asked, almost incredulous.

Ross was suggesting Sullivan make her a vampire.

"You could," Angel chipped in. "I would do it, in fact, but we all know the consequences of that."

"What for?" Sullivan wanted to know. He couldn't understand their concern for a woman who had just set a trap for him. He knew that she'd made quite an impression on all of them that night she'd dropped by for a visit, but he didn't expect this.

"She's an untrustworthy bitch and always has been," Sullivan insisted.

"She was loyal to Loo," Ross said. "She risked her life for him."

"Loo had helped her," Angel added. "Loyalty breeds loyalty, Sullivan. What did you ever do for her?"

The truth about Sullivan and Kathy's former relationship had been made known to them after Sullivan discovered her treachery. Angel had a point, he supposed. But he didn't like being cornered like this. He fought back.

"Vannevar wouldn't allow it," he said.

"Vannevar's not here," Angel said, in a matter-of-fact tone. "Besides, if he finds out and doesn't like it, then it's up to him to end her life. Why should it be *your* decision?"

Angel's twisted logic only served to confuse Sullivan further. Argue as he might, he could sense that he was losing the battle. Despite her treachery, his friends liked Kathy, had enjoyed her company at the party the other night, and now were concerned for her.

"She doesn't have anyone else in the world, Sullivan," Angel said. "She would be your childe and loyal only to you—if you can earn it."

The war was lost. Ross and Angel had made Sullivan feel so guilty that he felt he had no choice but to accede to their wishes. He finally agreed to go through with it.

Left alone with Kathy in the living room, he knelt by the couch, looking down on her face. Her breathing was shallow, her pulse weak. The right side of her head was bundled in bandages: the same side he'd been injured on, Sullivan realized.

Gently he pierced her throat with his fangs, lapping at the blood that flowed slowly and weakly from the wound. Her pulse fluttered as Sullivan drank deeper, tasting the bittersweet life that had been Kathy's. Her blood grew gradually cooler as Sullivan drank on, her pulse growing faint. She grew paler and paler until at last, with a convulsive shiver, life passed from her body. With a final rush the last of Kathy's blood flowed into Sullivan's mouth, and with it her existence.

Sullivan rose slowly to his feet, staggering a moment, filled with the energy of another's life now totally consumed. Then, with his fingernail, he opened his forearm, a line of blood marking the cut he made, rivulets forming and running down toward his wrist. Gently he took hold of Kathy's head, and opening her mouth, allowed some of the blood to drip between her parted lips.

There was no reaction at first and Sullivan stopped for a moment to massage her throat, trying to insure the vitæ he gave her reached where it was needed. Then he fed her again.

This time there was a reaction. Kathy coughed once, then moved. Opening her eyes, she saw Sullivan's bloody forearm in front of her and suddenly sat up, grabbed his bloodied arm, and sank her teeth into it. Sullivan almost swooned as he felt the warm blood rushing back out of his body in a torrent.

Kathy was voracious and she sucked and swallowed as Sullivan grew faint. Finally, with an effort of will, he pulled his arm away, Kathy snapping after it with sharp, white teeth. Then she came fully awake, suddenly conscious of where she was.

"Sullivan?" she gasped, when she saw him standing in front of her.

"Hi," he said, trying to sound noncommittal.

February 11

**Stuck in a late-night traffic jam near
the approach to the Bay Bridge . . .**

"Damn it," Tomaine swore to himself as he nudged the Mercedes along through clogged traffic.

Auto traffic getting off and on the bridge was so busy round the clock that even the slightest problem resulted in backups and delays. Somewhere up ahead two motorists in a fender bender were making thousands late.

Angrily, Tomaine grabbed the cellular phone and punched a memory dial. He hated to use a radiophone when making a call like this, but it was a chance he was willing to take. Besides, what was life without a little risk.

The phone on the other end rang three times, then someone picked up.

"Hello," said a sleepy voice.

"Denton?" Tomaine asked.

"Yes," said the voice, suddenly waking up. Denton was a city councilman.

"You know who this is?"

The voice answered in the affirmative.

"I don't think we should go along with the mayor's decision to delay the *Festivo*. What do you think?"

The voice agreed, hesitantly.

"A lot of people got hopes riding on this affair. It's not right to cancel it out from under them."

Denton kept saying yes.

"I suggest you talk with Ms. Tildon. She always supports the public," Tomaine told him. "Do this right," he added, "and you might be in line for the mayor's job next election."

Denton thanked him and hung up.

Tomaine clicked the phone off and hung it back up.

That should take care of things, he told himself. He'd been trying to find out who was behind the *Festivo* for weeks. Failing, he had convinced Vannevar that the Sabbat was behind it and that it should be delayed. Now, with Denton breaking with Vannevar's mayor and leading the people against the decision, he would almost ensure that the Prince's mayor was finished in this town. Spreading the rumor about the Mexican communists, Tomaine felt, was an inspired stroke of genius. He hoped the controversy would draw the Sabbat out.

The traffic was still crawling. Tomaine blew his horn.

"Assholes," he muttered to himself.

18

That is not dead which can eternal lie,

And with strange aeons even death may die.

—Abd al-Azrad,
Kitab al Azif

Sullivan spent a few minutes with Kathy, but felt he had little time for idle chitchat. Leaving her to the care of the others, he began making preparations for the assault on the Grandfather. Angel tried to dissuade Sullivan, pointing out that he was still weak from reviving Kathy, but he was adamant. He wanted to take the Grandfather while the elder was still weak and unsuspecting. If Sullivan allowed the thing to muster its strength, he reasoned, there would be that much less chance of coming out with his life.

In the garage under the house he found a lawn mower and gasoline. Using beer bottles, he fashioned a pair of Molotov cocktails. Putting them in a bag along with the severed head of Loo, he got ready to leave the house.

"I'll go with you," Angel offered.

"No thanks," Sullivan said. "Too dangerous."

"That doesn't matter," Angel argued. "Besides, you need somebody to watch your back. I can guard the entrance to make sure that no one follows you in."

Reluctantly, Sullivan finally agreed, and soon the two

were in the Lexus, headed for the city. Ross and Will stayed behind to look after Kathy.

"Slow down," Angel complained as Sullivan wove in and out of traffic, still congested in certain parts of town even at three in the morning. "Let's get there in one piece, all right?"

There wasn't much time left before dawn—only a couple of hours—and Sullivan felt pressed by the clock. All during the drive he kept replaying the events of the night, seeing over and over the death of Loo, watching his brother die again and again. But it also gave him the strength to do the job before him. Thinking about how the Grandfather had played them one against the other all these years kept him angry enough to face what was coming. Regardless, he eased up on the car's accelerator, a little.

Once in the city, Sullivan brought the Lexus into Chinatown via a back route up Jackson Street. Traffic was light, but the street congested with delivery trucks bringing fresh produce, fish, and meats to the markets. Sullivan fretted, looking at the clock as they slowly crawled along. Finally, growing frustrated, he grabbed the bag out of the backseat, shut off the car, and got out.

"Let's go," he told Angel. "We'll go on foot."

"How'll we get back home?" Angel asked, looking behind them at the Lexus abandoned in the middle of the street. Already the horns of other drivers left trapped behind the empty car were honking.

"I don't know," Sullivan said. "We'll figure that out later." In truth, he wasn't considering it at all. Sullivan had little hope of surviving the night.

In the alley they found the back door to the fish shop locked, the store closed for the night. With a single boot Sullivan kicked the door in, shattering the frame. Inside, the shop was dark and quiet; it looked empty.

"Wait here," Sullivan said, lowering his voice. "The Grandfather's down there," he said, indicating the stairs leading to the basement. "Don't let anyone down after me."

Then he was gone, silently slipping down the steps into the darkened basement below.

There was no light in the underground and Sullivan

had to feel his way through the gloom, the air heavy with the by-now familiar scent of incense masking the foul odor of decay. Once in the passageway the darkness grew so thick that even Sullivan's sensitive eyes had trouble penetrating it.

After a few moments he reached the shadowy antechamber that led to the Grandfather's room. Here he paused, listening near the entrance. From the room beyond, the Grandfather's chamber, Sullivan heard the heavy, rasping breathing of the monstrous thing that was his elder, as well as the voice of David the ghoul. The ghoul was moving about the chamber, saying something Sullivan could not make out.

Sullivan crept forward, being careful not to bump the tables with their loads of carved jades and ivories. He stood near the curtain now: the silk tapestry dividing the antechamber from the Grandfather's quarters. It was quiet, David no longer speaking. Only the whistling sound of the Grandfather's breathing was audible. Sullivan hesitated a second, then parted the tapestry and stepped through.

The Grandfather squatted in its customary place at the far end of the chamber. Its mask was off, its hideous half-human, half-insect face revealed. The thing bent forward, looking down on the kneeling David who fed from one of the Grandfather's grotesquely twisted limbs. As Sullivan watched, the Grandfather moved slightly, dislodging some of the vermin feeding on its open sores, sending a score of maggots raining down on the kneeling David. The skin of the Grandfather was covered with pus-laden sacks, each looking as though ready to burst at a touch, draining and becoming another one of the myriad open sores covering the monster. Sullivan was revolted at the sight of the thing he had for so many years obeyed without question, and by David the ghoul, who drew inhuman vitality so willingly from the monstrous entity.

"Grandfather!" Sullivan shouted at it.

The thing looked up, cocking its head, peering at Sullivan. David stopped feeding and, getting to his feet, turned to face the intruder. The pair looked surprised.

Sullivan guessed they hadn't yet learned the outcome of the evening's events.

"Sullivan," said the Grandfather, slyly, changing its expression from one of surprise to inhuman friendliness. "What brings you here tonight."

"I brought you a present," he said, reaching into the bag. "Here," he said, tossing Loo's head across the room at the pair.

It sailed through the air, turning over lazily, bouncing on the stone floor and rolling over twice before coming to rest in front of the Grandfather, its eyes staring up at him.

The Grandfather stared at the head a moment, disbelieving, then looked up.

"Kin-Slayer!" the Grandfather bellowed, pointing at Sullivan with a long, horned finger. "Kill him!"

The Grandfather began gathering itself to spring, but it was too late. While the pair's attention was on Loo's head Sullivan had taken the opportunity to ready and light the two Molotovs and he heaved them one after the other at the monster. Both hit their mark, shattering on the hard cartilage and gnarled bone that made the Grandfather's exoskeleton. Flames shot up instantly as the gasoline spread and burned, setting alight the Grandfather's robes as well as the tapestries and hangings decorating the chamber. The Grandfather-thing roared in pain, twisting up to its full height of nearly twelve feet in a futile effort to escape the flames now engulfing it.

Sullivan dived for the doorway but failed to reckon on David, who beat Sullivan to the punch, knocking him off his feet with a flying tackle. Sullivan fell over backward, away from the exit he hoped to reach, David wrapped tightly around his legs. He tried desperately to get loose, kicking David mercilessly with his free foot, but the ghoul hung on for dear life, refusing to let go.

The Grandfather, wrapped in flames, staggered slowly toward them, the bright light from its flaring torchlike body illuminating the room with dancing light. Robes now burned clean away, the naked monster stumbled as it slowly walked toward them. Suddenly falling against the wall, it almost collapsed but managed to push itself back upright and came on, reaching toward the pair struggling on the floor. Hate twisted its face as pieces of burned flesh fell to the floor—a burning tower, a pillar of roaring flame, a walking funeral pyre filling the room with smoke dense as pitch.

Then a shadowy figure appeared in the doorway. David screamed as someone hit him from behind and Sullivan felt his ankle suddenly released. Instantly he was on his feet and stumbling out the door, just as the Grandfather took his final step and toppled over headlong—a crashing, burning *Hindenburg*, glowing ribs showing through incinerated flesh like so many twisted beams and girders. Falling atop the screaming David, the Grandfather crushed out the ghoul's life.

Staggering through the doorway, Sullivan banged into someone: the rescuer he had seen strike David from behind.

"Quick!" a woman's voice said. "Let's get out of here."

It was Kathy. She had saved Sullivan from the Grandfather and was now helping him escape the holocaust. She got Sullivan back to his feet while behind them the Grandfather-thing raised itself on one arm, let out a final roar, then collapsed in a heap in a shower of ash and sparks.

"How'd you get here?" Sullivan gasped, as they headed up the passageway to the shop's basement.

"Will brought me—after Ross helped me out. I got healthy on his blood."

She was still half tugging Sullivan along; he could barely keep his feet. Even as they reached the stairs they could see that the shop above them was already filling with smoke, ready to burst into flames.

"C'mon," she said. "It's getting near dawn."

Angel was waiting for them at the top of the stairs and helped Kathy pull Sullivan out of the building. Will was in the Hyundai, parked at the end of the alley, its engine running. Already, building fire alarms were ringing and Sullivan could hear distant sirens as firemen raced to the scene. The trio raced to the car but were surprised when a tall, cadaverous figure suddenly came running from the street around the corner.

It was Chi, looking weak and injured, but still with enough strength to try and save the Grandfather. Sullivan pulled himself up, prepared to fight the ghoul, but Chi passed them by with nary a glance. They watched him hurry down the alley, then, without a second's hesitation, plunge into the burning building through the shattered door. A moment later there was a roar as something inside the burning building collapsed, sending a cloud of smoke and ash pouring out the doorway.

"And good riddance to that one," Angel said.

Soon they were headed back to the Castro and a few minutes later, safe inside Angel's house. They found Ross asleep on the couch, resting from the blood loss he suffered to help Kathy gain the strength she needed to aid Sullivan.

Dawn was near and the three vampires quickly retired, leaving discussion of the night's events until later that evening. Kathy shared Sullivan's bed.

February 12

In a luxurious residential suite atop one of San Francisco's finest hotels ...

Lord Honerius held his glass of blood in toast with the Prince and Nickoli, Primogen minister of finance. They were enjoying their success.

"To the fall of the Grandfather, gentleman," said Vannevar, hoisting his glass, then taking another deep swallow. "And to our continued success."

The three had been congratulating themselves all evening but still Honerius sensed something was wrong. The Prince kept coming back again and again to the subject of Sullivan. Why had he survived, the Prince wanted to know. Years of forecasting had shown over and over again the death of the kin-slayer along with the demise of the Grandfather.

"I would not trouble myself too much about this, my lord," Honerius kept telling him. "You know as well as I the variables involved in such an undertaking as this. We should just be happy that we've succeeded and not worry about details. We have greater challenges ahead of us—the Sabbat, for one."

Evidence of the dark sect of vampires known as the Sabbat had lately surfaced. Practitioners of diablerie, the two cases discovered so far had been attributed to their presence. It was soon discovered that the Sabbat was behind the upcoming *Festivo dello Estinto*, forcing Vannevar to try and delay it.

"I have taken care of that for now," Vannevar brushed it off. "The *Festivo* is indefinitely delayed; the mayor is bound to his decision."

"He will lose votes," interjected Nickoli. "It is doubtful we can count on his reelection next year."

"No matter," said the Prince. "We can find another to fill his shoes. You have some promising young men groomed and in shape, I trust."

"Indeed I do," answered Nickoli, smiling.

"But let's talk about Sullivan," said the Prince, again returning to the subject Honerius hated. "Why did he live?" he asked rhetorically. "Because of the interference of another vampire, never foreseen by us—a woman who would not now exist if a certain Phillips had not, *by chance*, wandered onto our little scene."

"But I thought you liked Sullivan," Honerius said, trying a new tack, growing desperate now. "He still lives. You should be happy."

"Of course I'm happy," Vannevar said. "But that doesn't negate the fact that I suspect you of planning and plotting behind my back, Honerius."

"No, my lord," he argued.

"Enough!" the Prince commanded.

Honerius fell silent.

"Leave my sight," the Prince ordered him.

Honerius set down his glass and left the room. At the doorway he turned to give his customary departing.

"I wish you well, my lord. Have faith in the all-knowing father," he said.

"Save it," Vannevar scowled at him. "Just get out of here."

Defeated, Honerius took his leave.

"So what's to be done now with Sullivan?" Nickoli asked, after Honerius had left.

"We shall see," said Vannevar. "We need to bring Sullivan into the fold. I think I have a plan."

19

Strange to see how a good dinner and feasting reconciles everybody.

—Samuel Pepys, *Diary*

"Here—try this one on," Ross said, handing Sullivan a black sport coat.

Sullivan slipped on the tailored coat and checked himself in the mirror. The fit was good; he and Ross were nearly the same size.

"That looks fine," Ross smiled, hands on hips. "Let's find you some shoes, now."

Ross had brought a selection of his clothes from his Sunset house for Sullivan to try on. Tonight was perhaps the biggest evening in Sullivan's life and he wanted to look right. Ross had even brought a razor and Sullivan, for the first time in decades, was clean-shaven. Tonight, he had an audience with the Prince.

Vannevar had sent word to Sullivan, indicating he was pleased with the death of the Grandfather and happy to learn that Sullivan survived. He assured Sullivan that no charges would be brought against him regarding his recent actions and he had been cleared of any accusations of diablerie. In effect, he had been pardoned.

Furthermore, Sullivan was invited to attend a special

function being held at the Vampire Club on the city's north side, in the Marina. Word was out that the Prince intended to sanction Sullivan as an independent vampire, which would, incidentally, give him the right to retain a childe.

Approval of Kathy's status within the vampire world was essential to her continued existence. Kathy was currently in the other room with Angel, who was helping her with her makeup. She'd been out shopping earlier with Will and had come home with an armload of boxes and bags. She'd given Sullivan a preview of the skimpy black cocktail dress she intended to wear tonight.

While Sullivan tried on clothes, Will sat in a nearby chair, poring over books, as he had for the last few days, ever since the destruction of the Grandfather.

"It says here," Will spoke up, finger tracing the lines on the page in front of him, "that other worlds and places can be tapped by the wise magician, and from these worlds aid and succor drawn. Apparently," he said looking up, "that's what Chi was trying to do. I'm not exactly sure, but one book refers to creatures called 'Nyarlix' and describes something similar to what we saw crawling out of Chi's bowl."

Sullivan paid only a little attention to what Will was saying, busy trying on different coats, slacks, and shoes, and checking himself in the mirror.

"I don't know," Sullivan said, talking to Ross. "Maybe we should rent the tux, like we discussed."

"Don't worry about it," Ross advised. "Dressing for the occasion is a must, Angel tells me, but style is according to choice. Some will be in formal wear, others casual, while others will be making statements of their own."

Sullivan felt some trepidation at the thought of all the vampires he would meet tonight. Many of them he already knew, of course, from his years in the city, but never had he been with more than a few at a time. The Vampire Club catered exclusively to his kind and was known as a place where the undead could let their hair down by dropping the Masquerade for a few brief hours of relaxation.

Angel came into the room. "My, don't we look nice," he said admiringly, looking Sullivan up and down.

"Maybe better than we hoped for," Ross kidded.

Sullivan walked around the room in a little circle, getting the feel of the new clothes. The fabric seemed too delicate compared to his usual jeans and wool jacket and he felt a little uncomfortable realizing how easily it would snag or rip. He also worried about getting Ross's fine clothes dirty.

"Don't worry," Ross had told him. "They'll always clean."

Nonetheless, Sullivan had opted for the darkest clothing in the lot, hoping that any stains he picked up would show less.

Kathy suddenly appeared in the doorway.

"Ta-dah." She twirled around to show off the dress.

Will and Ross smiled when they saw her, and Angel applauded. Sullivan was dumbstruck.

With her hair swept back and her makeup subdued, dressed in a new outfit, Kathy once again appeared to Sullivan as an entirely new person, much as she had the night she'd first shown up at Angel's in the tailored suit. Sullivan began to realize he knew very little about this woman. Like a chameleon, she seemed to change with her environment.

And she looked radiant. Like all vampires, her skin was pale, even more so in the black dress, but glowing all the same with a vitality and energy more than human. Kathy's blue eyes flashed with excitement and anticipation. She was a long way from the dope-riddled whore he used to know.

It was nearing time to leave, and, after getting their coats, they were walked to the door by Angel and Will. Ross had his extra clothes thrown over his arm, ready to go home to the Sunset.

"Good luck," Angel told Kathy, kissing her on the cheek. "You two have a good time."

"Don't wait up for us," Kathy called back over her shoulder.

Ross said good-night and left in his BMW. Kathy and

Sullivan had the keys for Will's Hyundai, the Lexus having been abandoned in Chinatown the night Sullivan killed his Grandfather.

The death of the Grandfather had sent shock waves through the vampire community. Most, in fact, were glad to know the monster was gone, having feared the thing's presence in the city for over a century and a half. Still, the demise of the mysterious Asian vampire threatened the precarious balance of power in the vampire world. Vannevar had ridden through it well, though, seeming to emerge from all of it stronger than ever. Chinatown was already consolidating under the Dowager, and the Mission District had been parceled out to those who called most loudly for the execution or expulsion of Sullivan. The killing of an elder was no small matter; many elders quite naturally felt it set a bad example for their own offspring. The usual penalty for such a crime was death, but Vannevar had talked them out of it— though buying off those who complained most loudly was no inexpensive matter. The Prince had convinced the Primogen that Sullivan had actually done them all a favor and hence deserved to live. Feted with additional territories and privileges, they had finally voted to recognize Sullivan as a vampire in his own right, a title giving him the privilege to create and retain a childe.

"What's Vannevar look like?" Kathy asked as they drove north, making their way toward the Marina and the Vampire Club.

Sullivan described the Prince as best he remembered him. They had met only once before, years and years ago, when Sullivan had been formally presented after Vannevar's accession to the throne. He had been impressed by the Prince at the time, remembering him as tall and thin in the aristocratic manner. Thomas had been an officer in America's Revolutionary War and seemed to Sullivan to combine the intelligence and breeding of the upper class with the practical mind of a military man. As a mark of his origins, Vannevar still kept his chestnut hair tied back in a small queue. Meeting him that one time, Sullivan had been frightened by Vannevar's might, but admired him all the same.

In the Marina, Sullivan steered the car up the winding private drive toward the gated wall that surrounded the club and its adjoining apartment building, the Westminster. The plaque mounted on the stone wall read:

THE ALEXANDRIAN CLUB
FOUNDED 1917
PRIVATE
MEMBERS ONLY

He stopped at the guardhouse in front of the opened gate.

"Sullivan," he said. "And Kathy."

The ghoul on duty waved them through.

Sullivan had been here only a couple of times before. Open to all vampires of all clans and persuasions, the club was "neutral ground," where resentments were supposed to be forgotten, and violence forbidden. The club's building was actually a steel-hulled yacht, washed ashore during the 1906 earthquake. Righted, reinforced, and redecorated, it was opened eleven years later with much fanfare. Although owned by the Prince, it was operated solely by its foppish manager, Sebastian Melmoth.

A valet took the Hyundai at the front door, driving it into a lot already crowded with Mercedes, Cadillacs, and other luxury cars. Will's dark blue Hyundai looked positively cowed by the company.

Tex R. Cainen met the couple at the door. An old hand in San Francisco, Tex and Sullivan knew each other from earlier days.

"How's it been, buddy?" shouted Tex when he saw Sullivan. "I've been looking forward to seeing you again."

He slapped Sullivan on the back, then turned to Kathy.

"And who's this?" he asked, charmingly.

Sullivan made introductions and then followed Tex

into the Alexandrian Room. Here, mingled with the vampires and ghouls, were human retainers: some enthralled, others associating with the undead of their own free will. The Alexandrian Room existed specifically for these humans. The actual Vampire Club, downstairs, was off-limits to them. No mortal who entered that lower chamber ever returned alive.

Sebastian Melmoth was moving about the room, chatting with guests, making sure things were right. Small and slight of build, his longish silky brown hair was tied back with a red bow. Melmoth was dressed in a black leather vest and skintight leather pants with the butt cut out. Spying Sullivan and Kathy from across the room, he waved to them, calling out a cheery "Hello" while making his way to them through the crowded tables.

"Good evening," he said, when he reached them. "The Alexandrian Club pays welcome to its guest of honor this evening." He made a slight bow toward Sullivan. He then made a show of kissing Kathy's hand.

Sullivan had never liked Sebastian much. Sharp-witted and sharper-tongued, he'd always made a point of trying to make Sullivan feel inadequate. Now, since getting to know Angel, and discovering how Sebastian had more or less abandoned his own childe, he found he liked him even less. Despite all this, he managed to grunt a fairly friendly hello.

"Come," Melmoth said. "I'll show you to the party."

Taking Kathy by the arm, he showed them the way to the stairs leading down to the Vampire Club, Tex taking his leave to return to the front door.

As they descended the thirteen steps, Sullivan felt a quiver of fear. He had anticipated this evening for days, anxious to meet the Prince but at the same time never quite believing it was all true. The Vampire Club's law of neutrality was inviolate and Sullivan had no rational reason to believe Vannevar was out to get him, but he had walked into too many traps lately not to feel at least a little bit antsy.

In front of him Sebastian and Kathy chatted and joked casually. Sullivan tried to calm himself and followed along behind, finally reaching the huge wooden door marked "Private."

Melmoth opened the door and Sullivan was greeted by a wave of noise, light, and motion—all enhanced by the tang of human blood hanging in the air. The room inside was packed, filled with vampires of all ages, all clans, dressed in all manner of styles from antique to ultramodern. The buzz of conversation competed with recorded music pouring out of a hidden speaker system. Most of the revelers held crystal goblets of blood in their hands, taking occasional sips as they chatted and mingled. The blood they consumed was of varying types, Sullivan noted, sniffing at the air, and very fresh as well.

Standing aside, Melmoth waved the pair in and Sullivan and Kathy stepped into the swirling mix, immediately becoming caught up in the crowd. Faces appeared as if from out of nowhere, smiling, saying hello, many of them congratulating Sullivan and shaking his hand. Some of the vampires he spoke to he recognized but others he didn't. Only a few were old acquaintances.

Someone put a drink in his hand. Hungering, he took a swallow. The taste of fine whiskey—scotch—slid smoothly down his throat. Melmoth, he learned later, kept specially prepared stocks of blood, drawn from donors sated on liquors and other sorts of treats generally forbidden the vampire's select diet.

The crowd made way as Sullivan and Kathy walked through the club, working their way to the rear of the chamber. Here the last of the crowd stepped aside to reveal Vannevar Thomas, the Prince of San Francisco.

The Prince was standing, chatting with an older vampire, his arm around the waist of his beautiful mistress, Donna Cambridge. He was dressed in an older style. Sans coat, he wore a white shirt, open at the collar, with slightly puffed sleeves and French cuffs. His pants were black, his feet shod in black boots of soft leather. He looked much the way Sullivan remembered him: tall, thin, with strong eyes and a hawkish nose. Descendants of early American settlers, Vannevar claimed to have the blood of American Indians in his family background.

"Welcome," Vannevar called, seeing Sullivan emerge from the crowd. Setting down his drink, the Prince stepped forward to greet him with open arms, hugging Sullivan and slapping him on the back, then planting two kisses—French-style—on his cheeks.

Sullivan was taken aback by the greeting. He knew that Vannevar was supposed to have been pleased by what he'd done, but Sullivan had not anticipated this sort of reception.

"Come," the Prince said, putting his arm around Sullivan's shoulder. "Let me introduce you around. Donna?" he said, turning to his companion. "Entertain Kathy, will you?"

Leaving Kathy to the graces of the Prince's mistress, Sullivan let himself be escorted through the room while Vannevar introduced him to any number of important guests who were attending the party. Sullivan was surprised to find many of the Primogen here. Among others he met Nickoli, the Prince's Russian master of finance, and the Brujah clan leader, Tomaine. The Gangrel Primogen, Alicia McGreb, was pointed out to him, but she managed to avoid Sullivan for the rest of the evening, never making his acquaintance. The Prince informed him that she still suspected Sullivan in the death of Jacob, though Vannevar was quick to tell him not to worry too much about it.

At one point the Prince noticed Sullivan's glass empty and called Melmoth over to whisper something in his ear. Melmoth smiled and nodded, then disappeared before coming back a moment later with two large snifters of blood. Vannevar handed one to Sullivan.

"It's Napoleon brandy," he said quietly to Sullivan. "My special, private stock."

Sullivan nodded, and after taking a taste, complimented the Prince, though in fact he would have preferred beer.

Later, when the Prince was distracted for a moment with business, Sullivan, growing lost and bored with a conversation between the Toreador poet Virgil and the Malkavian shyster spiritualist Antonine Aristotle, suddenly realized that he'd lost track of Kathy. Scanning the room, he spotted her over near the wall, talking and flirting with a young male vampire unknown to him. Watching the pair, he was surprised by the twinge of jealousy he felt.

The Prince tapped him on the shoulder.

"It's time for a little entertainment."

The Prince escorted Sullivan to a row of chairs and seated him immediately on his right while servants cleared the center of the room of tables and chairs. Kathy came over and sat on Sullivan's right while Donna joined Vannevar on his left.

The already-dim lights came down even further and a spotlight was turned on the center of the floor. Music suddenly leaped from the concealed speakers: wild, gypsy music of bells, tambourines, and wailing violin. A female dancer leaped to the center of the floor, spinning lightly as the other vampires crowded around to watch the show.

Sullivan recognized the dancer as Carlotta, a vampire Sullivan had run into on the streets a half dozen times over the years. A member of the gypsylike wandering Ravnos clan, Carlotta was a dark-haired beauty with flashing eyes and a hot temper.

As the crowd looked on eagerly, Carlotta began seducing a young man from the crowd. Handsome, strong-looking, he was very obviously human. The man's glazed expression told of the spell of enchantment that held him, keeping him from realizing where he was or what was going on.

It was just as well, Sullivan thought.

As Carlotta continued the pantomime of seduction, rubbing and twisting against the man as though to warm herself, the Prince leaned over and whispered in Sullivan's ear.

"I have a proposal I'd like to make to you."

Sullivan, caught up in the dancer's show, leaned closer, keeping his eyes on the floor. Carlotta had both herself and the young man nearly undressed now, and was tantalizing and tickling her mesmerized partner with carefully placed flicks of her tongue and fingertips.

"It's an old line, I know" the Prince said. "But, frankly, I could use a man like you," he told Sullivan, never taking his eyes off the dancers.

The Prince was offering him a job, Sullivan thought to himself. Things were going well.

"Sure. What?" he asked the Prince.

Carlotta and her partner were down on the floor now, Carlotta atop the young man, straddling him, thrusting with her hips, her head rocking back and forth, long hair flying wildly.

"I need your strength, Sullivan," the Prince said, taking another sip of his blood and brandy.

Sullivan nodded.

The young man on the floor now began to writhe as though in agony, a groan escaping his lips as Carlotta continued to thrash above him.

"I want you to become my son, Sullivan. I want to adopt you."

Carlotta suddenly bent forward and sank her fangs into her partner's throat. The two of them writhed and twisted naked on the floor while she drained away his life.

Sullivan, stunned, was startled by the sound of his glass breaking on the floor. It had slipped, unnoticed, from his nerveless fingers.

February 18

At Angel's house in the Castro . . .

The doorbell rang.

"I'll get it," said Will, getting up from his chair.

Angel hollered something from the back room Will couldn't understand. He opened the door . . .

20

He who has a thousand friends has not a friend to spare,

And he who has one enemy will meet him everywhere.

—Ali ibn-Abi-Talib,
A Hundred Sayings

"You may, of course, keep Kathy as your childe," the Prince added, ignoring Sullivan's dropped glass.

Sullivan was at a loss for words. He turned and looked at Vannevar, who was now looking right back at him, smiling broadly.

Carlotta had finished her show and was standing before the rapt audience with arms held above her head, nude and bathed in blood. The crowd responded enthusiastically as she slowly turned before them. The young man lay pale and dead on the floor, his corpse soon dragged off by the club's attendants.

"What do you say?" Vannevar asked him.

Sullivan stammered out an affirmative, sure that there was some formal response he should give instead, irrationally worried that he might somehow blow his chance by blundering the response.

"Good! Good!" Vannevar said, slapping Sullivan on the back.

The Prince rose from his seat to address the crowd.

"My people," he said. "Gather before me. I have an announcement to make."

Silence fell as the crowd of vampires drew nearer, all eyes on the Prince.

"I have spoken at length with my friend here," he said, indicating Sullivan with his hand. "And he has agreed to become my childe—my adopted son."

The crowd responded enthusiastically, applauding, even giving oohs of envy, though Sullivan noticed a few faces obviously unhappy with the idea of Vannevar advancing his power and control any farther. It dawned on Sullivan that these vampires must view him as something of a threat—a force to be reckoned with. He sat up a little taller in his chair.

"Tonight we shall begin the Blood Bond."

A vampire who feeds three times from the vitæ of another Kindred becomes a part of that elder, subject to his wishes and commands—and forever loyal. This is what Vannevar was requesting of Sullivan and at the last moment the candidate found himself feeling hesitant. He was once blood bound to Kwon, as was Loo, but that ended when Kwon died in the aftermath of the 1906 earthquake. Sullivan was free of any such restriction after that, though he continued to serve the Grandfather and the Family with the utmost loyalty. Yet, to be adopted by the Prince was not only a great honor, but a source of great power, as well. He could actually be in line to rule the city someday, he realized.

Already the Prince stood before him, rolling up his sleeve, exposing the bare flesh of his arm. Sullivan got up out of his chair.

"Come forward, subject," Vannevar commanded him. "And draw strength and life from me. Feed upon my blood and vitality. Become one with me."

He lowered his arm as Sullivan knelt before him. The Prince closed his eyes as Sullivan bit into the flesh, drawing the vampire's blood into his mouth, swallowing it.

Though not particularly old himself, Vannevar had been embraced by an ancient vampire of great power.

None knew the limits of Vannevar's power and abilities and few dared test them. Even now this potent blood poured through Sullivan, infusing him with its power and strength as he gulped hungrily, even as Vannevar tried to bring it to an end.

"Enough!" the Prince finally said, pulling his arm away forcibly, breaking Sullivan's grip. Then he softened. "Enough for tonight at any rate, my son," he added, drawing Sullivan back up to his feet. "Twice more," he announced to the crowd, "and we will be one!" There was more applause and some cheers this time. Sullivan, still panting, excited by the experience, wiped his chin with the back of his hand and found it covered with the Prince's blood. He looked down to see Ross's good shirt and jacket likewise stained. Kathy appeared from out of nowhere, dabbing at him with a wet napkin.

"Looks ruined to me," she said seriously. Then cheerfully added, "Congratulations," and pecked him on the cheek.

The Prince took his leave soon after, making sure he first said good-night to Sullivan and Kathy, promising him they would meet again soon. Sullivan and Kathy stayed on a little longer but the get-together began thinning out and Sullivan, exhilarated by the night's events, wanted to get away himself. A short time later he and Kathy were driving away from the club in Will's Hyundai.

Well fed, and with hours to go before dawn, they had little to do and cruised around aimlessly for a while before Kathy suggested a drive through the central peaks for a view of the city. Sullivan agreed, wheeling the car around and heading in that direction.

Soon they were following the winding roads that curled up and around Mt. Sutro, Twin Peaks, and Mt. Davidson, nine-hundred-foot peaks sitting very nearly in the center of the city. Parking on Mt. Davidson, beneath the giant concrete cross that stands atop this mountain overlooking the cemeteries of Colma, they gazed at the glittering lights of distant downtown, miles away, relaxing after the night's events.

"So what does this all really mean?" Kathy asked at last, breaking the silence.

She had been through so much this last week, and, though adapting rapidly to existence as one of the undead, she'd hardly had time to learn what being a vampire was really all about. As it turned out, Sullivan himself wasn't sure what adoption by the Prince meant.

"I guess it means I work for the Prince, permanently."

Sullivan had never known anything but working for someone else.

"There's got to be more to it than that," Kathy said. "He's royalty. He's a prince. That must make you something."

Sullivan shook his head. He didn't have a clue. He kept thinking about what it would mean to be blood bound to the Prince. Unable to resist his sire's demands, Sullivan would be forced to do whatever was required of him—even laying down his life if necessary. Somehow he felt he'd had enough of dancing to other people's tunes. He felt unsure about what he should do.

Soon after, they left the mountaintop. There were still a couple of hours before dawn but they were both sure that Angel and Will would be waiting to hear what happened. Sullivan and Kathy were anxious to tell them.

Driving down the mountainside toward the Castro, they exchanged notes on some of the vampires they'd met during the evening. They both agreed that Vannevar was everything people said he was, and charming and agreeable to boot. As best he could, Sullivan described to Kathy the Primogen he'd met, telling her what they were like, and whether they were friends or enemies of the Prince. Vannevar had taken the time to fill Sullivan in as they went along, advising him this way and that in regard to different Primogen and other powerful vampires of the city. Sullivan had learned a great deal about the various power factions and webbed alliances that kept San Francisco's vampire society in a constant state of tension and consequent stability. At the time, Sullivan had felt privileged to be informed about such things, but since thinking it over, had found it all rather distasteful. He felt he had no mind for the kind of subterfuge and game-playing that kept Vannevar and the others constantly occupied.

"What do you think of Donna?" he asked Kathy. He hadn't had a chance to do much more than say hello and good-bye to the Prince's courtesan.

"She's all right, I guess," she answered. "Kind of stuck-up, maybe. I guess she figures that because she's with the Prince, she's hot shit."

Sullivan shrugged, grunting something noncommittal.

They were nearing home now. Sullivan hit the garage door opener on the dash and wheeled the Hyundai inside, beneath the house. Shutting the door, the two headed upstairs to the kitchen.

The first sign of trouble was the wreckage they found littering the floor: spilled condiments, a broken mixing bowl, and an overturned chair.

"Look," Kathy said, pointing.

There was a smear of blood on the kitchen door, and more splattered nearby on the floor.

Sullivan indicated to her to be quiet and then crept across the kitchen. He listened at the swinging door leading to the rest of the house but heard nothing. Slowly he pushed it open.

Angel's severed head was mounted on a wooden stake, set to face them when Sullivan opened the door. The dead vampire's eyes had been gouged out and replaced by two medallions bearing likenesses of Jesus. Angel's gaping mouth was stuffed with a mixture of garlic cloves and holy wafers.

Kathy screamed at the sight of it and turned around to face the other way, refusing to look at it.

Sullivan was shocked as well, but chose not to show it. Stepping out of the kitchen, he let the door swing shut, leaving Kathy behind. Slowly he circled the mounted head, staring at it, not believing his eyes. Then he remembered Will and began a search of the rest of the house. He found Will's body crumpled up near the front door, which was closed, but not locked. Will had been shot three times in the head, then his body torn and savaged to make sure he was truly dead. The main struggle had taken place in the living room: there were blood and pieces of broken furniture everywhere—probably where the intruder or intruders had encountered Angel.

Leaving everything as he found it, Sullivan methodically set fire to the house, igniting curtains and stacks of old newspapers until he was sure the flames had caught. Back in the kitchen he grabbed Kathy by the arm and pulled her downstairs and out of the house. They climbed into the Hyundai and, opening the garage door, drove off into the night as the first of the flames burst through an upper window.

"Goddamn it!" Sullivan swore, pounding his hand against the steering wheel. "Why?" They were headed west over Mt. Davidson. Ross's house was on the other side, on the western slope. There Sullivan was sure he and Kathy could find refuge.

Kathy was still crying, her face damp with blood-tainted tears.

"I still don't think you should blame Vannevar," she sniffed. "I don't think he had anything to do with this."

"Why not?" Sullivan shouted.

He'd blamed Vannevar right from the start, though the evidence against the Prince was skimpy at best.

"He'd just as soon get rid of Angel as any of the rest of them," Sullivan insisted. "You heard what Angel said about Vannevar being upset—why he wouldn't go tonight."

"Angel wouldn't have gone anyway," Kathy reminded him. "You know that." Kathy had more than once suggested that at least some of Angel's ostracism was self-imposed. She accused him of feeling sorry for himself.

"Exactly!" he said. "This way he knew he'd have me out of the house and Angel would be alone."

"Vannevar could have just as easily killed all of us," she reminded him.

Sullivan thought a minute, mounting his argument.

"He wants me to be blood bound to him," he said. "Just to keep me out of it." His rationale, he knew, was growing thin.

"If that were true," Kathy said, "he would have waited until after you were bound to him before killing Angel."

Kathy was right, Sullivan realized. No matter how he added it up, it didn't really point to Vannevar. But he wanted to blame him anyway. No matter who killed Angel, Sullivan reasoned, it was somehow due to Vannevar. Sullivan had been with the Prince all night long, watching him as he pulled the strings at the party, making all the puppets dance whichever way he chose. Even if some other vampire did it as retaliation against Vannevar, Sullivan still felt the Prince was responsible, due to the machinations Vannevar was always engaged in.

"I don't give a fuck!" he said. "If it wasn't for Vannevar and his shit, Angel wouldn't be dead. I won't have any more to do with him," he announced.

And that was that, but he realized he had no reason to be angry with Kathy.

"I'm sorry," he said.

She made no response.

"I said 'I'm sorry,'" he repeated.

Still she said nothing. Sullivan looked over to where she sat, expecting to see her pouting out the windshield, refusing to answer or look at him. Instead he saw her arched painfully back in her seat, eyes staring, her mouth wide open as though in the midst of a silent scream. Then her head snapped around unnaturally to face him and he saw the bloody wooden stake protruding from her mouth, jammed through the back of her head by someone now climbing up and out of the backseat: a vampire with a face horribly marked by burns, skin pockmarked. Sullivan recognized him—the madman Phillips.

"Die, whore! Servant of the devil!" Phillips screamed, twisting Kathy's head this way and that with the butt end of the stake sticking out of the back of her head. Kathy flailed and twisted, unable to free herself.

Letting go of the wheel, Sullivan lunged across the front seat at Phillips, grabbing the madman by the shoulders and pulling him off Kathy. Sullivan punched at him once, ineffectively, as the little Hyundai ran off the edge of the road and rolled over with a crash to lie on its back, wheels spinning in the air.

Sullivan watched as Phillips awoke, staring out at a dark night, the city spread out below him. The madman's feet dangled far above the ground. He was tied spread-eagle upon the gigantic cross made of concrete, ten feet above the ground. Sullivan stood below him, looking up at the helpless man with an evil grin. Kathy lay on the ground next to him, half-sitting up, rubbing the spot on the back of her head where Phillips had impaled her with the stake.

"Wake up, fucker!" Sullivan shouted up at Phillips. "It's time to face the light."

Phillips looked at his wrists. He was fastened securely to the cross with tire chains Sullivan had taken from the trunk of the wrecked Hyundai. Phillips was facing east, toward Oakland and the hills beyond where already the sky was turning gold. Soon the first rays of the sun would come beaming through the gaps between the hills.

"Too bad for you," Sullivan said. "I woke up first."

"Hell-spawn!" shouted Phillips, struggling ineffectively. "Blasphemer!" he sputtered.

"Fuck off!" Sullivan said as he helped Kathy to her feet. The two of them disappeared over the mountain, heading down the shady side toward Ross's house.

"You'll burn in Hell, Sullivan!" Phillips screamed after them. "And the whore too!"

But they ignored him, intent on beating the sunrise to Ross's house a few blocks away.

Phillips was still shouting curses when the first rays of the sun peeped over the hills and began to burn his skin. He continued to damn Sullivan and all his kind as his flesh cooked and his lips boiled and split. He was still condemning them all to Hell as his body puffed and swelled in the full light of the sun, finally bursting with a loud report, raining bloody smoldering fragments of the madman down on the ground around the foot of the cross—one of them a scorched skull with the fangs of a vampire.

PART

III

Wayward Son

21

Anarchy, anarchy! Show me a greater evil!

This is why cities tumble and the great houses rain down,

This is what scatters armies!

—Sophocles, *Antigone*

Civic Center Plaza in the heart of San Francisco had been packed all day with a buzzing, milling crowd. Angered over the cancellation of the *Festivo dello Estinto*, citizens had marched on City Hall bearing placards and shouting slogans. Many of the demonstrators were Hispanic: those Mission residents who would suffer most from the sudden cancellation of the event. But there were others as well, representatives from all over the city who decried the high-handed manner in which the government treated the people. Various city councilman had tried speaking with the demonstrators—as had the mayor himself—but to no avail. Nothing anybody said would budge the demonstrators from the Plaza. Police were ordered in but told not to antagonize the crowd. Despite hostility on both sides, altercations had been infrequent and there were as yet no arrests.

As night fell, the crowd became quieter, and those who had attended all day long grew tired and began drifting toward home. Police and officials breathed a sigh of relief as the situation began to defuse itself.

Across the way, in an alley off McAllister Street, a motorcycle gang waited in darkness. Engines off, headlights killed, the bikers watched the action in the Plaza from a distance.

"Looks like it's quieting down," said Dirk, in a matter-of-fact tone.

"A pity," said the rider with a red stubbly beard who sat next to him. A good-looking blonde with blue eyes straddled the bike behind the bearded rider. Dressed in a black mini and tights, she sat back with feet up on high-rider pegs and hands loosely draped over the shoulders of the biker she followed.

"Look," said the red-bearded Sullivan, pointing down at the Plaza. There, several police officers were moving wooden barriers into position to block off one of the side streets running off the Plaza, hoping to funnel the now-dispersing crowd out toward broad Market Street.

"Those fuckin' bastards are denying the people their rights," Dirk said, as though incensed beyond belief. "They're closing a public thoroughfare. They can't do that, can they, Sullivan?" he asked his partner.

"Nope," Sullivan said. "People got rights."

"Well, then, let's exercise our rights, eh?" Dirk said.

Standing up in the saddle, he stroked the big Harley into life. The rest followed suit and soon the alley was filled with the cacophony of nearly a dozen bikes as, lights on, they wheeled out of the alley and poured down into the crowded Plaza.

Wheeling and gunning their bikes through the crowd, the bikers forced demonstrators out of their way, the protestors parting to make a path as the bikers rolled over to where the police officers worked to barricade the street. Most of the bikers stopped a few yards back from the barricade but Dirk and Sullivan pulled right up to the light wooden fence, gunning their engines for effect.

"Get those things off the Plaza," the cop said. "Before I run you in. What you're doin' is against the law."

Dirk and Sullivan said nothing, merely looking at each other with simpleminded faces.

"Duh—gee, really?" Kathy asked the cop, sarcastically.

Dirk casually raised his right hand then dropped it. At the signal, one of the bikers behind them roared forward, lifting the front wheel of his bike into the air.

The cop saw him coming, shouted something, then tried to scramble out of the way. He just barely missed being hit by the barricade as the careening biker crashed through it, front wheel pounding down on the pavement as chunks of wood flew in all directions. Cops behind the line scattered and whistles were blown.

The rest of the bikers wheeled around, shouting, as the crowd in the Plaza surged forward, toward the source of the sudden disturbance. The police, panicking, tried to stop the crowd, assembling themselves into a line to defend the fallen, though pointless, barrier. The crowd, unable to stop because of those pushing from behind, crashed into the police line as Sullivan and Dirk raced away from the disturbance.

Violence erupted when two of the demonstrators were pulled off their feet and thrown to the ground by police, the crowd jeering in anger as they were handcuffed. The mob surged forward, this time of its own will, and citizens scuffled with police while the two hostages were wrested out of the hands of the cops and secreted back through the crowd. Police fell back and formed a wedge to drive toward the crowd and split the demonstrators. Screaming and shouting, the protesters fled back across the Plaza, trying to escape the police onslaught, while the bikers continued circling, shouting encouragement, making feints at the police lines, and driving the situation to a frenzy.

The cops, their small contingent in danger of being surrounded, fell back again toward the barrier, this time with the crowd in hot pursuit, while at the same time a police helicopter hove into sight over the dome of City Hall.

Sullivan and Kathy were racing around the outer edge of the crowd when Sullivan spotted a biker he didn't recognize coming the other way. Before he could react, the passenger on board swung a black baseball bat that caught Sullivan on the jaw, knocking him over and out of the saddle. Even as he hit the ground he recognized his attackers as some of Belladonna's Fish Wives: dyke bikers who made a habit of lending their muscle to the Prince and the Primogen.

Sullivan rolled over and was back on his feet in time to see his Harley wobble to a stop and fall, Kathy stepping off lightly, landing on her feet and avoiding the wreck.

The dykes spun around and were now coming back to take another shot at Sullivan. He let the passenger—a human—take her best shot at him with the black bat, catching the blow straight in the ribs. Hanging on to the weapon, with a yank he pulled the passenger out of her seat. Thrown off-balance, the Fish Wife crashed hard and was sent sprawling on the Plaza tiles. The human was hurt and crawled painfully away from the wreck, but the vampire rider was already up and getting to her feet.

Kathy came out of nowhere and cracked the Fish Wife across the forehead with a three-foot length of duplex motorcycle chain, laying her back down on the pavement nearly as quickly as she'd gotten up. Sullivan rushed up and, with a swift kick to the head, made sure she'd stay down for a while.

Sirens were screaming across the city now and the helicopter skimmed low over the Plaza, flashing its spotlights and using its PA system to order the crowd to disperse. Motorcycle engines continued to roar and Sullivan saw other Gutters now engaging in fights with the Fish Wives and their human retainers. The Wives were badly outnumbered, Sullivan saw, and, much to his satisfaction, getting the worst of it.

Dull thumps sounded from the other side of the Plaza and Sullivan watched two smoking canisters of tear gas arch over the crowd to fall amid the demonstrators. People screamed and fled the smoking bombs while, at the opposite end of the Plaza, additional police units arrived to begin preparing for another assault.

"C'mon," Sullivan told Kathy. "Let's get out of here."

They hurried to the fallen bike. Righting it, Sullivan saw the damage was minor, and with a single kick had it restarted. Kathy climbed on and they circled back to the fallen Fish Wife. Gasoline trickled onto the Plaza tiles where the motorcycle's fuel line had been ripped free of the gas tank. Sullivan slowed just long enough for Kathy to light a book of matches and throw it at the fallen machine.

The gas erupted in a tower of flame fifteen feet high, throwing flickering light across the Plaza as the crowd screamed again. The Fish Wife, caught in the flash of the explosion, jumped to her feet, dancing and beating at her flaming jeans.

Kathy laughed wildly as more thumps sounded and additional tear gas was fired into the now-rioting crowd. Sullivan swung the Harley around and raced out of the Plaza as the police helicopter once again swept low over the raging scene.

The Gutters met back up at the Gene Splice on the Haight. Here they would be safe till tempers cooled down. Sullivan and Kathy were the first back, taking seats inside the club, listening to the thrash band while waiting for the others to return.

Sullivan and Kathy had been running with the Gutters for nearly three weeks now. They had stayed with Ross only one night, then moved on, wishing to avoid drawing any unwanted attention to his home. Dirk had welcomed Sullivan and Kathy to the group and set them up with a haven in a house on Waller Street, a block south of Haight, which they shared with two ghouls. Kathy had rested a couple days, healing her wounds, but was soon fit as a fiddle. Sullivan had got hold of an old Harley and the two of them had been riding the streets at night—sometimes with Dirk and his Gutters, other times just the two of them.

Despite Kathy's arguments, Sullivan had ultimately spurned Vannevar's advances. Though he finally was forced to admit that others were probably responsible for the deaths of Will and Angel, in his mind he still held Vannevar accountable. Rumors were out that the madman Phillips had actually been lured into the Bay Area by one of the Kindred—possibly even a Primogen, some said. Sullivan was slowly learning that there was little that happened in this city by chance, and that the Prince had his hands in everybody's business.

Tonight's event had been a spur-of-the-moment thing. Awakening in the evening to discover that angry citizens had been mobbing City Hall all day, the Gutters were quick to throw their chips into the fray. The *Festivo* had finally been canceled after much wrangling back and forth in the City Council Chambers—and that left many citizens disgusted and angry. Reasons for the cancellation were obscure: one rumor suggested the city had been threatened by Mexican communists opposed to the religious orientation of the festival, though this was vigorously denied by officials.

Aside from popular disapproval, local businessmen stood to suffer as well, having purchased large and expensive inventories in anticipation of the event. Community groups were perhaps the most upset. Many of them had been promised much-needed donations by area businesses purchasing advertising space in the parade; these donations would now be lost. The mayor's ratings had fallen drastically and politicos were already predicting his defeat in next fall's election.

Today's demonstrators had been predominantly Hispanic, residents of the Mission who stood to lose the most, but many others attended as well, incensed and expressing their displeasure over the city's high-handed measures. The Haight was particularly well represented and already there was talk on the street of staging a spontaneous unofficial parade, despite the city's order to the contrary.

Dirk was next to show up at the club, followed soon after by other members of the gang. Dirk sat down next to Sullivan and for a while the two of them watched Kathy dancing with a young human who had been trying to put the moves on her, not realizing what he was messing with. Dirk was alone these days, Veronica having left him just a short time after Sullivan had met her. Despite his charm, Dirk had never been particularly successful in romance.

"Heard anything from the Prince lately?" Dirk shouted in Sullivan's ear, trying to make himself heard over the din of the music.

Sullivan shook his head no, then leaned over to Dirk to shout back, "I think he's given up on me finally."

Dirk grinned and sat back in his chair.

The rest of the gang had all returned by now, most of them huddling at a corner table, laughing, exchanging stories.

"How's Kathy doing?" Dirk nudged Sullivan, nodding in the direction of the young woman making her way toward the door, her young escort bearing a glazed expression.

Although Kathy had willingly followed Sullivan when he hooked up with the anarchs, it was no secret she was continually urging Sullivan to make amends with the Prince.

"She's okay," Sullivan answered him. "She gets pissy now and then, but it'll be all right."

He watched her as she hustled her meal out the door. She'd return in a few minutes, full and satiated, glowing with health. Sullivan never failed to experience a pang of jealousy watching her leave with other men, a feeling he didn't quite understand.

Kathy had seemed to adapt quickly to the anarch lifestyle, though she still expressed doubts. She made it no secret that she thought their lives would be better with Sullivan working for the Prince. She had liked the clothes, the car, and enjoyed the more stable, rooted lifestyle. "Bourgeois," Dirk had called it. A new word in Sullivan's vocabulary, he felt he instinctively understood its meaning and currently applied it to everything with which he found fault—much to Kathy's annoyance. During a recent argument at the house she had called Dirk "a bad influence."

"Don't let her talk you into settlin' down," Dirk said, leaning over to Sullivan's ear, smiling. "They're all that way."

Sullivan grunted and shrugged, smiling back.

"Bourgeois," he said.

Dirk laughed.

March 9, early morning

On a street named Beacon, atop Billy Goat Hill . . .

"What is the word from the street?" Selena asked the wild-eyed Sabbat woman coming down the stairs.

"More than three dozen arrests, several wounded, no deaths," Loonar reported as she crossed the chamber.

Loonar's eyes were yellow, with the vertical pupils of a goat. Her snow-white hair, ratted out in all directions, was streaked with red the color of blood.

"The anarchs do our work well," Selena said, as Loonar scampered to the dais, where a captive male lay naked: food for Selena and her visitor.

"The people of the Mission are angry," Loonar said, between mouthfuls of blood. "They talk of staging the *Festivo* regardless."

"And well they might," Selena said. "What with so many sponsors withholding money."

The Sabbat had made good use of its connections influencing numerous sponsors to first promise and now withhold desperately needed monies.

"And what of Sullivan?" Selena asked.

"He was there," answered Loonar.

We could use someone like that, Selena thought to herself.

22

Curse God, and die.

—Job

The next evening the trio found them-
selves at a loss for something to do. Several suggestions
were made, including a nighttime ride through Marin
County, but nothing sparked their interest. Before long
they were cruising aimlessly through the city, much like
other nights, searching for diversion.

Eventually they headed north to check out the crowds
along Fisherman's Wharf. At the corner of Powell and
Jefferson Kathy hopped off Sullivan's bike to head out on
her own, leaving him and Dirk to their own devices. The
two of them slowly cruised west along busy Jefferson,
watching the sidewalks thronged with nighttime tourists.

"There's two," Dirk said a couple blocks later, nodding
at a pair of teenage girls standing by the curb.

The pair had been gawking at the bikers but now
looked away, pretending they had no interest as Dirk
pointed them out. Dirk and Sullivan pulled up to the
curb and started the small talk.

Later, after a walk along Pier 39 and a few moments
spent watching the sea lions on their rafts, Dirk and

Sullivan left the two girls sleeping peacefully on a secluded bench at the darkened end of the pier, relieved of some of their blood but none too worse for the experience. Tourists passing by earlier had thought the four of them no more than a pair of youthful couples necking in the dark.

Retrieving the bikes, the two headed down toward Ghiradelli Square, where they planned to meet Kathy.

Waiting for her to show up they took seats on a bench overlooking Aquatic Park and the Hyde Street Pier. The Pier featured a number of authentic historic ships including an old square-rigged brig similar to one Sullivan had sailed on long ago. He was looking at the brig, thinking about ships and the sea, when Dirk interrupted him.

"You heard anything more about Vannevar?"

Sullivan shrugged and grunted, "No."

A rumor had been going round that Vannevar was thinking of canceling Sullivan's sanctions. Unhappy with Sullivan's sudden refusal of adoption, the Prince was reputed out to get him. Most doubted Vannevar could muster enough support actually to outlaw Sullivan, the political situation was too precarious, but he could undoubtedly refuse to allow Sullivan to keep his childe, Kathy.

"For my money," Dirk offered, "I don't think he'll do it. He's smarter than that. Why piss you off? What would be the point?"

"Just to make a point," Sullivan answered.

He figured Vannevar would have to punish him somehow, just to save face. Sullivan's resentment toward the Prince had steadily grown over the last few weeks as more details of the plots and counterplots implemented by the Prince and his cohorts to destroy Delfonso and the Grandfather emerged. The thought of being used by Vannevar rankled him.

Kathy finally showed up, escorted across the square by a middle-aged tourist in a polo shirt and polyester trousers—one of Kathy's favorite types. Sullivan was always amused by how she managed to get them to walk her home when it was all over. The tourist appeared a bit weak and pale, but Kathy was fresh and strong, flushed with blood.

"Hi," she said, arriving on the scene, sending the tourist away with a wave of her hand, not bothering with introductions.

"Everything go all right?" Sullivan asked as the tourist staggered off in a daze.

"Fine," she said.

It was still early, barely midnight, and, looking for something to do, the three decided to visit the Vampire Club; Sullivan had not been back there since the night he met the Prince. Mounting the bikes, they were soon roaring up through the streets of the Marina, headed for the Club.

Tex met them at the door, surprise showing on his face when he spied Sullivan, Dirk, and Kathy.

"Hi, Sullivan," he said, cheerily enough. "Dirk. Kathy. How ya'll been?"

"Fine," Sullivan said. "Great, actually. We're headed down to the Club."

"Wait a second," Tex said, taking Sullivan by the arm, pulling him aside in a friendly way. "Look," he said in a low voice, so only Sullivan could hear, "the Prince is down there with some friends. Maybe it's not a good time . . ."

"Oh, fuck him," Sullivan said, yanking his arm away from Tex. He was feeling a little full of himself. The two girls Sullivan and Dirk picked up earlier had been flying on cocaine. They had offered some to the vampires, which was, naturally, refused, but the girls had been tooting all night long and their blood was charged with the drug. Even now Sullivan could feel it coursing through his system. He felt it, recognized it from the old days in the city, and was enjoying it.

"It's a free country, ain't it?" he asked, belligerently. "My friends and I just want to have a drink, all right?"

Tex just sighed, stepping aside to let him pass. Dirk winked at Tex on the way by.

"It'll be all right," he assured the doorman. "We'll keep an eye on him."

Sebastian Melmoth met them in the Alexandrian Room.

"Mr. Sullivan," he said, somewhat icily. "What brings you here tonight?"

"We just want to spend some time downstairs," Sullivan answered, pushing by Melmoth.

"Of course," Melmoth answered. "Let me show you to a table." He hurried in front of Sullivan, in order to lead the way.

Downstairs, Melmoth put them at a corner table, as far away from the Prince and his party as possible. Vannevar, accompanied by Donna, was sharing a table with a couple of Tremere vampires. Sullivan barely knew the one—a woman named Anastasia, new in town. The other was Don Benedict, one the old Dowager's "suck-ups," whom Sullivan had seen around Chinatown many times. Benedict and Anastasia glanced over their shoulders as the anarchs, boots clumping and chains clanking, walked noisily to their table. They sat down heavily, laughing and joking for the benefit of the Club, Dirk propping his feet up on the table and shouting for a drink, but Vannevar paid them no attention.

Kathy and Sullivan slid in behind the table, sharing the bench along the wall. A waiter appeared and drinks were ordered, Sullivan asking for blooded whiskey.

The Club seemed much different from Sullivan's last visit; that night had been a gala affair. Tonight the Club was quiet: groups of vampires huddled at tables spotted round the room, heads gathered together in whispered talk.

Vannevar and the others were discussing something in low voices; Sullivan couldn't make out what. Occasionally Vannevar would make some sort of joke and the others would all laugh.

"Bourgeois fuckhead," Sullivan mumbled to himself as he stared at the Prince's table. Then he ordered another whiskey.

The anarchs tried to liven the place up, talking loudly, pounding their empty glasses on the table and shouting "Barkeep!" and constantly pestering the waiters to turn up the music. They began talking loudly about the recently canceled *Festivo* celebration, pointedly, perhaps foolishly, baiting the Prince. Everyone knew full well that the festival had been canceled by order of the Prince, and that Dirk, Sullivan, and the rest of the anarchs were responsible for the Civic Center Plaza riot following the cancellation. Untouchable in the Club, they felt free to annoy the Prince as much as they could get away with it. Whiskey and cocaine running through his veins, Sullivan felt himself nearly invulnerable.

"Yeah, it's too bad about the *Festivo*," he said, loudly enough to be heard by everyone in the Club, even over the music.

Conversation died. The music still played, seemingly louder in the otherwise now-silent room. Dirk and Kathy exchanged glances, wondering.

"Yeah," Sullivan went on, staring at the blood in his glass, swirling it around. "It's too *fuckin'* bad people aren't allowed to have a little fun once in a while."

Sullivan looked over at Vannevar, who had so far ignored the anarchs. At this last comment the Prince looked up, gave Sullivan a killing glance, then turned back to his guests.

Not good enough, eh? Sullivan thought to himself, getting up from the table to start walking over toward the Prince.

Kathy guessed right away what he was up to.

"Dirk! Stop him!" she said.

Dirk got up and tried to take Sullivan by the shoulder.

"Leave me alone!" Sullivan growled at him, throwing Dirk's arm off. "I know what I'm doin'."

Dirk took a step back and let Sullivan have his way, looking back at Kathy and shrugging helplessly. Sullivan turned back toward the Prince's party and wobbled over toward the table. Vannevar watched him approach, the Prince's eyes now grown dark and malignant.

"So what's the matter?" Sullivan demanded. "Ya got nothin' to say for yourself—big shot?"

"You're drunk, Sullivan," the Prince said evenly. "Go home."

"Fuck you," Sullivan said, and threw his drink in the Prince's face.

Sullivan's action took even the Prince by surprise, the blood striking him full in the eyes, splashing down over his shirt and coat, and spattering his companions. The vampire Prince leaped to his feet, glowering ominously while the very ground beneath the Club rumbled darkly. Donna gasped, but Vannevar calmed himself, doing nothing. Ghoul bouncers appeared on the scene, as if from nowhere, but Dirk and Kathy already had Sullivan by the arms and were half dragging, half carrying him up the steps and out of the Club. Sullivan continued to shout, but the Prince remained silent, staring after them as Donna attempted to wipe the blood from his face.

Melmoth met them at the top of the stairs, already aware of what happened.

"Get him out of here," he told Kathy, in a tizzy. "Get him out of here right now!"

"Fuck off," Kathy said, shoving Melmoth out of the way. She and Dirk had Sullivan back on his feet and were trying to push him in the direction of the front door.

"That's it," Melmoth said, chasing after them. "You're banned, Sullivan. Don't come back to my club again!"

Sullivan twisted away from Dirk and Kathy and spun around, his fist catching the yammering Melmoth on the nose. Melmoth sat down hard on the floor, hands flying to his face.

"Oww!"

"Fuck your club," Sullivan yelled at him as Dirk and Kathy once again began hustling him toward the foyer.

"And that was for Angel!" he shouted as they pulled him out of the Club. "Bourgeois fuck—" the front door slamming behind them cutting off the last of the epithet.

Out in the parking lot it didn't get any better. Sullivan

accused Dirk and Kathy of getting in his way and called them both "fucking pansies." Kathy got pissed and Sullivan ended up taking off by himself, roaring away on the Harley, looking for somewhere he could lose himself awhile.

He ended up at Ocean Beach. Parking the Harley in the sand, above the high tide line, he walked down to the water and began strolling the shore, occasionally stooping to pick up a rock and toss it at the incoming breakers. The cocaine and whiskey were still heaving through his system but he felt he was starting to cool down. Nonetheless, he couldn't bring himself to regret his actions tonight. He knew that daring the Prince in public was a sure way to bring himself grief, but it just didn't seem to matter much anymore.

Fuck Vannevar, he thought to himself. Let him make trouble. Let's see what it would cost the Prince to get rid of him.

A late-night fog was coming in off the ocean, a wispy gray cloud that slowly consumed the beach, dampening the air and veiling the coast from sight. The Harley, only a few hundred yards away, was soon lost in the mist, and the Great Highway was only a ghost of itself, blurry headlights racing along, paralleling the shoreline, the sound of the automobiles themselves lost in the din of the rolling breakers.

Sullivan, watching the water, thought he saw something moving beneath the waves a few yards offshore. Then it began to emerge—someone, or something, was rising from the water, gliding toward him as it did.

It was a woman—dark-haired, dark-eyed, staring right at him. As she drew closer, she rose above the waters, skimming over the tops of the waves as though by magic. Sullivan rubbed his eyes, shook his head, but she was still there, drawing closer all the time. She raised her naked arms, reaching toward him, and she parted her lips to reveal long, tapering fangs. Sullivan felt woozy, as though the drugs and alcohol had suddenly returned full force, then the feeling passed and the woman was suddenly in his arms.

"I've been looking for you, Sullivan," she said through sultry lips. "My name's Selena."

Soon the pair were riding away from the beach on the Harley, heading south.

March 9, late evening

In the chambers of
the city council, during a
nighttime session . . .

Council Chairperson Margaret Tildon beat her gavel on the wooden block in front of her, the sound ringing sharply through the crowded hall.

"Order! Order!" she shouted, trying to make herself heard over the buzz of the angry crowd.

The galleries were packed with citizens attending the meeting, here to witness the emergency session called by the council to discuss the issue of the delayed *Festivo*. Civil disturbances and angry letter campaigns had stirred them to action. Even those loyal to the mayor, facing an angry constituency, were considering voting against him, overriding his cancellation of the event.

"I will have order or I will ask the police to clear the building!" Tildon shouted over the noise.

Gradually the crowd quieted down, the noise subsiding to a murmur. Tildon had already expressed her support for reinstatement of the *Festivo* and the crowd was willing to listen to her.

"We have heard the issue discussed from all sides and I think it's time we call a vote," she announced.

"I second the motion!" shouted Councilman Denton, jumping to his feet, trying to be the first to second the motion.

Denton, long an ally of the mayor, had suddenly broken with his old friend to support the people, taking their side in the *Festivo* issue. He had persuaded three others on the council to agree with him and had successfully cultivated enough voter pressure to swing most of those still undecided.

A quick vote was taken: the measure overriding the mayor's decision passed with only one dissenting vote, one abstention. A shout of joy went up among the audience and the council members were roundly applauded. The building quickly emptied out.

In the shadows of a large pillar, the Brujah Primogen, Tomaine, waited until most of the crowd was gone before getting ready to leave.

He had monitored the meeting and vote from the rear of the building. Pleased with the job Denton had done getting the *Festivo* reinstated, he told himself he would have to find some way to reward his loyal councilman. Perhaps, he thought, he could run him for mayor next election now that the Prince's man was doomed.

Outside, Tomaine headed for the special lot where he'd parked his Mercedes. The burglar alarm on the car made a "boop" noise as he shut it off, unlocked the door, and climbed in. Now, he told himself, he only needed to track down the source of the *Festivo*. The whole thing reeked of Sabbat, just as he'd told Vannevar, and he was anxious to know exactly who they were.

23

The dead govern the living.

—Auguste Comte,
Catéchisme Positiviste

Before leaving the beach, Selena had explained to Sullivan why she'd come.

"We seek your aid, Sullivan," she told him. "We need your strength."

"Who does?" he asked, his mind strangely cloudy.

"Those with the courage to face the truth, Sullivan. Those who no longer have reason to fear the likes of Prince Vannevar."

She explained that she belonged to a secret society of vampires who, like himself, saw through the facade created by the Prince and the precious Camarilla. She spoke the last word as though spitting poison from her mouth.

"I'm an anarch," Sullivan said, proudly.

"Anarchs are children," Selena said. "Without someone to complain to they are lost. They need the Camarilla as badly as the Prince does. Tell me, what has an anarch ever done aside from whine about the way things are, then demand those in power do something to change it for the better? Only a fool would admit to being manipulated by another, and only an idiot asks that same person to help them. We, on the other hand, prefer to help ourselves."

She revealed that she and her followers were the force behind the *Festivo dello Estinto* canceled by the Prince.

"He fears us," she told him. "We have more power than he."

"You can get to Vannevar?" Sullivan asked.

"We plan to eliminate him."

Sullivan steered the motorcycle south along the Great Highway. Nearing the city's zoo at the far southwest corner of San Francisco, Selena directed Sullivan to park his bike in the empty lot across the street. They walked to the high iron fence and in turn both easily vaulted over the top. Once inside, they could smell the odors of the zoo's many animals, occasionally hearing snuffles and grunts from the night.

"What are we doing here?" Sullivan asked. He'd never visited the city's zoo.

"A little object lesson," Selena replied. "What do you know about Darwin? About evolution?" she asked him, taking him by the hand to lead him along the darkened path.

Sullivan admitted he knew little. The name was familiar to him—a nineteenth-century naturalist—but he was unsure of what Darwin had actually discovered.

"We're supposed to be descended from gorillas, or something," he finally offered.

"Well, something like that," Selena answered, smiling slightly at Sullivan's ignorance. "But the theory I had in mind was the concept of 'survival of the fittest,'" she said. "The proposition that the strong, the most deserving, should rise to their natural position of dominance in the world."

Sullivan was familiar with that theory; he saw it in action everywhere, from aboard ship to the political situation in the city: the strongest were always dominant. He told Selena so.

"Then why," she asked, "are the Kindred forced to hide ourselves and our true natures from the world, from the humans who should, by rights, fear and respect us?"

Sullivan had no answer. He'd always avoided humans for fear of discovery and death. Vampires, once known, were usually soon destroyed. Actually, as he told Selena, he tended to think of vampires as more of a curse, a plague upon mankind.

"That's what the lords of the Camarilla would wish you to believe," Selena explained. "That is how they control you. But, in truth, we are the dominant species. We stand at the top of the food chain."

They were nearing the pit holding the lion exhibit.

"See," Selena said, pointing toward a large male, prowling silently across the paddock in the dark. "That is your true nature, Sullivan. A lord, a mighty warrior."

She turned to look at him.

"Not a pimp, selling whores to humans, scraping profits off drugs and other human vices. That is the life of a scavenging hyena, an animal despised by all."

Sullivan felt embarrassed. He knew that much of what Selena said was true. He somehow felt ashamed of himself, a rare emotion.

"Come," she said, leading him away from the lion.

"You know," she continued, "in earlier times vampires were worshiped as gods by the humans. They paid us reverence, protected and fed us. We were their masters and the world was better for it. In those days you didn't find reeking cesspools of humanity like the Tenderloin. We did not allow such things to exist. Those who lived and died under our rule led ordered and peaceful lives."

They passed a glass enclosure housing three sleeping koalas: gifts of the Australian government. Sullivan stopped a moment to peer at the furry creatures, then continued on, following Selena. He objected to her reasoning.

"People don't die voluntarily," he said. "People just don't hand themselves over willingly."

"But they once did," Selena said. "Once upon a time death was not viewed as the end of everything. Life and death were both parts of the natural cycle. People today live in constant fear of death. They do everything they can to make their world safe and secure but all their security does is provide them with more time to think about dying. They worry continuously about their always approaching and inevitable dooms. We could teach them to appreciate—even love—death."

Sullivan thought of something Delfonso had talked about—the thousands of humans who once marched to their deaths in the ancient Aztec city-state of Mexico, patiently waiting in line for the chance to have their living hearts torn from their bodies and offered up as sacrifices to their "gods."

"I don't believe it," Sullivan said. "They just didn't understand the truth."

"The fact is that neither they nor you understand the truth, Sullivan. Death is natural. Death is right. Death is good."

They had entered the building housing the zoo's reptiles and now stood before a glass enclosure housing a huge African rock python.

"Animals don't kill for spite, or out of meanness, like people do," she explained. "Only out of necessity. And the fear you think you see in the antelope's eyes as it is pursued by the lion is not fear, but excitement—life being lived to its fullest. Once the lion has taken its prey and the antelope knows the game is lost, it relaxes. The scientists say it slips into shock to protect itself from the horror of death, but the state is transcendent. Even the lowliest of animals is given a moment wherein the true meaning of life is realized."

Sullivan was getting lost, although her words seemed to ring true.

Selena suddenly snatched up a nearby garbage can and hurled it at the pane of glass protecting the python's cage, shattering it. She stepped in through the opening, carefully picking her way through the shards of glass.

"Even the serpent is gentle," she said. "It actually hugs its victims to death."

The coiled python watched warily as Selena approached. It moved to retreat as she drew near, but Selena was too fast and she darted out a hand to catch the monster behind the head.

"Behold," she said, dragging the snake out from behind its clump of artificial rocks.

The snake, unable to free itself from Selena's grip, changed tactics, abandoning retreat and lashing forward with its body, wrapping the naked Selena in bands of great, heaving coils that circled her breasts, waist, hips, and one leg. The coils tightened, binding Selena unmercifully as a soft moan of delight escaped her lips. Sullivan watched, fascinated, as the blunt tip of the snake's tail, now rigid, stroked suggestively up and down the inside of Selena's thigh.

When the snake had done its utmost to crush its victim, about the time Selena appeared ready to pass out and Sullivan was about to leap to her aid, she opened her eyes again. Turning the snake's head toward her, she gazed deep into its cold eyes. Its tongue flicked out and back in, tickling at Selena's lips. She forced its head back, exposing the broad, creamy scales of the serpent's throat. Her fangs lengthened, then she sank them into the snake's neck and began to drink.

Sullivan watched the python grow limp, its huge coils falling away from Selena one by one to reveal her naked form beneath. Sullivan had drunk the blood of animals on occasion, but only mammals. He had not heard of vampires consuming the blood of reptiles.

The tip of the snake's tail quivered, then relaxed. Selena dropped the head of the dead snake to the floor of the cage.

"Come," she said, stepping out of the coils piled around her, taking Sullivan by the hand. "I have a place where we can stay after the sun rises." She led him away.

A shabby-looking motel down the street offered them a room. Selena, now somehow dressed in a white chemise, obviously had some sort of arrangement with the place. The clerk, possibly a ghoul, recognized and provided her with a key for a "special" room at the rear of the complex.

Once in the room, Selena curled up next to Sullivan on the queen-size bed and explained how she thought he could help her overthrow the Prince.

"If you accepted his offer of adoption," she cooed, "you would be very near to him and know all he does. Knowing in advance what his plans are, we could work to counteract them."

"I would be a spy," Sullivan said.

"A hero," Selena corrected him. "Working to bring down the oppressive regime. You would liberate our people, Sullivan, and you would not go unrewarded."

Sullivan thought little of rewards. He had never really wanted much out of life.

"It's impossible," Sullivan said, frightened even to think about it. "Vannevar has all sorts of powers. He would see right through me and know what I was up to. Besides, the Blood Bond would force me to reveal the truth."

"I can protect you against all that," Selena reassured him. "I control magicks far more powerful than the Prince can even imagine. I can cloud the thoughts in your mind, hiding them from the Prince and his Primogen cronies. You would be perfectly safe, as long as you acted out your part."

Selena had told Sullivan she was Tremere, explaining the sudden and inexplicable "costume changes" she'd made throughout the evening, though it was unclear to Sullivan whether they were actual conjurations or mere illusions. At any rate, she was quite powerful and no doubt capable of protecting Sullivan from exposure. But he had never really considered revenge against the Prince and the thought disturbed him. Pestering Vannevar and defying his orders in the manner of Dirk was as far as he yet dared imagine. Could he actually be part of a plan to overthrow his enemy? Recalling the earlier events of the evening, he winced. The thrown drink had clearly been a mistake.

"I don't think I could get back in his good graces," Sullivan said, remembering the malevolent look in Vannevar's eyes, the blood streaming down his face.

Selena laughed.

"Believe me. That's no problem."

Sullivan looked at her questioningly.

"Word travels fast," she explained. "News of someone's openly insulting the Prince carries like wildfire. I know all about it. The fact is," she continued, "that Vannevar likes you. He seems to have grown fond of you. With proper presents and apologies, you could win him back. After all, he feels he owes you something."

She was right and Sullivan knew it. With a little luck he could talk his way back into the Prince's confidence. But what kind of present could win him back?

"We will provide the Prince with evidence exposing one of his Primogen rivals as a traitor to the Masquerade. The evidence is compelling enough that most of the Primogen will have to concede to Vannevar's demands."

She leaned over Sullivan and opened the top drawer of the nightstand, withdrawing a small, leather-bound journal, worn and partially scorched. She handed it to Sullivan.

"What's this?" he asked, opening it up. It was a journal, filled with crabbed handwriting Sullivan could barely make out. The book smelled of smoke, an odor he recognized from somewhere.

"That belonged to Phillips, the hunter," she explained. "It's his journal and explains in great detail the voice that led him to San Francisco."

Sullivan squinted at the pages. The ink was faded, the crabbed handwriting nearly illegible. He could make out no more than a word here and there. Remembering the madman, and the death of Angel, his insides tightened, the old anger smoldered up again.

"Honerius, you know, is responsible for Phillips's interference," she told him. "The evidence is in the diary."

Honerius! The old Tremere. It wasn't Vannevar, but all the same, one of his Primogen, another one just like him.

"Honerius led Phillips here? Why?"

"Just a wild card for him to play with," Selena told him. "It was all part of the bigger plan cooked up by Vannevar and Honerius, but a portion of which Honerius chose not to inform the Prince."

"Honerius turned him into a vampire, too?"

"Him, or one of the others, no doubt," she said. "They all play the same games, lying and deceiving one another."

Sullivan stared at the book in his hand, remembering Angel and Will.

There was a knock at the door; Sullivan looked up sharply.

"No worry," Selena said, sliding off the bed. "It's room service."

She went to the door.

"I ordered us up a little treat before bedtime."

She opened the door a crack and Sullivan saw the night clerk standing outside. He handed Selena a cloth sack the size of a pillowcase. Something wriggled inside it.

Selena thanked the clerk and shut the door after him, locking it. She carried the sack over to the bed and set it down in front of Sullivan.

"I saw you admiring these earlier and made arrangements to have one sent up."

She reached in the sack and drew out a small koala bear. Frightened, the creature clutched at her arm as it would the branch of a tree, whimpering in fear.

"Awww," she said sympathetically, tickling the animal under the chin.

Then she lifted it to her mouth and bit its throat. The koala squirmed feebly, then relaxed. Selena drank a bit, then handed the unresisting animal to Sullivan, still seated on the bed.

"Here," she said. "It wants you."

Sullivan took the little creature in his hands. He had been feeling hungry and the sight of the creature's blooded throat awakened the feeling again. Gently, he bent forward and drank from the creature's throat. It put tiny arms around Sullivan's neck, holding him tightly while he swallowed deeply. Finally, the little thing relaxed in death, it's arms dropping to its sides as Sullivan drained the last of its blood. It tasted sweet and warm, pure and innocent—delicious.

"There," Selena said, taking the limp carcass from Sullivan and placing it back in the sack. "You see now what I mean. Death need not be violent and terrible."

Sullivan wasn't sure, but he knew the blood of the tiny innocent creature had tasted better than any he remembered, and not like an animal's at all.

"I think I understand," he said.

But of vengeance on the Prince and Primogen he was sure. In the remaining hours before dawn, Selena and Sullivan finalized their plans.

March 10, morning

At the Federal Building in downtown San Francisco, in the basement forensics laboratory of the FBI . . .

Forensics specialist P. Arthur Rowley looked again at the skull that had been brought to him by Agent Simmons for identification. Though at first glance it looked obviously human, the strange formations of the brow and jaw indicated some sort of degenerative, perhaps inherited disease. Most remarkable were the upper canines. Nearly twice normal length, they proved to be retractable, fitting into special sockets in the upper jaw. Rowley had never seen anything quite like it.

Rowley read again the Special Alert in his hand. A standing order, it was one of many that Rowley had received in the two years he'd worked here. This particular alert, however, had issued from the Special Affairs Division in Washington, D.C. A shadowy department with only a few personnel, Special Affairs was rumored to be involved with a certain type of serial killer. Specifically, cultists of varying sorts.

The alert requested reports be filed regarding specific sorts of evidence that might be found on crime scenes. Among the many odd items listed were suspects and/or forensic evidence of humans with enlarged upper canines.

Dutifully, Rowley made several photographs of the skull and faxed them to Washington along with a short report addressed to the head of the Special Affairs Division, Director George F. Thomasson. Thirty minutes later a fax came back, requesting that Rowley package and deliver the skull to a courier, who would call within the hour. The evidence would be delivered directly to Washington.

24

Oh, what a tangled web we weave,

When first we practice to deceive!

—Sir Walter Scott, *Marmion*

Arrangements were made early the next evening. Much to Sullivan's surprise, one phone call was all that was needed. Leaving a message with a secretary, the call was returned less than an hour later by the Prince himself.

Sullivan had apologized profusely, pleading youthful indiscretion while the Prince listened patiently and quietly. He perked up, however, when Sullivan mentioned the evidence he'd obtained regarding Honerius's double-dealing.

"You have the evidence in your hands?" he asked Sullivan.

"It's all right here," he told him.

"I would have to see it first, of course," Vannevar told him.

Vannevar sent a courier to the motel to retrieve the journal. An hour and a half later the Prince phoned back to tell Sullivan he would accept the offer. The evidence was sound enough to help him to depose Honerius, and in return the Prince promised to forgive Sullivan's transgressions and again extend him the offer of adoption.

Sullivan gratefully accepted and was told to attend a meeting being held downtown later tonight. There Sullivan's reacceptance of the adoption would be made formal and public. Sullivan thanked the Prince and hung up.

"Everything's set?" Selena asked, sitting next to Sullivan on the edge of the bed.

"Yeah," Sullivan answered her. "He says everything looks fine." But he worried about the cold, distant tone of the Prince's voice. It did not seem as warm and friendly as it had the night of the party at the Vampire Club. Despite accepting Sullivan's apology, Vannevar sounded suspicious.

An hour later Sullivan was headed into the downtown, riding the Harley. The address given him was deep in the Financial District, on Montgomery Street near Pacific.

The address turned out to be one of the many small banks located in this neighborhood. Made of brownstone, pillared and porticoed, the two-story structure bore the title of the First Pan-Pacific National Bank.

Sullivan wheeled the motorcycle up the ramp of the four-story parking structure across the street, where he had been told to park. The place was nearly empty, only a handful of parked cars scattered among the various levels. The attendant at the gate told Sullivan to park on the roof, in the special motorcycle slots. Upstairs he left the Harley parked in the open night air before riding the elevator back down to ground level and crossing the street to the closed, darkened bank building. A button by the door was marked "For Night Service." Sullivan pressed it and waited. A few seconds later a scratchy voice sounded on the intercom.

"May I help you?"

"Sullivan," he said. "Here by invitation."

"Come right in," said the voice, and an electric buzzer sounded, signaling that the front door was unlatched.

Sullivan pulled open the door and entered. Inside the lights of the bank were dimmed, the tellers' booths abandoned and lonely-looking. A tall, slender man approached from the darkened rear of the bank, his heels clicking on the tiles. Sullivan could tell it was a ghoul.

"Good evening, Mr. Sullivan," the ghoul said. "The others are waiting for you. Come this way." He gestured with his arm in the direction from which he'd come. "The elevators are back there."

Sullivan followed the ghoul to the rear of the building. There stood a pair of elevators; the doors of the right-hand one opened at the touch of the button.

"Please step in," the ghoul said.

The old feeling of walking into a trap settled over Sullivan, but he didn't hesitate, stepping in and turning around to face the doors closing behind him. The ghoul punched a button and the elevator began descending into the earth.

Two floors down the doors opened and Sullivan got out, the ghoul pointing him toward a door at the far end of the hall before closing the door and ascending. Alone, Sullivan walked the length of the hall and, after a second's hesitation, raised his hand and knocked at the door.

It opened almost immediately. It was the Prince.

"Good evening, Sullivan," he said evenly. "Do come in."

Sullivan searched the Prince's face for some sign of friendly recognition but found nothing. Regardless, he smiled and nodded, stepping into the room.

Others were waiting. Sullivan had heard the buzz of conversation when the door was opened but was surprised to find himself in a room full of Primogen. Looking around at the half dozen vampires collected here, he quickly spotted the old Dowager; the Brujah leader, Tomaine; Nickoli, the financier; Serata, the Toreador; Bloody Mary; and old Honerius. Apparently Vannevar had not taken action against him, yet. Alicia McGreb, the Gangrel, was noticeably absent.

"You've met everyone, I presume," Vannevar said, showing him into the room.

Sullivan nodded assent, the others indicating yes, few of them making more than a small effort to nod in Sullivan's direction.

Sullivan was confused. He had not expected to attend a meeting of the city's Primogen. He'd assumed Vannevar desired a more or less private meeting, perhaps attended by one or two trusted friends. Any one of the elders in this room was more than powerful enough to tear Sullivan to shreds, if they desired as much. Again, Sullivan wondered if he had been led into a trap. Perhaps the assembled Primogen intended to extract information from him. Certainly there were no signals coming from the Prince.

"As you all know by now," Vannevar began, pitching his voice so as to be heard above the conversations, "Sullivan has had second thoughts concerning my earlier offer of adoption."

The Primogen turned to look at the younger vampire. Sullivan felt the combined weight of their gaze.

"Many feel that he has overstepped his bounds, and deserves to be punished."

Vannevar turned to look at Sullivan.

"What about you, Sullivan? What do you think would be the proper punishment for a wayward childe?"

Sullivan froze, not knowing what to say. He didn't like the direction the conversation was taking.

"I don't know," he stammered. "I really didn't mean any harm . . ."

"He really didn't mean any harm, folks," Vannevar said, sarcastically. Turning back to speak to the Primogen again, he asked: "What do you think about that?"

Sullivan felt sweat forming around his collar. His nerves jangled as the tension grew. He had been a fool to come here.

Then the Prince turned back to face him.

"But all is forgiven," he said, opening his arms and drawing Sullivan to him. "Boys will be boys, I guess," he said, patting Sullivan on the back.

Sullivan fed from the blood of the Prince again, as he had at the Vampire Club, kneeling before his lord, drawing sustenance from the extended forearm while the assembled Primogen looked on. But it was not like the evening in the Vampire Club. That night the blood had tasted warm, powerful. Tonight it seemed cold, thin, almost as though Vannevar was trying to keep its real strength away from

Sullivan. As he fed, he sneaked a glance up at the Prince and was frightened by the hard, cold look in Vannevar's eyes. There was nothing warm about this exchange.

Finished, Sullivan got to his feet while Vannevar rolled his sleeve back down. Then he began.

"Thank you again for coming tonight," he told the assembled Primogen. "I deeply appreciate your being able to attend on such short notice. But witnessing the return of Sullivan to our fold was not the main purpose of our meeting. I have other news for you."

The Primogen waited for the Prince to go on. Most looked impatient, the Brujah Tomaine, bored.

"Some of you have questioned the wisdom of my accepting Sullivan's apologies, particularly in light of events at the Club last night."

Vannevar looked back over his shoulder at Sullivan. His face turned away from the Primogen, no one but Sullivan could see the malice that face held. He turned back to the Primogen.

"But it turns out that Sullivan has done us a great service. He has brought me evidence of a traitor in our midst. One who would undo the Masquerade and bring destruction on us all."

Though not a sound was heard in the room, Sullivan could feel the tension. Not meaning to, he glanced toward Honerius and thought he saw fear in the eyes of the old Tremere. But, looking around, it seemed he saw at least a little concern in the eyes of all those present. They all had their secrets, he supposed. Tomaine seemed the most composed, still jangling his car keys in his pocket, impatient for the meeting to be over.

Vannevar produced the diary from within his coat: the scorched diary of Phillips.

"We have all been concerned over the sudden and unexpected appearance of the madman Phillips in our midst. I might point out we all owe Sullivan a debt of gratitude for destroying him, by the way. But most important, it was evident to all that this deranged killer had somehow been lured here, and by one of our own.

After considerable investigation only the question of who introduced him remained to be answered."

He held up the book.

"This diary," he said, "contains that answer. It was the property of Phillips, written by him describing the voice that he heard in his head, the voice that led him here. Let me read to you. Page nine: 'The voice came again, in the night, guiding me. But this time, as it departed, the voice wished me well, telling me to have faith in the all-knowing father.'" Vannevar trailed off without commenting further.

All eyes had turned on Honerius, now visibly agitated. The quote was one of his favorite catch phrases, known to all the Primogen.

"There are at least a dozen more examples such as these," Vannevar said. "Need I go on?"

"The evidence seems pretty flimsy to me," Serata said. "I don't think there's enough to convict a man of Honerius's rank and esteem."

"If you don't believe me," Vannevar said. "Read the truth for yourself."

He tossed the diary out onto the floor. It landed in front of the Primogen, but not one of them made a move to pick it up. The challenge went unanswered.

"He has betrayed the Masquerade," Vannevar said.

The door opened and four ghouls appeared. Unspeaking, Honerius went to meet them. They led him away, to what fate Sullivan dared not guess.

"And we all have Sullivan to thank for this," Vannevar said, after Honerius had been led from the room.

All eyes turned back toward Sullivan, eyes that bored holes through him. Sullivan could almost taste the hate and fear. He knew they viewed him as a traitor and a potential enemy. Why in hell was Vannevar doing this to him?

"Without Sullivan's intervention," the Prince kept harping, "I would never have learned the truth about Honerius—his violations of the rules of the Masquerade and the danger he has put all of us in."

Then, as though kidding, though it was abundantly obvious he was not, he added, "So watch your steps out there. I may have Sullivan keeping tabs on you."

Then he laughed.

"Meeting adjourned," the Prince announced, smiling broadly.

The Primogen began shuffling toward the door, some muttering softly among themselves.

Sullivan followed along behind them, hoping to get out of the room before the Prince asked him to stay. He didn't want to face Vannevar alone.

He was appalled. Why had the Prince done this to him? It was bad enough that Vannevar had revealed the source of his evidence, naming Sullivan, but then he had seemed to go out of his way to implicate him in the eyes of the rest of the Primogen.

Outside of the room he found himself in the company of the assembled elders, waiting for the elevators to descend. No one spoke to him. It dawned on Sullivan there was no way to avoid riding upstairs with one or more of the Primogen. He waited until the elevators loaded up, then chose the right-hand one occupied by Tomaine and Serata, avoiding the Dowager in the other car. The doors closed behind them and Sullivan waited out the interminable ride up two floors to ground level. Neither of the Primogen said a word, but Tomaine did poke Sullivan in the ribs once and give him a smile.

Easy for him to laugh, thought Sullivan. An elder like Tomaine could take care of himself against even the most powerful vampires. Someone of Sullivan's stature didn't stand a chance.

Out on the street the vampires scattered in different directions, only a couple of them heading for the parking structure, where they'd left their automobiles. None were parked on the top level, where Sullivan had left the Harley.

Riding the elevator to the roof, he felt a sickness growing in the pit of his stomach. Vannevar suspected him, obviously, and out of retaliation had jeopardized

Sullivan's existence with the other Primogen. As long as he remained under the protective wing of the Prince he was safe, but if Vannevar withdrew the protection, he once again would become a hunted man.

Still thinking, he stepped out of the elevator, not paying particular attention to his whereabouts. He was only a step or two out the door when he felt a hand on his shoulder. He was hauled back, spun around, and thrown violently up against the wall.

It was Vannevar.

"What kind of shit are you trying to pull?" the Prince demanded.

Sullivan tried to straighten up, get his feet back under him, but Vannevar, with almost no effort, slammed him back against the wall with one hand. Sullivan's shoulder blade cracked painfully on the bricks.

"Nothing," he tried to explain. "What do you mean?" He was fumbling for words.

Vannevar grabbed him by the chin, held his face up where he could see it. The Prince's eyes glowed in the darkness, searching Sullivan's face, looking for the signs of deceit. Sullivan, terrified, tried to remain expressionless, hoping desperately that Selena's enchantments would protect him from the Prince's scrutiny.

Vannevar released him, stepped back.

"Watch your step, Sullivan," he warned him. "Be careful what you do."

The Prince disappeared in a swirl of mist, leaving Sullivan shaken and alone.

"I'm fucked," he mumbled to himself as he got on the Harley and rode off.

Back at the motel Selena was waiting to hear what happened. She made him tell her every detail of the meeting, including the reactions of the Primogen to the fall of Honerius.

"I'm in deep," he told her. He was scared.

"Don't worry," she reassured him. "The Prince will fall, and with him the Primogen, and we will have you to thank." She went on. "Tomorrow," she promised him, "I will take you to our secret headquarters."

Strangely, Selena's presence seemed to calm him. Slowly he shook off the feelings of dread, once again confident in his decision. He rested easily.

March 11, morning

At the Federal Building in downtown San Francisco, in the office of Director Brower . . .

"What?" Simmons protested, almost incredulous. He couldn't believe what the boss was telling him.

"You heard me," Director Brower told him. "You've been ordered off the case. The word comes straight from Washington."

"But I think I'm closing in on something," he complained.

"Sorry, but that's the order," Brower told him, putting the faxed brief away. "Furthermore," he went on, "you're ordered to report to Washington yourself, tomorrow."

"Tomorrow?"

"You and Rowley both."

"Why Rowley?"

"Goddamned if I know, Simmons. Look, don't give me grief over this, okay? I've already got Rowley stamping up and down about that damned skull downstairs."

The skull had arrived back in San Francisco that morning, delivered by courier. A memo enclosed with the skull indicated that some mistake had been made: no one had requested the skull be sent to Washington and it was being returned. Rowley swore up and down that it wasn't the same skull he'd sent them.

"I can't leave tomorrow," Simmons told him.

"Why not?" Brower asked. "I've got seats booked already for the both of you."

"Send Rowley on," Simmons told him. "I've got some family matters to take care of before I go out of town."

"Jesus Christ, Simmons. All right. I'll wire Washington and tell them you've been delayed a day. They won't like it, but tough shit."

"Thanks," Simmons said, getting up from his chair to leave.

"Stay off the case," Brower warned him, not looking up from the report he was filling out.

"Gotcha," Simmons said, going out the door and shutting it behind him.

25

We have made a covenant with death, and with hell are we at agreement.

—Isaiah

They left the motel the next evening after sunset. Riding on the back of the Harley, Selena directed Sullivan over the mountains and into the foothills below, onto a street called Beacon on the lower slopes of Diamond Heights, overlooking Billy Goat Hill and Noe Valley below.

"It's just ahead, on the right," Selena said, pointing to an isolated Methodist church a few doors up. Painted white, it looked to be at least a hundred years old. In good condition, it obviously was still in operation, reasonably maintained and recently painted. Colorful banners and a collection of plastic playground equipment announced its current role as a community day-care center. Sullivan killed the engine and coasted the motorcycle up the drive.

Selena, getting off the bike, noted a look of concern on Sullivan's face as he eyed the church.

"It's okay," she said. "Just wheel your bike up here off the street."

Unlocking an ancient iron gate, she held it open while

Sullivan pushed the motorcycle into the backyard and parked it on the kickstand. Selena locked the gate behind them.

The yard was overgrown with trees and secluded from its nearest neighbors. Sullivan noted a small burial plot behind the church—a rarity in San Francisco.

"We've been here a long time," Selena explained. "The church was built late in the last century, a good distance from the city then."

Sullivan nodded. He remembered when this southern part of the city was nearly unpopulated, but couldn't recall a church. He followed Selena down a short flight of stone steps leading to a heavy wooden back door and the building's basement beyond. Descending, Sullivan felt another wave of the recurring dizziness he'd been suffering most of the evening.

"The church here has functioned in a number of different roles over the years," Selena said, unlocking the heavy door.

It creaked as she pushed it open.

"It was originally Baptist, I think."

He followed her down a flight of dark stairs made of stone. Reaching out, he touched the wall, finding it soft and somehow insubstantial to his touch.

"Not everything here is as it appears to be, I'm afraid," Selena said, not looking around, merely sensing Sullivan's actions. "We have protected ourselves with many magicks—disguising reality, hiding ourselves from the others. Some of our enemies suspect our presence, but our hiding place has never been found. You yourself, though you visit now, will not find us again unless we wish it."

The stairs curved round, then emptied out on a large, well-lit chamber decorated with hanging silks. Various passages in the walls led to other chambers. A dais occupied the center of the room, piled with pillows. Selena lay down on the bed, inviting Sullivan to join her.

He lay down next to her, half-sitting up, but she leaned all the way back, stretching her arms above her head, allowing Sullivan to gaze at her body, now visible through a gown somehow grown transparent. He gently stroked her belly, moving his hand to her breast as Selena sighed. He leaned over and kissed her lips, pinching and twisting her nipple between his fingers. She kissed back, hotly, then nipped his upper lip, drawing a little blood. She pulled away, sitting up, licking the red drops from her lips, a lascivious smile on her face.

"We need sustenance," she said, clapping her hands twice.

A young male ghoul appeared from one of the passages and was told to bring them food. A moment later he returned, accompanied by a young woman, naked but for a short skirt tied round her waist. The woman, obviously unaware of her surroundings, was led to the dais and laid down between Selena and Sullivan. Together they shared her, drawing blood from her arms, legs, belly, and throat.

After what seemed like hours, and with the woman drained to near death, they broke off, leaving her to rest, nearly unconscious.

"How are we going to overthrow Vannevar?" Sullivan asked Selena. "How many of us are there?"

"Not many," she said, "But we are strong and determined. We will at last be free to indulge ourselves and take our rightful place as rulers of this world. We shall be revered as we should be. We shall all become gods and I, perhaps, queen."

A faraway look came over Selena's eyes as she spoke. Sullivan saw the lust behind her eyes, the greed, the hunger for power. Still absentmindedly stroking the sleeping woman's belly, his fingers suddenly felt something strange, coarse and wrinkled to his touch. He instinctively pulled his hand back but, looking down, saw nothing unusual about the young woman, though again he had felt the by-now familiar wave of dizziness he often experienced in Selena's presence.

When he looked back up Selena was looking him in the eye.

"Feeling all right?" she asked.

"I'm fine," Sullivan said, though feeling uneasy.

"I've arranged another treat for you," she said, clapping her hands.

The ghoul appeared again, this time carrying a wicker basket covered with a piece of flannel. He set the basket at Selena's feet then turned and left the chamber. Selena reached into the basket and drew forth another of the wiggling koalas from the zoo.

"You seemed to enjoy the one last night so much," she said, "I made arrangements to obtain another."

She handed the furry animal over to Sullivan who, with little hesitation, began to feed from it. It relaxed in his grip, seemingly fainting as Sullivan hungrily drained its life.

A noise came from up the stairs: someone coming in the door.

"Selena?" a woman's voice called down, accompanied by footsteps on the stairs.

"Careful," Selena called. "We have company."

"No problem," the voice answered, then two figures appeared at the bottom of the steps.

A youngish, red-haired woman in a black leather jumpsuit had entered, a young man on her arm. The man wore the same dazed look of confusion borne by the young woman Sullivan and Selena shared. The red-haired woman was quite obviously a vampire—one of Selena's cabal, no doubt.

"I love what you've done with the place," she complimented Selena, looking around the chamber as she showed her young man to a chair and sat him down.

"You like it?" Selena asked.

"It's lovely," said the woman. "But I need to talk to you a moment—in private."

"Excuse me, dear," Selena apologized to Sullivan, getting up off the dais. "I must see what Loonar wants. This will only take a minute."

Sullivan watched her as she walked away, disappearing through one of the passages into the chamber beyond, already in conversation with the red-haired woman. He looked over at the male visitor who, sitting nearby, stared dumbly ahead, then glanced back at the naked woman sleeping next to him.

There was a scrabbling sound at the upstairs door, followed by the familiar creak of its opening. Sullivan heard shuffling sounds, then a series of thuds as something heavy fell down the stairs.

Sullivan was shocked by the naked, blood-covered corpse that flopped and tumbled down the steps. He set the limp koala down and jumped to his feet as the carcass finally came to rest, sprawled on the chamber floor in front of him. It was mutilated, bruised, and covered with bite marks. Shuffling footsteps told him someone, or something, was following the body down the stairs.

A small, black-robed figure hopped down the last of the steps and into view. Face deathly pale, hair a shock of snow-white, the dirty, grime-coated figure jumped back a step when he saw Sullivan.

"Who are you?" he hissed.

A sinuous black tongue slid out of the vampire's mouth. At least a foot long and forked on the end, it licked the side of his face before retreating back into the vampire's mouth.

"I'm with Selena," Sullivan said, nervously. The room was wavering before his vision. The dizziness was back; then it passed. He tried to focus his eyes, but the very walls seemed blurry and indistinct.

"Hmmpf," the little vampire responded, blinking red-rimmed eyes at Sullivan.

Sullivan watched in disbelief as the room around him seem to melt, changing shape and color, the tapestries evaporating to reveal raw stone walls beneath, the soft, gentle light fading to a stagnant gloom.

"I suppose you're here to join us then," the vampire said. "I'm Gregori."

Sullivan didn't answer, left speechless as he discovered the lavish chamber where he'd spent the evening was, in reality, a blood-soaked dungeon ornamented with severed body parts, human entrails strung from inverted crosses, floors stacked with rotting human heads, and tables crowded with bowls of coagulating blood. The good-looking young man had become what he really was: a wine-soaked derelict, and the young woman sleeping on the pillows was revealed as an ancient bag lady covered with sores. Next to her, almost dead, lay an unconscious infant—Sullivan's koala! The enchantment had fallen away and, free of Selena's spell, Sullivan was discovering the truth hidden behind her illusions.

"You want to become Sabbat, huh?" Gregori asked, cackling, his snake tongue lashing in and out.

So it was Sabbat! Sullivan thought to himself. Stories about the diabolical sect were many, though Sullivan had never known anyone who'd actually had contact with them. Driven mad by diablerie, the Sabbat were rumored to demand an initiation rite that required a candidate be buried alive. The Sabbat reputedly had control of much of Mexico, having slain most of the Camarilla in that country and from there were threatening much of North America. They were known to be laying plans for eventual world domination. Apparently, Sullivan had stumbled into a nest of them right here in the middle of San Francisco.

He heard voices coming from the far passage and the sound of approaching footsteps. Selena and her companion were returning.

Walking closer to Gregori and the corpse, Sullivan began inching toward the stairs, acting as though he were interested in inspecting the dead body the mad vampire had dragged home.

"Looks good, huh?" Gregori asked, licking his lips with his snake tongue.

Sullivan took one more step then, without warning, turned and bolted up the stairs leaving the Sabbat vampire to stare after him, baffled by the stranger's sudden odd behavior.

Reaching the top of the steps, now slippery with human blood, Sullivan fumbled at the door latch while he heard Selena screaming from below:

"Stop him, Gregori, you fool!"

Throwing the door open with a bang, Sullivan ran for the Harley but then, remembering the gate, checked it and found it securely locked. Voices shouted behind him as the Sabbat chased up the stairs after him. With a pang of regret he vaulted the fence, abandoning his Harley to the Sabbat.

March 11

In a luxurious residential suite atop one of San Francisco's finest hotels . . .

Donna Cambridge waited for the arrival of her unexpected visitor. The call had come from the downstairs desk announcing the arrival of a Kathy Sikowski. The caller bore no invitation.

"Send her up," Donna had told man at the desk.

A moment later the front door chimed. Donna straightened herself up, walked across the foyer, and opened the door.

"Good evening," she said to the blond-haired woman dressed in leather standing outside. "Please come in."

"Hi," Kathy said, stepping inside the apartment. "I think we need to talk . . ."

26

Circumstances rule men; men do not rule circumstances.

—Herodotus, *Histories*

Sabbat! Sullivan thought to himself as he fled the church, racing down the hill into Noe Valley.

The Sabbat were nearly unknown in this part of the country—or at least that's what most believed. Like the Camarilla and its Masquerade, the Sabbat had been spawned by the terrible Inquisitions of the Middle Ages. But unlike the Camarilla, which pursued a secretive line and a more or less peaceful coexistence with humans, the Sabbat believed themselves superior to the race of mankind and, therefore, the rightful rulers of this world. If allowed their way, the Sabbat would force all mankind into slavery, obeisant to their whims and desires.

Fortunately, the Sabbat's numbers were comparatively small. All the same, vast reaches of territory had fallen under Sabbat control in Eastern and Northern Europe, the Eastern U.S., and lately much of Mexico. It was from here, Sullivan reasoned, that Selena's pack had originally come, and probably from where they took their orders. Fond of religious trappings—generally misused in blasphemous ways—it was not uncommon for Sabbat packs

230

to locate their headquarters under a church like the one on Billy Goat Hill.

Sullivan slowed down after a while, feeling sure he'd gotten away cleanly, but a few minutes later, while working his way north on Castro street back toward the Haight, he realized he was being followed. Surprised to discover an unnatural presence lurking behind him, dogging his footsteps, Sullivan embarked upon a zigzag course, cutting through alleys and smaller streets, seeing if the presence fell off—but it followed him everywhere.

Now sure he was being stalked by one of the Sabbat, Sullivan attempted the trick he had used with such success against Domingo so long ago. Dodging around a corner, he ducked into the first darkened storefront and waited.

Before long a shadowy figure appeared at the end of the street, obviously the person who was after him. It moved silently, but with a noticeable limp. At first Sullivan assumed it was Gregori, but then he realized this person was much taller, his true height disguised by the slouching gait he affected. And it wasn't a vampire, Sullivan thought.

The stranger stopped a dozen yards away, a silhouette in the night. He lifted his head and sniffed the air.

"Sullivan?" it whispered.

Sullivan recognized the voice. He stepped out of the doorway, back onto the sidewalk.

"Chi?" Sullivan asked the stranger. "What are you doing here?" He'd thought the old ghoul was dead.

Chi limped forward, dragging a leg, one arm held across his stomach, bent and twisted unnaturally.

"Thank God I found you," Chi said, reaching Sullivan.

Nearer, and in better light, the ghoul's pathetic condition was more clearly revealed. Aside from his obviously injured leg, his bent right arm looked useless—broken and burned, the hand twisted into a frozen claw. The ghoul's spine was injured as well, forcing him into a hunched posture, and his face was marked by still-healing burns. He had been frightfully injured by the collapse of the building in Chinatown the night of the fire.

"I have been searching for you since the Grandfather's demise," he told Sullivan.

Sullivan first thought had been that the ghoul sought revenge, but in his present condition Sullivan could not see where Chi could pose him any real threat. Besides, he had always been fond of the old ghoul and had no wish to harm him. He noticed how haggard and drawn he looked, thin even for Chi.

"Are you hungry?" Sullivan asked him.

The grateful look in the ghoul's eyes told him the answer. Sullivan led him into the darkened storefront and there restored some of the ghoul's strength, feeding him with a meal of blood offered from his own veins.

A few minutes later they found a pay phone and called a cab to take them back to the Waller house.

"How did you find me?" Sullivan asked Chi during the ride back.

"It was difficult," Chi said. "The Sabbat keeps its head-quarters and the church hidden by many strong magicks, obscuring it from perceptions both normal and magical. If they wish to remain unseen, unnoticed, only the strongest of spells can penetrate their veil. If their presence is unknown, discovering them is almost impossible."

Sullivan recalled the strange feelings of dizziness he'd suffered in the presence of Selena. He had lived in a world of illusions, he realized, recalling how they had suddenly faded away, revealing the truth beneath. He remembered, with a shock of horror, the nearly dead infant he'd left lying on the dais—and of the other "koala" he'd devoured in the motel the night before. He shuddered.

"I was under some sort of spell?" he guessed, remembering the drowsy young man Carlotta had danced with and slain that night at the Vampire Club.

"Without doubt," Chi answered. "I attempted many things hoping to break the hold she had on you, but it was not until the chance appearance of Gregori that I was able to collapse the illusions she'd kept you under. He did not know you were there and hence was unprepared to help maintain the veil. If he had been warned, he could have helped Selena delude you. As it was, his interruption, combined with my constant assaults, allowed the truth to be revealed to you."

"They're up to no good," Sullivan said.

"The Sabbat never are," Chi answered, laconically.

"No," Sullivan corrected him. "I mean they have something planned. They intend to overthrow the Prince somehow." He was trying to remember some of the things Selena had told him while he was under her spell, but his memories were blurry.

Chi had already guessed.

"It must be the *Festivo*," the ghoul said, thoughtfully. "That would explain the Prince's cancellation of the event. Vannevar must have guessed that the Sabbat was behind it."

"What do you think they're trying to pull?" Sullivan asked Chi.

"The Sabbat makes use of such events to run amuck, creating terror and death. It would help undo the Masquerade."

The cab pulled up at the Waller address and let the two out. Sullivan unlocked the front door and they went into the house. The place was empty, the two ghouls he and Kathy shared the place with, Roger and Wag, evidently still out for the night. He checked for signs of Kathy but found none. The room they shared looked undisturbed. Sullivan wondered where she was, realizing he'd completely forgotten about her while under Selena's spell.

When he came back downstairs, Chi was waiting for him.

"Are we alone?" he asked.

"Apparently," Sullivan told him.

Assured of privacy, Chi, with great gravity, began speaking to Sullivan.

"You are the last member of the Family," Chi told him. "And I have come to serve you."

As fond as he was of the old ghoul, Sullivan was not sure he wanted him in his life. Chi belonged to an earlier, different time. Sullivan wasn't the same person anymore.

"I'm not really in need of a servant," he told Chi, trying to be gentle. "Things aren't the same as before."

Chi listened, but his position remained unchanged.

"It's not that simple, I'm afraid," he told Sullivan. "You are the last of the Family. You inherit the Family's destiny whether you wish to or not."

Sullivan listened but didn't buy it.

"I told you I'm through with the Family," he said. "I thought that would be clear by now," he observed, thinking of the night he assassinated the Grandfather.

"Your fate is tied to his, Sullivan. Like it or not, your future is inextricably bound to the Family's, as foretold by the signs. I will serve you throughout," Chi told him. "I have been loyal for centuries."

Sullivan had been thinking about leaving town. Caught between the Sabbat, a suspicious Prince, and an angered Primogen, he felt his best chances were to move to another city and try to start a new life, but his thoughts kept turning back to Kathy. He remembered the night he'd left her standing in the parking lot with Dirk. He argued with Chi that the two of them should leave San Francisco, as soon as arrangements could be made. Perhaps he could take Kathy with him, he said.

"You can't spend your life running from responsibilities," Chi told him. "Like everyone, your fate is inescapable. The wise man looks to meet his fate head-on."

Sullivan wanted to object, but couldn't muster the effort. He had to admit he was tired of running away. He remembered the basement of the church, thought of the infants they had brought him disguised as koalas, and his insides twisted painfully.

"You know that Selena was responsible for Angel's death," Chi finally said.

"You lie," Sullivan said. He couldn't believe anyone anymore.

"It is true," Chi told him. "I learned of it myself."

He went on.

"I've never lied to you, Sullivan. I have always told you the truth. I defended you before the Grandfather, arguing you were not the kin-slayer, but he would not listen. He insisted, and as with all prophecies, his actions brought it to fruition. You were not at fault."

Sullivan listened but didn't answer. He was thinking of Angel, and Will—and of the slain infants.

Chi seemed convinced that the two of them might be able to destroy the Sabbat and its headquarters. Chi controlled magicks with which he believed he might defeat Selena. She did not know that Chi was with Sullivan and they might take her by surprise. Chi felt that if they could uncover and destroy the Sabbat pack, the Prince might forgive Sullivan.

"I doubt that," Sullivan said, remembering his deception, the thrown drink at the Club. He had insulted Vannevar in front of his peers. No man could forgive that.

Their conversation was interrupted by someone coming in through the front door. It was Roger, home for the night.

"Sullivan!" he said, unexpectedly finding his roommate sitting in the living room after his inexplicable absence. "Where the hell you been?"

While Roger spoke he simultaneously checked out the stranger, Chi, sitting quietly in the corner.

Sullivan introduced the two, then asked Roger about Kathy.

"Haven't seen her either," he said. "Someone told me she's staying over at Dirk's house."

The thought disturbed Sullivan. For the first time, he realized he was jealous.

"She's okay, then?" he asked.

"As far as I know," Roger told him.

Dawn was growing near and Sullivan and Chi retired to the room upstairs, Sullivan sleeping alone in the bed while Chi rested sitting upright in an armchair.

Roger awakened them early that evening, just as the last of the sun disappeared below the horizon.

"Get up, Sullivan," Roger was saying, shaking the vampire by the shoulders.

"Huh?" Sullivan said, drowsily.

"The FBI came by today looking for you."

"What?" Sullivan said, his mind suddenly clearing. "Who?"

"The feds," Roger said. "An agent came by late this afternoon asking about you."

"What did he want?" Sullivan asked.

"He wouldn't say."

"Shit!" Sullivan swore, swinging out of the bed.

Chi was already up and about, wide-awake. Without being told, he knew that he and Sullivan had to get out of the house and away from here.

"He wanted to know where you were," Roger said. "I told them that you used to live here but that you moved out a few days ago."

Roger obviously knew little else; the agent had been cagey. Roger gave Sullivan a card the man left with him. It said the agent's name was Simmons.

"I don't know why they're after me," Sullivan protested.

He didn't need Roger to tell him that didn't make any difference.

"We've got to get out of here," Sullivan said. "Can we borrow your car, Roger?"

Roger willingly handed over the keys to his old Ford and soon Sullivan and Chi were heading south, away from the Haight, toward Ross's house.

March 12, near midnight

At the Powell Street BART station in downtown San Francisco . . .

The broad-shouldered black man rode the elevator up two stories from the lower recesses of Hallidie Plaza to ground level. At the top he stopped to check his directions, tilting his glasses slightly better to see the hastily scribbled notes.

"Take bus nos. 6, 7, or 77 out Haight Street to Clayton. Address—1718 Waller Street."

The tip had come in to him just the other day. He hoped his sources were accurate. Even a *ronin* had obligations and could not afford wasted time and effort.

He waited at the bus stop only a few minutes before the No. 6 Parnassus pulled up. He got on board.

27

There are a thousand hacking at the branches of evil to one who is striking at the root.

—Henry David Thoreau,
Walden, 1, "Economy"

Arriving at Ross's house, Sullivan was shocked when he found the front door standing partially open, the splintered frame evidence that someone had forced their way in.

"Wait here," Sullivan told the ghoul, and slipped into the house. There were signs of a struggle but no one was about. Though still plenty worried, he was relieved to find that Ross was not murdered.

He called Chi in and snapped on a couple of lights. That's when he saw the note on the table.

Hi, Sullivan. Bet you didn't think we knew about Ross.

It was signed:

Selena.

"Damn!"

Sullivan threw down the note.

"They have taken your friend?" Chi asked.

"Yes," Sullivan said dejectedly, sitting down heavily on the couch. "Selena's got him."

If Sullivan still entertained any thoughts of leaving

town, they now deserted him. He knew he had to try and save Ross.

"We've got to take them out," he told Chi.

The ghoul smiled to himself.

"A wise man meets his fate head-on," he said again.

The two had only a few preparations to make, readying Chi's brass bowl the most time-consuming of the tasks. Within an hour of their arrival they were ready and about to leave when a knock came at the front door.

Sullivan looked up, startled.

"Who's that?" he asked, looking at Chi.

The ghoul shrugged.

"C'mon," Sullivan said, pulling Chi out of the living room, back into the darkened hallway.

Sullivan peeked around the corner as a second knock sounded. The door, its latch broken, swung open a few inches with the repeated blows. Sullivan saw a man dressed in a plain suit standing on the porch and ducked back around out of sight.

"Mr. Yount?" the man asked through the partially open door.

There was no answer.

"Mr. Yount? I'm Special Agent Simmons, with the FBI. Are you here?"

Sullivan heard the agent moving around. No doubt he'd spotted the signs of a struggle. He waited as the agent, now quiet, moved nearer their hiding spot.

When Simmons got near the hallway, Sullivan suddenly stepped out into view. The agent, startled, took a step or two back, fumbling for the ID in his coat pocket.

"Simmons!" he said. "FB—"

Sullivan was on top of him before he got the last letter out, decking the agent with a single blow to the jaw. Sullivan knelt down and checked the man's pulse. It was strong and regular.

"We've got to do something with him," Sullivan said. He couldn't allow anything to interfere with their plans tonight.

Rummaging through the kitchen, he found a roll of duct

tape and proceeded to bind up the unconscious agent, gagging him with a dishtowel taped over his mouth.

The agent secured, Sullivan moved to the front window and peeped out through the curtains.

"He's got a car here," Sullivan said. "It's parked out front. We'd better take it with us."

Chi had already rifled the agent's pockets and found the keys.

"Here," he said, handing them to Sullivan.

They wrapped the still-unconscious Simmons in a quilt from the couch, and, after first checking to make sure no one was on the streets, hustled the disguised body out the front door and loaded it into the trunk of Simmons's departmental sedan.

"Let's go," Sullivan said, slamming shut the trunk and climbing in behind the wheel while Chi got in the passenger side. "Let's get this over with."

"What are we to do with Agent Simmons?" Chi questioned Sullivan as they headed over the mountains toward Billy Goat Hill.

Sullivan didn't have any idea.

"Leave him in the trunk for now," he said. "Somebody'll find him soon enough, I guess." Considering what they were going up against, Sullivan really wasn't planning on surviving the night.

They found the neighborhood quickly enough but, even after driving up and down Beacon Street several times, failed to locate the church.

"Where the fuck is it?" Sullivan swore as they made their third pass by the same spot. Chi had warned him about this, but Sullivan had found it hard to believe, or even imagine.

"They are well guarded," Chi said. "They have put up extra protection I fear, in anticipation of the coming *Festivo*. Do not worry," he added. "You can be sure Selena expects you to find her."

They finally parked the car on a side street and continued the search on foot. Chi felt his magic might be more efficacious outside the car.

"We must search more slowly, more carefully," Chi told him.

They tracked up and down several streets, hunting vainly before finally turning a corner and spotting their goal. "There it is," said Chi.

The church stood in the spot Sullivan remembered, though he was sure they had passed by this same area several times in the car. There had been no church then, but now it stood before them.

They approached quietly, sneaking along the line of bushes to the old iron gate. It was unlocked and opened easily, allowing Sullivan and Chi to slip into the back-yard. Sullivan quickly scanned the area, vaguely disappointed to find no trace of the Harley.

Chi waited out of sight around the corner of the building while Sullivan quietly descended the half dozen steps to the back door. He hesitated a moment, then knocked loudly, three times.

"Who comes before the Gate?" asked a voice from the other side of the door.

It was Gregori, the snake-tongued vampire.

"It's me. Sullivan. I've come back. I had time to think it over."

There was a moment's hesitation before the door opened with a creaking groan, revealing the white-faced Gregori standing behind it.

"Welcome to Hell," Gregori said, grinning nastily at Sullivan. Then he shouted down the stairs: "One named Sullivan comes before the Gate of Hell, demanding to be allowed in. What should I tell him?"

He spoke the ritual of entering. A response came back: "Tell him that all are equal in Hell, and that he seeks his own doom."

It was the voice of the red-haired Sabbat woman Sullivan had seen the night before, the one named Loonar.

Gregori turned to smile at the visitor, but Sullivan had already made his move. Clamping a big hand around the smaller vampire's throat, he pinned Gregori back against the wall, then drove the wooden stake he'd kept concealed into the squirming vampire's abdomen. Gregori writhed in Sullivan's grip, not strong enough to free himself and his windpipe crushed so tightly in Sullivan's hand he couldn't make a sound.

Sullivan leaned all his weight into the stake, forcing it up and through the vampire's body, searching for Gregori's heart while blood poured from the wound, flooding over Sullivan's hand, spattering on the floor. The snake-man's tongue whipped out and wrapped itself around Sullivan's wrist while Gregori flailed away with his fists, but his struggles were of no avail. Sullivan, finally finding the vampire's heart, pierced it with the wooden stake and Gregori went limp, his tongue slowly unwinding from Sullivan's arm to hang slack from his gaping mouth.

Sullivan lowered the paralyzed Gregori quietly to the floor, the wooden stake protruding grotesquely from his abdomen at a funny angle. Chi stepped through the doorway, taking up a position near Sullivan. The ghoul had already prepared himself and even as he stepped inside he began to uncover the brass bowl he carried before him.

As before, once uncovered, smoke began issuing from the vessel: dark smoke that rapidly took form and substance, becoming black lashing tendrils that grew and stretched. The rest of the creature slowly began emerging from the bowl, black as night, a shapeless sack of a body with a toothless, palpitating maw and a dozen or more thin, whiplike tentacles. It rolled, or spilled, out of the bowl, hitting the floor with a soft plopping sound—a creature now much larger than the vessel it emerged from. At a magical sign from Chi, the monster fled rapidly down the stairs, disappearing out of sight around the bend while Chi and Sullivan followed as closely behind as possible.

Even before they reached the lower chamber Sullivan heard a scream—Selena's—and the shout of the other Sabbat woman. Reaching the bottom of the stairs they found the Nyarlix had done its work—gone straight for Selena and attacked. Even now the thing had her in its coils, its sinuous tentacles feeling, squeezing, probing—

searching for an entry to her body. But Selena's magic was strong and even though the creature held her tight enough to prevent her moving, the Tremere's spells kept the monster from doing her as much harm as it intended.

Behind Selena hung Ross, suspended from the sealing by chains around his ankles. He was pale, lifeless-looking; numerous bite marks on his throat and arms showed where the Sabbat had been drinking his blood. Sullivan could not tell if he was alive or dead.

But there was no time to think about it. The other Sabbat woman, spying Sullivan and Chi, abandoned her mistress to throw herself across the room at the intruders. Sullivan saw she aimed for Chi. If attacked, the ghoul would lose control over the Nyarlix and the monster would probably abandon its victim, seeking easier prey—perhaps the ghoul himself. In any case, if Selena was freed to turn her magicks on them, all would be lost.

Sullivan launched himself at the Sabbat woman, knocking her aside and pulling her to the floor just as she was about to lay hands on Chi. While Sullivan wrestled with her, the ghoul never flinched, keeping all his attention concentrated on the task before him, his one good hand weaving magical signs, manipulating the Nyarlix in an effort to penetrate Selena's powerful defenses.

Sullivan and the Sabbat rolled across the floor, over and over, the woman fighting with an insane fury Sullivan hardly expected and could barely match. She clawed at his face, kicking and biting madly while she shrieked and howled. She sank her teeth in Sullivan's shoulder and, in his efforts to pull her mouth away, she managed to wriggle free of his grasp and dart away.

"After her!" Chi hissed, barely able to divert his attention from the struggle at hand. The Nyarlix had by now forced some of its tendrils up and under Selena's skin. Her head was bulging, marked by thick dark veins that pulsed and throbbed. Her once-beautiful face was distorted—with pain, with rage, with frustration—swollen and broken by the monster's incessant attacks.

"Do not let her get away!" Chi cried, his own face

twisted by the effort he expended withstanding Selena's constant magical counterattacks.

The Sabbat woman headed out one of the passages and down a stone spiral staircase that led to lower chambers. In a flash Sullivan was after her, flying down the stone steps, pursuing her deeper and deeper into reaches unknown to him.

The woman was fast and Sullivan could not gain on her, now and again catching a fleeting glimpse of her tattered and ragged robes disappearing around the curve of the staircase as he chased her deeper and deeper into the earth.

After what seemed endless turns, they reached the bottom, where the stairs emptied into a passageway of arched stone. The Sabbat woman never slowed, running straight down the dim passageway toward a distant chamber glowing with red light. Sullivan was right on her heels.

"Zarastus, hear me!" shouted the Sabbat woman as she ran toward the chamber. "It is I, Loonar, your servant. I ask salvation!"

She plunged through the opening, straight into the chamber. Sullivan noticed a shimmering effect as she crossed the threshold, saw something move in the darkness beyond, heard Loonar scream. Then the room disappeared, leaving Sullivan standing before a blank wall.

"Damn!" he swore, feeling the stones before him, solid under his hands. Loonar had escaped—or had she? The scream he'd heard just before the room disappeared hadn't been one of salvation.

He tried again to find an opening but soon gave up and, anxious to aid Chi, hurried back up the stairs.

Halfway up the stone staircase a tremor passed through the earth, the stairs shifting back and forth under his feet as Sullivan pounded up the seemingly endless steps. Before subsiding, the oscillations grew so strong he was forced to steady himself against the walls with his hands while he ran.

A second tremor hit just as Sullivan reached the top of the stairs and the chamber above, this time rattling the building to its foundations. Ignoring the shaking, Sullivan raced toward Ross, still hanging from the ceiling.

Chi sat on the floor looking exhausted. Selena was gone, the Nyarlix lay nearby, occasionally pulsing, a thick purplish fluid running from its toothless maw. Chi had warned Sullivan that the creatures could not survive long in this environment, alien to their systems.

Reaching Ross, Sullivan felt for a pulse.

"He's still alive," Sullivan shouted to Chi.

Chi grunted something indicating satisfaction and began getting back to his feet.

"Is Selena dead?" he asked the ghoul.

"No," groaned Chi as he reached Sullivan's side, helping him lower the limp Ross to the floor. "She escaped at the last minute. I nearly had her." He was distressed.

Ross's breathing was regular, though he looked extremely pale. Laid out on the dais, he began to revive. He opened his eyes and saw Sullivan.

"Surprise, surprise," he half mumbled when he saw his rescuers. "I guess I owe you one, Sullivan."

Again a tremor passed through the building, beginning gently, rocking the basement, but growing stronger with each pulse as objects began to tip over and smash on the floor.

"We have to get out of here," warned Chi. "Selena has abandoned this place. It will soon collapse."

Sullivan had thought it a typical earthquake, nothing to be overly alarmed about, until Chi's warning.

"The Sabbat will allow this place to self-destruct, destroying any evidence of their presence. We must get away."

Even now the walls were starting to sway, cracks zigzagging through the mortared stone as dust began filtering down from the floor above and chunks of masonry broke loose and fell to the floor. Deep, torturous groaning sounds echoed up from the circular staircase that led to the chambers below.

Sullivan helped Ross up to his feet and half-carried him up the stairs. At the top they had to step over the still-paralyzed form of Gregori lying on the floor, eyes wide-open and mouth agape. Sullivan turned and kicked the vampire down the stairs, just as another great shudder rocked the building.

Safe outside, they watched from a distance as the final tremor rolled through the area. Other buildings swayed, but the church literally flailed about as the lower chambers folded in on themselves. The foundations gone, one corner of the church sank a good six feet into the ground, crashing noises coming from within as desks, tables, chairs, and every other object not fastened down slid across the floor and crashed into the interior walls. Even as they watched, a portable typewriter shot through a front window, ejected by the force, smashing through the glass to land upside down on the front lawn.

The three of them headed back to the car, Ross with one arm draped over Sullivan's shoulder. On the way, Sullivan told Chi of his experience downstairs and the cry for the thing called Zarastus.

The old ghoul stopped his hobbling when he heard the name. "Zarastus?" he asked, searching Sullivan's face.

"That's what the Sabbat woman called him," Sullivan said.

Chi turned dark and thoughtful. They continued their way back to the car, but while they walked Chi thoroughly questioned Sullivan about the experience. Sullivan wanted to know what Chi was thinking.

"There are many legends," Chi told him. "About elder vampires—creatures so old and powerful they become monstrous things, no longer bearing any trace of the humans they once were. Most of these creatures met their ends ages ago, but there have always been stories about a few that survived, living locked away in places now forgotten. Zarastus was one of these. He is worshiped by Sabbat."

Sullivan knew little about the ancient legends; he was more concerned about the immediate future.

"Selena still lives," Sullivan said. "She'll be at the *Festivo* tomorrow night."

"No doubt," Chi said.

"We've got to get word to Vannevar," Sullivan said,

remembering the vile practices she had tricked him into engaging in. "She has to be stopped. I can't let her continue."

They rounded the corner onto the street where they'd left the stolen federal vehicle. Spotting the trunk partially open, Sullivan grabbed the old ghoul by the shoulder and pulled him back out of sight. The three of them hid around the corner.

"Simmons is gone," Sullivan hissed to them. "Damn!"

Chi peeked around the corner.

"I don't think so," he said. "I think he's still in the trunk."

Sullivan looked around the corner, saw again the trunk standing open an inch or two. Then he saw the dark pool of blood on the ground beneath the trunk. Something was wrong.

Leaving Ross where he would be safe, the two crept up silently behind the car, wary of a trap. Opening the trunk, Sullivan looked in to find Agent Simmons lying where they'd left him. He was dead, his throat and torso ripped open, what was left of his face bathed in blood. Sullivan looked away, almost sickened by the sight.

"Selena," he said.

Chi continued to examine the corpse, unflinching.

"Perhaps not," he said. "There is much blood here. Little, if any, was consumed." He noticed how the strong layers of duct tape were ripped and torn away.

"Who else could it be?" Sullivan said.

Chi had no answer.

"Let's get out of here," Sullivan told him.

Ducking back the way they had come, they picked up Ross and hurried away from the scene. On foot, they struck out south, toward the lowlands, but a moment later Sullivan noticed the sky in the east turning gray, brightening. Dawn drew near.

"What's going on," he asked, looking at the eastern sky in disbelief.

They hadn't been that long at the church, he reasoned. It felt as though it should be no more than two or two-thirty in the morning.

"The sun is nearly up," Chi said. "I fear we won't make it back to the Haight in time."

"But we were only there ten or fifteen minutes," Sullivan said.

"I battled Selena for several hours while you were gone," Chi told him. "Perhaps time does not pass the same in regions near where Zarastus dwells," he said, cryptically.

Sullivan needed an emergency haven, and fast. The sun was already turning the sky its characteristic pinkish gold.

They were near Dolores Park, on the western edge of the Mission. For the most part open meadow, a narrow stand of eucalyptus trees running next to the trolley tracks provided the most likely spot for a temporary hiding place. The park was a popular place during the day but the area near the tracks was generally unvisited. Regardless, the risk was great.

"Try and get word to the Prince," Sullivan told Chi and Ross as he hurriedly dug himself a shallow hole in the ground. "Tell him I sent you. Tell him what's going on."

Sullivan crawled into the shallow grave and Chi began heaping the dirt back on top of him, helped by the still-tired Ross. By the time the sun was up Sullivan was covered over and drifting into sleep. The last thing he heard were the two's footsteps heading off toward the city and the low rumble of a passing trolley.

March 13, shortly before sunrise

In a basement apartment in San Francisco's Tenderloin District . . .

Selena rested on the faded, worn couch. She was angry, mad over the loss of the church, but she couldn't help but feel grateful to her host.

Tomaine sat down beside her.

"Feeling better?" he asked.

Though healing fast, Selena was still marked and scarred by the attack of Chi's monster. She felt weak, drained.

"I can arrange for more sustenance, if you wish?"

He'd found her fleeing from the church, wounded, needing aid and comfort. He'd taken advantage of her plight to make friends.

"Thank you," she said. "That would be good."

She needed to rebuild her strength for the *Festivo* tonight. Even if her pack was lost, she would attend. She would have her revenge on the Prince and the city.

Tomaine returned a few moments later with a late-night passerby he'd picked up off the street. It took only a few minutes for Selena to drink him dry.

"To the *Festivo*," Tomaine said, raising a glass of blood he'd drawn from the victim before he expired.

"To the *Festivo*!" Selena responded.

28

A little Madness in the Spring

Is wholesome even for the King.

—Emily Dickinson,
"No. 1333"

Sullivan awoke to the sound of foot-steps above him. Lying in the dirt, listening, he tried to identify them. Humans, he thought to himself. More than one.

He'd hoped Ross and Chi would return for him by sunset but it wasn't them he heard moving overhead. He grew panicky. Perhaps someone was hunting him. It was dark enough to rise, he felt.

He flexed and threw himself up into a sitting position, the loose dirt covering him flying in all directions. He was hoping to take any would-be attackers by surprise.

At the sight of a vampire suddenly leaping up from his grave the three children playing nearby screamed in unison and panicked, fleeing off across the park toward a group of adults standing a couple of hundred yards away.

Sullivan, realizing his mistake, scrambled up and out of the grave and headed out of the park, anxious to get away before any of the terrified children returned with angry parents.

He found a pay phone on Church Street and called the Prince's number; there was no answer. Sullivan wondered. Ross and Chi wouldn't have been able to get word to the Prince before sunset. Even now they might be on their way down to the park to pick him up. Sullivan hung up and tried Dirk. Again the same thing—no answer.

He hung the phone up and left the booth. He looked around, saw none of his companions, and decided to head down to Mission Street and the parade. He knew Selena would be there, somewhere.

The parade was scheduled to begin shortly after sunset, running up Mission Street from twenty-fifth Street to eventually end at Twelfth, where food and beverages were sold. Sullivan reached the route at the main intersection of Mission and Twenty-fourth, arriving just a few minutes after the first of the parade's attractions had passed by.

Crowds packed the dusky sidewalks, cheering and shouting as marchers, floats, and bands trooped by. All the paraders were dressed in costumes, masks, and makeup, and even most of the revelers had decked themselves out. Those few lacking any costume at all were far outnumbered by those who'd done themselves up to the hilt. The theme was death and skulls; skeletons and grim reapers abounded. Spotting any undead roaming through the crowd, Sullivan realized, would be tricky.

A float was passing by: a flatbed trailer made up to look like a scene from hell. Tortured souls, dressed only in the briefest of loincloths and sarongs, stood atop the float bound to stakes while red-and-yellow cellophane flames blown by the breeze licked at their legs. The condemned souls alternately wailed in agony and smiled for the crowd.

Others, on foot, surrounded the float, dressed as devils and demons, bearing pitchforks and spiked clubs. Reminiscent of the Mission's Carnavaal, those in the parade sang and danced as they marched, many of them barely covered by the skimpy costumes they'd chosen for the evening.

Sullivan turned left and headed up Mission, in the

direction of the parade. Staying near the rear of the sidewalks, where the crowd was thinnest, he pushed and wiggled his way through the packed audience, all the time keeping his eyes peeled for Selena.

Many were drinking, having a good time. Crowds stood on corners, exchanging beers and joints, chanting and carrying on.

A woman's scream caught Sullivan's attention. He looked across the street to see a young, dark-eyed Hispanic woman being pursued by a man in a black, cowled robe. Her pursuer carried a huge scythe in his hand.

Sullivan's first instinct was to try and stop it, but then the robed figure caught up with the woman and, grabbing her around the waist, pulled her to him for a kiss. Sullivan relaxed again. He was beginning to understand how the Sabbat could make use of something like the *Festivo*.

A block later he spotted Selena, walking on the other side of the street in the company of a young male in a black leather jacket. Selena was dressed in skimpy, red-spangled samba outfit and a domino mask, a pair of huge bat wings fastened to her back. The arched, black wings, Sullivan decided, must be some of Selena's magic.

The man turned to talk to Selena and Sullivan saw his face. His skin was dead white, hair gray. His red-rimmed eyes were small and evil-looking. It was the anarch Smash, Sullivan realized, apparently now joined to the Sabbat.

The pair were now talking to a small girl standing on the sidewalk. Dressed in a witch outfit, the little girl listened attentively to the two adults. Then he saw them lead her away from the crowd, into a nearby dark alley.

Sullivan pushed his way through the thick crowd, ignoring the shouts and curses of the bystanders. He broke through into the street and, dodging around the parade, reached the other side, where he'd seen the trio disappear.

The alley was L-shaped, the two Sabbat and the child nowhere to be seen. Sullivan hurried down to the corner of the alley and peeped around. Smash was on his knees in front of the little girl, saying something to her. She stared up at him with wide eyes, uncomprehending. A few steps behind them stood Selena, watching intently, her hands clasped together, her gigantic bat wings moving and rustling behind her.

Sullivan rushed them, not stopping to consider the consequences. Smash, now almost at the little girl's throat, looked up as Sullivan pounded down on him, just in time for Smash to get kicked in the face and knocked sprawling to the pavement. Sullivan lunged at Selena but was pulled down by Smash, who, already back on his feet, tried to get atop him. Selena stepped back, out of reach, cackling and giggling as the little girl, now free of the spell, ran from the alley.

"Back again, Sullivan?" she laughed. "You haven't learned anything, have you?"

Sullivan couldn't answer. Struggling with Smash, it was all he could do to keep the vampire's fangs away from his throat. The vampire was now much stronger than Sullivan remembered.

"Perhaps Smash will teach you a lesson," she said.

He was getting the best of Sullivan, forcing himself up and on top of his chest. Sullivan barely heard Selena, who now fled the alley, disappearing out the other end, heading back to the streets.

Sullivan tried to ward Smash off with his forearms, blocking the vampire's blows, but he felt himself losing the fight. The Sabbat backhanded one of Sullivan's arms away and slashed at his face with filthy claws.

Sullivan shouted in pain, his cheek ripped wide open, the vicious rake narrowly missing his eye. He grabbed at the lapel of the punk's leather jacket, trying to throw his attacker off, but the vampire was too strong and the tough leather only ripped under Sullivan's hands.

Smash had the heel of his right hand under Sullivan's chin now, pushing back with all his strength, forcing Sullivan's head back, exposing his throat. Sullivan had one arm on the Sabbat's shoulder, using it to try and keep the attacker away, but it did no good. Smash, more powerful than Sullivan, slowly bent toward his victim's throat, fangs exposed, eyes glowing evilly.

There was a sudden explosion of noise in the alley, the roar of an engine, then Sullivan felt the Sabbat knocked off him. Sullivan kicked wildly, pushing himself away, sitting up in time to see a motorcycle rider turning about, ready to make another pass at Smash, quickly on his feet again. The punk ignored Sullivan, readying himself to take on the mounted challenger.

Sullivan recognized Dirk and called out. Dirk ignored him, already racing back toward the Sabbat punk, club in hand.

Sullivan wanted to stop him. Dirk had no idea how strong Smash had become. He shouted again, tried to get back to his feet, but wasn't fast enough. Dirk bore down on the Sabbat who, at the last minute, stepped aside, and, grabbing Dirk's club, pulled the rider right off his seat. The bike tipped over with a crunch and stalled out.

The Sabbat grabbed hold of Dirk as he came off the seat and, cupping his right hand under Dirk's chin, sank his fangs into his neck.

Sullivan was by now on his feet and coming to Dirk's aid. He crashed into the two of them, knocking the Sabbat off-balance while at the same time grabbing hold of the punk's straw-dry hair and pulling his mouth away from Dirk's throat.

Releasing Dirk, the Sabbat turned back on Sullivan, twisting around in Sullivan's grip and knocking him to the ground, atop him again.

But this time Dirk was there and, leaping on the Sabbat's back, locked an arm around his throat and pulled back, keeping the snapping jaws away from Sullivan's throat.

The Sabbat's hands flew to Dirk's arms, trying to break the hold. Sullivan, still underneath him, grabbed the Sabbat's head with both hands and drove his thumbs into the vampire's eyes.

Smash howled in pain as Sullivan, grimacing, crushed

the two eyeballs in their sockets, sending blood squirting back in his face.

In agony, the Sabbat threw Dirk off and staggered to his feet, clutching at his face, screaming. With Smash unable to see to defend himself, Dirk and Sullivan moved in for the kill, first breaking Smash's legs out from under him with the club then, after he was down, tearing out his throat and decapitating him.

The distant crowd at the far end of the alley, captivated by the parade, had noticed nothing. Dirk and Sullivan quickly loaded the Sabbat's corpse into a handy Dumpster.

"Good thing I stumbled onto you, huh?" Dirk asked.

"Thanks," Sullivan said as he closed the lid on the broken, mangled body. "He nearly got me." He dabbed ineffectually at his torn cheek. "How'd you find me?."

"Chi called sometime during the day and left a message saying you'd be down here and maybe in trouble. What's going on? I thought that old fart was dead?"

Sullivan quickly filled him in on what had happened since he'd left Dirk and Kathy standing in the parking lot a few nights ago. Dirk listened.

"Where's Kathy?" Sullivan finally asked, fearing the answer.

"With the Prince, I guess," Dirk told him. "At least that's where she said she was going. She spent one night at our house, then disappeared. She was intent on seeing Vannevar and pleading your case. I haven't heard how it turned out."

"I heard she was with you," Sullivan said.

"Not a chance," Dirk said. Then, thinking better of it, added, "Well, I thought about it, but she's really not my type."

Sullivan was relieved.

"Selena's still out there," he said.

Dirk wasn't sure about going after her.

"She's way too powerful, man," he complained, shaking his head.

"I gotta try," Sullivan said. "She'll blow the Masquerade." But he was really thinking mostly of Angel and Will.

Dirk, as usual up for almost anything, saw his friend's concern and finally agreed.

"Where do you think she is?" he asked.

Sullivan figured she was somewhere with the parade, probably working her way toward the termination point at Twelfth Street, where a large crowd awaited the finish of the *Festivo*.

Dirk pulled his bike back up and restarted it, clearing the flooded carbs with a few quick twists of the throttle, the air splitting with the crackle of the motorcycle's exhaust. Sullivan got on behind and Dirk rolled back out of the alley, toward the crowds.

The sidewalks were plugged. Finding a gap in the metal barriers marking the parade route, Dirk and Sullivan rode the motorcycle out into the street, rolling along the edge of the parade, searching for Selena.

They slowly worked their way through the parade, Dirk occasionally goosing the throttle and veering to avoid a cop attempting to get the unauthorized bikers off the closed street.

"See anything?" Dirk asked as they began to draw near the front of the parade.

Sullivan craned his neck, standing on the pegs to see over the heads of the crowd. He scanned the sidewalks and saw nothing. He'd kept close watch on alleys running off the street but had not seen anything of Selena there, either.

Then he spotted her, up ahead, riding atop one of the floats. Dressed in her skimpy costume, and with her bat wings, she was the favorite of the cheering crowds. Selena waved gaily back to them. It was the float representing Hell that Sullivan had seen earlier, and, as he watched, Selena approached one of the bound victims and bent forward, biting the man's neck and drinking his blood as he moaned in ecstasy, bound helpless to a post.

The crowd cheered wildly, assuming it all part of the show, the blood spilling down the man's chest a mere special effect created for their amusement. Selena periodically broke off to wave and smile at the crowd before turning back to her feeding.

"There she is!" he shouted to Dirk, slapping him on the shoulder. "Let's go."

Dirk accelerated the big machine, weaving through and around the parade marchers toward the Hell float a block ahead. A cop guarding the barrier saw them flash by and gave pursuit. They ignored him.

Selena saw the pair approaching on the motorcycle and laughed as Dirk drew up alongside the slow-moving float.

"Come for some more fun," she laughed down at Sullivan. Then she abandoned her first victim and lightly scampered over the artificial rocks to one of the other bound "doomed souls."

The crowd laughed in appreciation of her antics.

Dirk rolled up near the side of the float as Sullivan got up out of the saddle and leaped the short distance between the bike and the float. Watching him, the crowd broke into applause at the successful stunt. A cop came running from the sidelines after Dirk, who scooted away.

Landing off-balance, Sullivan fell, then got back to his feet while Selena laughed haughtily from the top of the float.

"Catch me if you can," she teased Sullivan as he began climbing up after her.

Another cop had come out of the crowd and was hopping on the back of the float as well, sure that Sullivan was some drunken reveler out to cause trouble. Sullivan saw him coming and backhanded him, knocking him off the float to fall heavily on the street below. The crowd laughed and hooted at the officer's distress, then broke into another cheer as Selena began drinking blood from a second victim.

Sullivan was almost on her now, within a few inches of grabbing Selena, when she suddenly turned on him. Glaring at him, she extended the open palm of one hand.

Sullivan saw a brief flash of light in her eyes and, feeling as though he been hit by a giant fist, he tumbled over backward, sliding and bouncing down the side of the float to fall on the street on his back.

Dirk was there to pick him up.

"See? She's got magic," Dirk said, pulling Sullivan to his feet.

"Where'd she go?" Sullivan asked, checking the slowly retreating float and not seeing her there.

"She jumped off and headed down the side street," Dirk told him, helping him get off the street, out of the way of the parade already starting to back up because of the delay.

"There's cops coming," Dirk said. "We got to get out of here."

The two of them hustled off away from the parade route, following the street Selena had taken, abandoning Dirk's bike back where he'd left it.

She led them on. They would catch fleeting glimpses of her as she turned up darkened residential streets and down narrow alleys. Sullivan stayed right on her tail, Dirk lagging behind him a step or two.

"We don't really want to catch her, do we?" he kept asking.

Sullivan ignored him.

She suddenly appeared just fifty yards in front of them, peeking at them from around the corner of an alley. She giggled then ducked back out of sight. Sullivan stepped up his pace, Dirk tried to stay with him.

A horrifying scream came from the alley—a woman's scream. Then another shriek quickly choked off, dying away in a bubbling gurgle.

Sullivan rounded the corner.

Selena was dead, her naked body ripped to shreds by the huge black wolf that stood over her carcass, snarling now at the two vampires who interrupted its killing.

"Sssullivan," the Garou growled when it saw him.

It was Hayes, from Oakland.

"Time has come," spoke the wolf as it crept forward, stepping over the torn body of the dead Tremere as it transformed to the most deadly form of the Garou—Crinos. Hayes now stood a towering nine feet tall.

Sullivan and Dirk instinctively knew there was no hope in running. The huge beast would pull them down from behind after a couple of bounds. They instead started to spread apart, Sullivan on the right, Dirk moving to the Garou's left.

The animal ignored Dirk, never taking its burning eyes from Sullivan. Its ears flattened as it drew nearer, the face growing broad, lips curling, revealing huge ivory canines that put Sullivan's to shame.

Dirk made a feint toward the Garou and it stopped momentarily, snarling at the interloper before turning its attention back to Sullivan.

Sullivan glanced about for a weapon: a mistake. Hayes saw his attention diverted and sprang at him, striking Sullivan in the chest and shoulders and knocking him over backward to the pavement.

Sullivan went down with his knees pulled up, trying to fend off the raking claws. The werewolf locked its jaws on Sullivan's forearm and, tossing its head, threatened to rip his arm from its socket. Sullivan was yanked about like a doll in the hands of an angry child.

Dirk grabbed a metal garbage can, lifted it over his head, charged down on the enraged beast, and began beating it in the back with thunderous blows that nevertheless seemed to cause the Garou no harm.

Hayes ignored the first two or three blows but then suddenly turned and, releasing Sullivan, went after Dirk. Dirk tried to run but the Garou bounded after him, knocking him flat to the ground with a powerful swipe of its paw. Dirk, knocked half-senseless, could do little more than try to lift himself up, but the werewolf abandoned him, quickly turning back to Sullivan. It lowered its head and growled.

Sullivan was sitting up, his good right arm down on the ground trying to push himself back to his feet. His left arm was held at a funny angle; beneath the shredded sleeve of his jacket, shiny white bone showed through ripped and mangled flesh. Sullivan's hand slipped out from under him and he fell back down in a sitting position.

Hayes took a single step forward, then stopped. The animal turned its head, looking somewhere behind Sullivan.

"Devil!" the Garou hissed, stepping back as though in fear of what it saw.

Sullivan craned his neck around to look. He saw the Prince.

Vannevar advanced, speaking to the Garou. "You have no business here, Hayes," Vannevar said gravely, walking steadily forward as Hayes retreated. "Why have you come?"

The werewolf, growling, spit, "Leech! You must die!"

It tried to leap at Vannevar but was somehow restrained; it couldn't move. The Prince kept advancing, eyes glaring, hand extended. The Garou cowered at his approach.

Then the werewolf suddenly jumped in the air, writhing, and twisted about as though in pain.

Vannevar stared steadily at the beast, glowering down at it as, snarling, Hayes curled into a ball and began clawing at his own abdomen. Sullivan watched as the animal ripped at its stomach, tearing out entrails and chewing them as though they were the cause of its agony. Finally, intestines trailing on the ground, the monster died. Within moments the body had transformed itself back to that of Hayes, the Oakland Reverend.

Dirk was up, leaning against the wall for support, but Sullivan was still down. The Prince kneeled down and examined his wound, announcing that it would heal. Carefully, he helped Sullivan back to his feet.

He saw Kathy standing there. She had come with the Prince. Supporting him on the other side, the two helped Sullivan back to the white stretch limo waiting at the end of the alley. Chi was sitting in the backseat.

29

To that high Capital, where kingly Death

Keeps his pale court in beauty and decay,

He came.

—Percy Bysshe Shelley,
Adonais

His arm in a sling, Sullivan sat on the expensive silk divan watching the other guests at the party. Aside from Sullivan's own friends, several others, including some of the Primogen, had chosen to attend the gathering in the Prince's apartment atop Nob Hill.

Kathy was with Donna Cambridge near the bar, talking and joking with Vannevar and Nickoli. Ross stood at the large picture window, next to the Brujah Tomaine, the two of them identifying landmarks in the panorama of the city spread out below them. Ross, though still pale, was recuperating nicely. Chi sat on a nearby couch, engaged in a heated discussion with Joseph Cambridge, a towering Nosferatu whose diseased legs were supported by iron braces. Joseph was the older brother of Donna.

Dirk, invited, had declined to come. After the Prince had saved the lives of the two in the alley that night he had given Sullivan the choice of running with Dirk, or joining him as the Prince's adopted son. Sullivan had hated to turn his back on Dirk but had already reached the conclusion that Dirk's lifestyle was not for him; he needed more structure. Chi had said, "Try as you might, you cannot avoid entanglements. You are only free to choose *which* will entangle you." He had decided he would meet his fate head-on.

Dirk had left them that night in the alley, angered over his friend's choice. Sullivan had not heard from him since.

Kathy had done Sullivan the biggest favor: going to the Prince and pleading his case. Kathy claimed Vannevar had a soft spot for Sullivan and was easily persuaded to forgive him his mistakes. Donna had taken Sullivan's side as well, it turned out. She and Kathy had seemingly become fast friends. As for Sullivan's activities with the Sabbat, it was known he had been under the influence of Selena's magic and not wholly responsible for his actions. Besides, his final destruction of the Sabbat pack—and ultimately, Selena—had brought him back into favor. He had been forgiven.

The group at the bar broke up, walking over toward Sullivan.

"It's time," Vannevar said to him, smiling.

"Already?" he asked.

"See, Vannevar," said Tomaine, joining them, "he still has doubts." He turned to Sullivan. "You're sure you don't want to come work for me?" he asked him jokingly. "No blood bonds."

The Brujah had a sense of humor, and enough charm that he could occasionally get away with pulling the Prince's leg. Tonight was a happy occasion and the Prince was in a good mood. Regardless, Vannevar had already warned Sullivan not to trust Tomaine. The Prince had his doubts about him.

"Stand aside, Brujah," Vannevar joked with him. "This is *my* son you're talking to." He helped Sullivan up off the couch, onto his feet. "Come on," he kidded. "Let's get this thing over with."

Vannevar sat down in a chair and rolled up his sleeve. Sullivan knelt before him. Vannevar exposed his forearm and Sullivan leaned forward. He nipped the flesh and

began to drink, the warm, vibrant blood of the Prince filling him with a kind of ecstasy. As he drank, the Prince
placed his other hand on the back of Sullivan's head,
knotting his fingers in his short hair.

"My son," he said, closing his eyes.

March 16

Somewhere deep in the Asian continent, in a darkened room. . .

Something dark and malignant shifted its bulk. Upon
hearing the final report from the West Coast of America
it grunted, satisfied. So far, all was going according to
plan.

The Best in Science Fiction and Fantasy

A FISHERMAN OF THE INLAND SEA by Ursula K. Le Guin. The National Book Award-winning author's first new collection in thirteen years has all the majesty and appeal of her major works. Here we have starships that sail, literally, on wings of song... musical instruments to be played at funerals only...*ansibles* for faster-than-light communication...orbiting arks designed to save a doomed humanity. Astonishing in their diversity and power, Le Guin's new stories exhibit both the artistry of a major writer at the height of her powers, and the humanity of a mature artist confronting the world with her gift of wonder still intact.
Hardcover, 0-06-105200-0 — $19.99

L OVE IN VEIN: TWENTY ORIGINAL TALES OF VAMPIRIC EROTICA, edited by Poppy Z. Brite. An all-original anthology that celebrates the unspeakable intimacies of vampirism, edited by the hottest new dark fantasy writer in contemporary literature. *LOVE IN VEIN* goes beyond our deepest fears and delves into our darkest hungers—the ones even our lovers are forbidden to share. This erotic vampire tribute is not for everyone. But then, neither is the night....
Trade paperback, 0-06-105312-0 — $11.99

A NTI-ICE by Stephen Baxter. From the bestselling author of the award-winning *RAFT* comes a hard-hitting SF thriller that highlights Baxter's unique blend of time travel and interstellar combat. *ANTI-ICE* gets back to SF fundamentals in a tale of discovery and challenge, and a race to success.
0-06-105421-6 — $5.50

Today . . .

HarperPrism

An Imprint of HarperPaperbacks

SMALL GODS by Terry Pratchett. International bestseller Terry Pratchett brings magic to life in his latest romp through Discworld, a land where the unexpected always happens—usually to the nicest people, like Brutha, former melon farmer, now The Chosen One. His only question: Why? **0-06-109217-7 — $4.99**

MAGIC: THE GATHERING™—ARENA by William R. Forstchen. Based on the wildly bestselling trading-card game, the first novel in the *MAGIC: THE GATHERING™* novel series features wizards and warriors clashing in deadly battles. The book also includes an offer for two free, unique MAGIC cards.

0-06-105424-0 — $4.99

SEAROAD:Chronicles of Klatsand by Ursula K. Le Guin. Here is the culmination of Le Guin's lifelong fascination with small island cultures. In a sense, the Klatsand of these stories is a modern day successor to her bestselling *ALWAYS COMING HOME*. A world apart from our own, but part of it as well.

0-06-105400-3 — $4.99

CALIBAN'S HOUR by Tad Williams. The bestselling author of *TO GREEN ANGEL TOWER* brings to life a rich and incandescent fantasy tale of passion, betrayal, and death. The beast Caliban has been searching for decades for Miranda, the woman he loved—the woman who was taken from him by her father Prospero. Now that Caliban has found her, he has an hour to tell his tale of unrequited love and dark vengeance. And when the hour is over, Miranda must die.... Tad Williams has reached a new level of magic and emotion with this breathtaking tapestry in which yearning and passion are entwined.

Hardcover, 0-06-105204-3 — $14.99

and Tomorrow

WRATH OF GOD by Robert Gleason. An apocalyptic novel of a future America about to fall under the rule of a murderous savage. Only a small group of survivors are left to fight — but they are joined by powerful forces from history when they learn how to open a hole in time. Three legendary heroes answer the call to the ultimate battle: George S. Patton, Amelia Earhart, and Stonewall Jackson. Add to that lineup a killer dinosaur and you have the most sweeping battle since *THE STAND*.
Trade paperback, 0-06-105311-2 — $14.99

THE X-FILES™ by Charles L. Grant. America's hottest new TV series launches as a book series with FBI agents Mulder and Scully investigating the cases no one else will touch — the cases in the file marked X. There is one thing they know: The truth is out there.
0-06-105414-3 — $4.99

THE WORLD OF DARKNESS™: VAMPIRE— DARK PRINCE by Keith Herber. The ground-breaking White Wolf role-playing game Vampire: The Masquerade is now featured in a chilling dark fantasy novel of a man trying to control the Beast within.
0-06-105422-4 — $4.99

THE UNAUTHORIZED TREKKERS' GUIDE TO *THE NEXT GENERATION* AND *DEEP SPACE NINE* by James Van Hise. This two-in-one guidebook contains all the information on the shows, the characters, the creators, the stories behind the episodes, and the voyages that landed on the cutting room floor.
0-06-105417-8 — $5.99

HarperPrism
An Imprint of HarperPaperbacks